NEW DIMENSIONS 8

# New Dimensions

## SCIENCE FICTION

### NUMBER 8

Edited by ROBERT SILVERBERG

HARPER & ROW, PUBLISHERS

NEW YORK

HAGERSTOWN

SAN FRANCISCO

LONDON

FIRST EDITION

Designed by Sidney Feinberg

LIBRARY OF CONGRESS CATALOG CARD NUMBER: 77-11774

ISBN: 0-06-013792-4

78 79 80 81 82 10 9 8 7 6 5 4 3 2 1

# CONTENTS

# INTRODUCTION

This is the eighth in a series of annual collections dedicated to presenting the most original and exciting science fiction being written today. All stories in *New Dimensions* are published here for the first time. The contributors range from long-established professionals to brilliant beginners; the one thing they have in common is a desire to explore new territory, to discover effective new ways of approaching the ideas, images, and assumptions of classic science fiction. Old formulas, clichés, and stale concepts are unwelcome in these pages; *New Dimensions* seeks writers whose visions are unique and vigorously expressive.

The editor of *New Dimensions* is Robert Silverberg, himself one of science fiction's best-known writers, whose novels and stories include *Dying Inside, The Book of Skulls, Nightwings, Born with the Dead, The Stochastic Man, Shadrach in the Furnace,* and many others. Mr. Silverberg, who lives in California, has won science fiction's prized Hugo and Nebula awards for literary excellence many times, is a past president of the Science Fiction Writers of America, and was American Guest of Honor at the World Science Fiction Convention held in Heidelberg, Germany, in 1970.

NEW DIMENSIONS 8

JACK DANN *has collaborated in the editing of several unusually stimulating science fiction anthologies* (Wandering Stars, Faster Than Light, Future Power), *has written a number of fine short stories and novellas, among
them "The Dybbuk Dolls" in the fifth* New Dimensions, *and is currently at work at an ambitious cycle of
novels telling of the wanderings of the young galactic
voyager Bo Forester. He returns now to* New Dimensions *with a quiet, sinister story that may be the most
shattering portrait of the near future since Fritz Lei-
ber's "Coming Attraction" more than a quarter of a
century ago.*

■

# Jack Dann

■

# A QUIET REVOLUTION
# FOR DEATH

*No other epoch has laid so much stress as the expiring
Middle Ages on the thought of death.*

—J. HUIZINGA

It is a lovely day for a drive and a picnic. There is not a hint of
rain in the cerulean sky, and the superhighway snakes out
ahead like a cement canal. The cars are moving in slow motion
like gondolas skiffing through God's magical city.

"What a day," says Roger as he leans back in his cushioned
seat. Although the car is on automatic, he holds the steering
stick lightly between his thumb and forefinger. His green Chev-
rolet shifts lanes and accelerates to 130 miles an hour. "This is
what God intended when he made Sunday," Roger says as he
lets go of the steering stick to wave his arms in a stylized way.
He dreams that he is an angel of God guiding the eyeless
through His realms.

The children are in the back seat where they can fight and
squeal and spill their makeup until Sandra becomes frustrated
enough to give them some *Easy-Sleep* to make the trip go
faster. But the monotony of the beautiful countryside and the
hiss of air pushing past rubber and glass must have lulled Sandra
to sleep. She is sitting beside Roger. Her head lolls, beautiful
blonde hair hiding her beautiful face.

"I'm practicing to be an angel," shouts Bennie, Roger's oldest
and favorite son. The other children giggle and make muffled
shushing noises.

Roger turns around and sees that his son has painted his face

3

and smeared it with ashes. He's done a fair job, Roger thinks. Blue and grey rings of makeup circle Bennie's wide brown eyes. "That's very good, indeed," Roger says. "Your face is even more impressive than your costume."

*"I* could do better if I wanted to," says Rose Marie, who is seven and dressed in a mock crinoline gown with great cloth roses sewn across the bodice.

But Bennie is nonplused. He beams at his father and says, "You said that everyone,—even kids,—must have their own special vision of death. Well, my vision is just like yours." Bennie is twelve. He's the little man of the family, and next year, with God's help, he will be bar mitzvahed, since Sandra is half-Jewish and believes that children need even more ceremony than adults.

Rose Marie primps herself and says "ha" over and over. Samson and Lilly, ages five and six respectively, are quietly playing "feelie" together. But Samson—who will be the spitting image of his father, same cleft in his chin, same nose—is naked and shivering. Roger raises the car's temperature to 79 degrees and then turns back to Bennie.

"How do you know what my vision is?" Roger asks, trying to find a comfortable position. His cheek touches the headrest and his knee touches Sandra's bristly leg. Sandra moves closer to the door.

"You're nuts over Guyot Marchant and Holbein," says Bennie. "I've read your library fiche. Don't you think I'm acquainted intellectually with the painted dances of death? Well, ha, I know the poetry of Jean Le Fèvre, and I've seen the holos of the mural paintings in the church of La Chaise-Dieu. I've read Gédéon Huet in fiche and I've even looked at your books —I'm reading *Totentanz,* and I'm almost finished."

"You must ask permission," says Roger, but he is proud of his son. He certainly is the little man of the family, Roger tells himself. The other children only want to nag and cry and eat and play "feelie."

Sandra wakes up, pulls her hair away from her face, and asks: "How much longer?" Her neck and face are glossy with perspiration. She lowers the temperature, makes a choking noise, and insists that this trip is too long and she's hungry.

"I'm hungry, too," says Rose Marie. "And it's hot in here and everything's sticky."

"We'll be there soon," Roger says to his family as he gazes out the large windshield at the steaming highway ahead. The air seems to shimmer from the exhaust of other cars, and God has created little mirages of blue water.

"See the mirages on the highway," Roger says to his family. What a day to be alive! What a day to be with your family. He watches a red convertible zoom right through a blue mirage and come out unscathed. "What a day," he shouts. He grins and squeezes Sandra's knee.

But Sandra swats his hand as if it were a gnat.

Still, it *is* a beautiful day.

◆

"Well, here we are," says an excited Roger as the dashboard lights flash green, indicating that everyone can now get out of the car.

What a view! The car is parked on the sixteenth tier of a grand parking lot which overlooks the grandest cemetery in the East. From this vantage ground (it is certainly worth the forty-dollar parking fee) Roger can view beautiful Chastellain Cemetery and its environs. There, to the north, are rolling hills and a green swath which must be pine forest. To the west are great mountains which have been worn down by God's hand. The world is a pastel pallet: it is the first blush of autumn.

The cemetery is a festival of living movement. Roger imagines that he has slipped back in time to fifteenth-century Paris. He is the noble Boucicaut and the duke of Berry combined. He looks down at the common folk strolling under the cloisters. The peasants are lounging amidst the burials and exhumations and sniffing the stink of death.

"I'm hungry," whines Rose Marie, "and it's windy up here."

"We came up here for the view," Roger says. "So enjoy it."

"Let's go eat and put this day behind us," Sandra says.

"Mommy lives in her left brain, huh, Dad?" says Bennie. "She suffers from the conditioning and brainwashing of the olden days."

"You shouldn't talk about your mother that way," Roger says

as he opens the trunk of the car and hands everyone a picnic basket.

"But mother is old-fashioned," Bennie says as they walk toward the elevators. "She thinks everyone must conform to society to tame the world. But she is committed only to appearances; she cares nothing for substance."

"You think your father's so modern?" Sandra says to Bennie, who is walking behind her like a good son.

"You're an antique," Bennie says. "You don't understand right-brain living. You can't accept death as an ally."

"Then what am I doing here?"

"You came because of Dad. You hate cemeteries."

"I certainly do not."

But the argument dies as the silvery elevator doors slide open to take them all away from left-brain thinking.

◆

"Let's take a stroll around the cemetery," Roger says as they pass under a portiere which is the cemetery's flag and insignia. Roger pays the gateman who wears the cemetery's colors on the sleeves and epaulets of his somber blue uniform.

"That's fifty-*three* dollars, sir," says the gateman. He points at Bennie and says, "I must count him as an adult; it's the rules."

Roger cheerfully pays and leads his noisy family through the open wrought-iron gates. Before him is Chastellain Cemetery, the "real thing," he tells himself—there it is, full of movement and life, neighbor beside neighbor, everyone eating, drinking, loving, selling, buying, and a few are even dying. It is a world cut off from the world.

"This is the famous Avenue d'Auvergne," Roger says, for he has carefully studied Hodel's *Guidebook to Old and Modern Cemeteries.* "Here are some of the finest restaurants to be found in any cemetery," he says as they pass under brightly colored restaurant awnings.

"I want to go in here," Rose Marie says as she takes a menu card from a doorman and holds it to her nose. "I can smell aubergine fritters and pig's fry and *paupiette de veau* and I'm sick of Mommy's cooking. I want to go in here."

The doorman grins (probably thinking of his commission) and hands Roger a menu card.

"We have a fine picnic lunch of our own," Roger says, and he reminds himself that he's sick of French food anyway.

As they stroll north on the beautiful Avenue d'Auvergne which is shaded by old wych-elms, restaurants give way to tiny shops. Farther north, the avenue becomes a dirty cobblestone street filled with beggars and hawkers pushing wooden hand-carts.

"I don't like it here," says Rose Marie as she stares at the jettatura charms and lodestone ashtrays which are arrayed behind a dirty shop-window.

"You can find all manner of occult items in these little shops," Roger says. "This cemetery is a sanctuary for necromancy. Some of the finest astrologers and mediums work right here." Roger pauses before a shop which specializes in candles and oils and incense made of odoriferous woods and herbs. "What a wonderful place," Roger says as he takes Sandra's hand in his own. "Perhaps we should buy a little something for the children."

A hunchbacked beggar pulls at Roger's sleeve and says, "Alms for the poor," but Roger ignores his entreaties.

"The children are getting restless," Sandra says, her hand resting limply in Roger's. "Let's find a nice spot where they can play and we can have our picnic."

"This is a nice spot," Bennie says as he winks at a little girl standing in an alleyway.

"Hello, big boy," says the girl, who cannot be more than twelve or thirteen. "Fifty dollars will plant you some life in this body." She wiggles stylishly, leans against a shop window, and wrinkles her nose. "Well?" She turns to Roger and asks, "Does Daddy want to buy his son some life?" Then she smiles like an angel.

Roger smiles at Bennie, who resembles one of the death dancers painted on the walls of the Church of the Children.

"C'mon, Dad, please," Bennie whines.

"Don't even consider it," Sandra says to Roger. "We brought the children here to acquaint them with death, not sex."

8

"That smacks of left-brain thinking," says the little girl as she wags her finger at Sandra. "Death is an orgasm, not a social artifact."

"She's right about that," Roger says to Sandra. Only youth can live without pretense, he thinks. Imagining death as a simple return to nature's flow, he hands Bennie a crisp fifty-dollar bill.

"Thanks, Dad," and Bennie is off, hand in hand with his five-minute friend. They disappear into a dark alley that separates two long tumbledown buildings.

"He shouldn't be alone," Sandra says. "Who knows what kind of people might be skulking about in that alley?"

"Shall we go and watch him, then?" Roger asks.

"It's love and death," Rose Marie says as she primps her dress, folding the thin material into pleats.

"I want to go *there*," says Samson, pointing at a great Ferris wheel turning in the distance.

Roger sighs as he looks out at the lovely gravestone gardens of the cemetery. "Yes," he whispers, dreaming of God and angels. "It's love and death."

◆

Sandra prepares the picnic fixings atop a secluded knoll which overlooks spacious lawns, charnelhouses, cloisters adorned with ivory gables, and even rows of soap-white monuments. Processions of mourners wind their way about like snakes crawling through a modern Eden. Priests walk about, offering consolation to the bereaved, tasting tidbits from the mourners' tables, kissing babies, touching the cold foreheads of the dead, and telling wry jokes to the visitors just out for a Sunday picnic and a stroll.

"All right," Sandra says as she tears a foil cover from a food cylinder and waits for the steam to rise. "Soup's on. Let's eat everything while it's hot." She opens container after container. There is a rush for plates and plasticware and the children argue and fill their dishes with the sundry goodies. Then, except for the smacking of lips, a few moments of silence: a burial is taking place nearby, and everyone is caught up in profound emotion.

"It's a small casket," Roger says after a proper length of time has passed. He watches two young men clad in red lay the casket down on the grass beside the burial trench. "It must be a child," Roger says. A middle-aged man and woman stand over the tiny casket; the man rocks back and forth and rends his garments while the woman sobs.

"You see," Bennie says after he has cleaned his plate. "That kind of crying and tearing clothes is for the old left-brain thinkers. *I* wouldn't mind dying right now. Death is wasted on the old. Look at Mommy—she's haunted by silly dreams of immortality. Old people are too perverse to joyously give themselves back to nature." Bennie stands up, looking ghoulish and filthy in his death costume.

"And where are you going?" Sandra asks.

"To dance on the fresh grave."

"Let him go," Roger says. "It is only proper to continue great traditions."

◆

The sun is working its way toward three o'clock. There is not a cloud in the sky, only the gauzy crosshatchings of jet-trails. A few birds wing overhead like little blue angels. Roger sits beside his lovely Sandra, and they watch Bennie as he dances stylishly with the two young mourners clad in red. Roger is proud and his eyes are moist. Bennie has stolen the show. He has even attracted a small crowd of passersby.

This is a sight that would have made Jean Le Fèvre turn his head! Roger says to himself as he watches Bennie work his way through a perfect *danse macabre*. The mourners are already clapping. Bennie has their hearts. He has presented a perfect vision of death to his spectators.

"Wave to Benjamin," Roger says to his family. "See, he's waving at us." Roger imagines that he can hear the sounds of distant machinery. He dreams that God has sent angels to man the machinery of His cemetery.

And with the passing of each heavenly moment, the noise of God's machinery becomes louder.

◆

But God's machines turn out to be only children, hundreds of noisy boys and girls come to join in the Sunday processions. They're here to burn or bury innocents and bums and prostitutes, to learn right thinking and body-knowing, and share in the pleasures and exquisite agonies of death's community. The children seem to be everywhere. They're turning the cemetery into a playground.

As Roger watches children playing bury-me-not and hide-and-seek between the tombstone teeth of the cemetery, he thinks that surely his son Bennie must be in their midst. Bennie might be anywhere: taking a tour through the ossuarium, lighting fires on the lawns, screwing little girls, or dancing for another dinner.

"We should not have permitted Bennie to leave in the first place," Sandra says to Roger. "He's probably in some kind of trouble." She pauses, then says, "Well, *I'm* going to go and look for him." Another pause. "What are you going to do?"

"Someone has to remain with the children," Roger says. "I'm sure Bennie is fine. He'll probably be back."

Sandra, of course, rushes off in a huff. But that's to be expected, Roger tells himself. Bennie was right: she is perverse. After a few deep breaths, Roger forgets her. He stretches out on the cool grass, looks up at the old maple trees that appear to touch the robin's-egg sky, and he feels the touch of God's thoughts. He yawns. This bounty of food, fresh air, and inspiration has worn him out. He listens to the children and dreams of tractors.

A fusillade echoes through the cemetery.

"Daddy, what's that noise?" asks Rose Marie.

"The children are probably shooting guns," Roger says. He opens his eyes, then closes them.

"Why are they shooting guns?"

"To show everyone that death must be joyous," Roger says. But he can't quite climb out of his well of sleep. He falls through thermoclines of sleep and dreams of tractors rolling over tombstones and children and trees.

◆

"When is Mommy coming back?" asks Rose Marie.

"When she finds Bennie," Roger says, and he buttons the collar of his shirt. There is a slight chill to the air.

"When will that be?"

"I don't know," Roger says. "Soon, I hope." He watches the rosy sunset. The western mountains are purple, and Roger imagines that rainbows are leaking into the liquid blue sky.

Another fusillade echoes through the cemetery.

"Maybe Mommy was shot," Rose Marie says in a hushed tone.

"Maybe," Roger replies.

"Maybe she's dead," says Rose Marie, smoothing out her dress, then making cabbage folds.

"Is that so bad?" Roger asks. "You must learn to accept death as an ally. If Mommy doesn't come back, it will teach you a lesson."

"I want to ride on the Ferris wheel," Samson says. "You promised."

"If Mommy doesn't return soon, we'll go for a ride," Roger says, admiring the cemetery. Even at dusk, in this shadow-time, Chastellain Cemetery is still beautiful, he tells himself. It is a proud old virgin, but soon it will become a midnight whore. It will become a carnival. It will be Ferris wheels and rides and lights and candlelight processions.

Lying back in the grass, Roger searches for the first evening stars. There, he sees two straight above him. They blink like Sandra's eyes. He makes a wish and imagines that Sandra is staring at him with those cold lovely eyes.

In the evening haze below, the candlelight processions begin.

*Perhaps it's going too far to say that the theme of this story is a* New Dimensions *preoccupation, but the first issue did contain Thomas Disch's "Emancipation: A Romance of the Times to Come," and here, only eight years later, is another story about a pregnant man. There is otherwise not much similarity between the two: Disch offers a parable of displaced sexual identities in the century ahead; Dern provides a sharp, even profound, insight into the psychology of human-as-mother in today's society. Nevertheless, would-be contributors are warned that the concept may be exhausted for some time in these pages.*

DANIEL DERN *is no stranger to the sort of alienation his gravid protagonist experiences—not that he has ever been pregnant, so far as I know, but he* was *a literature major at* MIT, *which may be nearly as strange a situation. After graduation he dabbled in the world of computers, wrote an unpublished novel, sold some stories to* Analog, If, *and various science fiction anthologies, and began writing folk-music reviews. These days, he serves as a technical consultant in a variety of fields while writing fiction and reviewing music on the side. "My current projects," he reports, "include a Database Management Primer, an urban transit operator's manual, plus plans for a series of travel books, doing a newsletter or two, writing a musical adaptation of an s-f novel, and finishing a few more stories. Who knows, I may also rewrite my novel." Not much room in that schedule for visits to the obstetrician.*

∎

*Daniel P. Dern*

■

# YES SIR THAT'S MY

I try to imagine, amid our early-morning tussling, what it must be like, in her body, how it feels, to have foreign flesh pushed within me; how strange it is, that in pressing two bodies so close together another body could be formed and plucked from me. And that would be the meaning of it all, a meaning so clear that all attempts to subvert it would seem distasteful, no matter how necessary. And I would stay home and cook and wash dishes while she went out to hustle her bustle nine to five (assuming rotation rather than revolution) and the moon would go round the earth and I would feel mysterious and burbling (so they say); but I'll never understand, all I can do is hold her tight as one of us bucks above the other, and smile, feeling that I *do* understand something, and that I must pretend the rest. Or make do, accepting that there are some things I will never understand.

We drift back to sleep, and then the alarm is going off, *brrp, barrupp*, ho, time to get up. I blink hard, tap the switch for silence, and walk my fingers up the arm across my chest to her neck, chin, nose. Her face tells me she has cramps, slight ones; I kiss her gently and place my palms below her stomach for a moment, then turn her on her side and rub her back, paying special attention to the diagonals behind her kidneys, where the warmth is most needed. We get up, and in the shower she pinches my waist; *you're getting fat,* she says, so I promise to skip lunch and jog, which satisfies her. Then, as we clear away breakfast and she leafs through her papers for the morning's appointments, she curses and snaps the briefcase shut, biting her upper lip between the teeth.

13

*What's wrong?* I ask. She has to go to the clinic, some special test they want her to take, a urine sample, sugar levels, whatever. *Can I help?* I offer. She goes and dials a number on the phone, chews on a nail while they leave her holding. I put the dishes away and knot my tie. *Yes,* she tells me; I can bring it in for her. In fact, they want my sample, too, while I'm there. One moment. She shuffles through the shelves. Here, this will do. Hang on.

◆

Lawyers—even bright-eyed, red-haired, long-nosed lawyers —have to start their days early. Especially when they're just out of law school, as my wife is, and don't own or run the office, which she doesn't. Us photographers have it easier. No model is going to show her body, much less her face, before ten, and all the adfolks I know believe it's immoral to start drinking before ten-thirty. So all I have to do, unless there's work left over from the day before, is know what to set up and check over my equipment and hope it's merely another long day in the studio and not some bright sales maven's idea of inspiration to make me go out on location chasing long-legged dreams in this New York's most unlikely folly of a cold, cold winter. Never mind my solidified sinuses and blue-tinged fingers—do you know what those subfreezing temperatures do to my *film?* Not to mention my shutters? Give me a CIA special Besseler Topcon Super D and I'll shoot your frozen beauties; just spare, if you will, my poor gray Hasselblad.

So while she makes ready to go off to help honest, outraged prostitutes bring suit against the police department in arresting sellers while ignoring purchasers—tort for tart, she calls it—I hunt up a book to accompany me to the clinic, knowing there will be a wait. "Feel better?" I ask as she leaves. She nods. "See you tonight."

Her family's got this hyperglycemia habit; we check her every so often but luckily haven't nabbed her metabolism yet. She shows traces, however, so she eats real careful. Me, I got my own worries. Now they find another new test, or it's a golden oldie, or maybe they just want to keep us worried, whatever the reason, off I go, maybe we'll learn something new today.

♦

The doctor's office is typically clogged; squalling rug rats quiver in their mothers' laps; lizard-skinned septuagenarians sit motionlessly; I twiddle a *Reader's Digest,* taking two and three readings to decode each joke. Vaguely I remember my first visits as a child: brown block toys, the bristling smell I now know to be ammonia, the anticipation of pain. My eyes take in the paragraph once again; I know there is humor in there, but it evades me with Middle-American cunning.

A starch-white nurse gargles my name.

I quickstep down the hallway and return with filled bottle and vial, extract from my pocket the home brew. Tests, yes, mumble check babble the doctor mutters, see you at pay the next week call you. Still cringing from the shot my childhood memories awaited, I rebundle and trudge off.

It's a problem day, they keep sending models with skin tones half a zone off, too dark, too light, I'm tempted to send them back saying, not cooked enough, another turn on the spit please. Finally we slide the last film back off and call it a day. That's all girls see you tomorrow and don't break that smile.

The phone is ringing when I unboot in the doorway; I ignore it, knowing you never make it in time. Settling back with a light drink and heavy novel, I brood over Eleanor of Aquitaine until another car rattles in the driveway.

She is perturbed, I can tell; I start tea and gentle her as she uncloaks. *The doctor called,* she recites, *they want me in for testing.*

I hold her and ask, *did they say why;* she shakes her head. Tea, news, dinner, work, wine, shower, and bed. I hold her again and whisper not to worry. She cries out as she clutches me, and in relaxing, weeps.

The look upon her face next evening is stranger still: *They thought I was pregnant, but I'm not; they want to see you tomorrow at ten.*

♦

Penetration, relaxation, penetration, relaxation—whose arrogance is it to classify this act "invasion"? For every woman demanding *out, out,* is there not a male whose inner voice screams, *keep it in, don't let anything escape,* and then roll away before feeling becomes a fact. Lock it in, lock it out; it is the violation of surfaces that distresses. I cannot imagine what it would be to have her squirt inside me, fill me and lie by my side empty and drained. Nor the inexhaustible transport of her release; this jealousy will never be reconciled. What soft, bleary smile might I drift with after such elevation, and the warm knowing shit-eating grin that would mist my eyes till noon?

I cannot know, only cause; rod and tongue march around her flesh like Jericho horns until she crumbles.

◆

The office is still fey; they pluck fluids from me, prod me, ray me, invade me, with stiff lights and cold devices up every orifice, and gather like flies to prognose.

It is evident, it is impossible; I am *enceinte.*

◆

A blessed event! Will it be a boy or a girl? Shall I knit booties and crave pickles? What are the rules in such circumstances? *Man Expecting,* tabloids would hawk. *Hubby Takes Turn— Mom Stays Mum.* Men's faces grow pale; women guffaw. They have to be carried; their deep laughter overcomes them. The rich chortling echoes down the hallways and explodes in amazed whispers. I sit there, stomach twisting; I am not amused.

◆

*Ectopic pregnancy,* they chant. *Parthogenetic reproduction, reverse ovarian drift.* Not impossible, not odd. Perfectly explainable. Nature not putting all her eggs in one basket. *Liberoparous hominem. Homo anticipatus.* Their professional mumbo-jumbo permits them to gloss over the miraculous with blasé jargon, but I am not fooled. They are staggered and still reeling from the blow; all their fancy words are just a mask for their fright. I loosen my belt thoughtfully; I've got love in my tummy.

How do I tell her? Am I going to be a father or a mother? Will she be suspicious, suspect another woman? Is she willing to accept this child? My God, suppose she refuses—am I prepared to sacrifice this flesh of my flesh, say yes to the silver knife and sucking tube? Not with my child you don't!

Then again, this could be more than a mild disruption in my life: by what right would the church and others decide what I will do with my body?

Thoughts avalanche faster than I can cope: what about my job, my career? Is it all right for me to work, can I get paternity leave?

I wonder if my medical plan will cover the hospital bills.

And will my dry breasts blossom in time to suckle my child?

◆

First she is amused, then startled, then shocked. As she slowly believes, her emotions do a tango. The lawyer's cool surfaces, mixed with spousely concern. Unbelief returns; she cannot grasp the truth. Jealousy. Confusion. Love. Fear. Joy. Humor. Concern. Doubt. She proves equal to the situation; she is no more capable of accepting it than I am.

We sit and think.

A strange, loving look suffuses her features. Never before has she been gentle in this way. It is a deep loving we make late that evening, almost irrelevant to pleasure. I hold her close and weep.

◆

My belly is swelling; we have abandoned tobacco, alcohol, aspirin. Loose trousers hide my precious paunch; even so, I get comments—*Too much beer, old fellow? Better get to work on those pounds, boy.*

I banter back and look chagrined. Conveniently, the clinic has maintained my delicate condition *entre nous* and *sub rosa* and no doubt *oy vey iz mir,* but I still fear someone will discover me.

Is it embarrassment or the inevitable pursuit by the media and fanatics that encourages my furtiveness? It is not yet too

late for this all to turn out a bad dream, or at least a creative
tumor.

◆

No one could be more loving, more supportive than that
bright-eyed, red-haired, long-nosed lawyer who is my wife.
"The entire legal establishment is prepared to defend you," she
assures you. "At least, I pledge myself without cost in your
cause, no matter how prolonged. So long, Mom, and all that.
Here is a list of precedents I have made up for you already."

Spencer Tracy never received so magnanimous an offer from
his legal-minded screenmate Kate; happy am I to have such a
wife, to care for the swelling life within me.

◆

The doctors are very puzzled.

"It's not a parthen," they declare. "It's clearly got both your
chromosomes. Confess, sly scoundrel, how did you do it? Did
Johns Hopkins pull this fast one? What perverse position did
your wife and you employ that fatal night? Talk, or we shall
publish!"

I stay silent, aware of my rights. Their bluster cannot budge
me. I know they are relieved that Christmas will come only
once this year.

◆

She is gentle with me now, allowing me the bottom in all but
our most energetic moments. Even so, my tongue is more convenient. We do not go out much; our evenings are preoccupied
with reading and talk. We have much to discuss; all these years
she has been a woman and I have failed to take interest except
in the obvious. Suddenly I am very concerned; the rights of
mothers, Lamaze and painless birth, proper nutrition, obliga-
tions to the state—I find I am less alert to the outside world than
I used to be; my mind drifts at unlikely moments and fills with
thoughts of sky.

To hide our fear, we joke: will she join me in the delivery
room, or pace frantically outside, choking on cigars?

◆

Someone has told the papers, the mercenary scoundrel. Peace is a forgotten concept; the household, the driveway, the entire block is littered with newssneaks. Our phone sounds like an ice cream truck. Our mailbox is overrun; indeed, the mailman has taken to doing our house as an entire bag drop. Luckily, no one has yet been violent.

The church is rather off-balance. Hurrah!

◆

I can feel movement already. My body feels light in spite of its new bulk; I rest my hands on my hairy navel and wonder whether some mistake has not been made. Surely the noble doctors could not be wrong?

Perhaps the women never really did it at all, it is only a lie spread and carefully maintained by some mysterious power structure. It is as likely as my being the only one.

The thought does not console me.

◆

Spring has exploded: the air is overpoweringly sweet. Birds sing, worms turn, leaves unroll . . . I feel a mysterious kinship with the earth, and cautious of my cargo I take to our garden.

Sitting in the class together, my wife and I attract strange glances, but everyone is too polite to talk to us. *I don't mind,* I would say, *come, do you believe in breast-feeding.* But beneath their distance I know I frighten them, so we do not press for company. *One, two, one, two,* we all chant together. *Breathe. Breathe. Relax.*

*You have given your fellow men another tool for oppressing us,* an angry woman writes. *Now you don't need us at all.* Uncertain, I ponder this. But: *You are a brave man,* another letter says, *to share our burden with us. I wish you well.*

I answer as many of these letters as I am able; their encouragement strengthens me. The others, the distressed mudslingers, I skim for originality and then feed to the trash.

◆

Business is booming, I can report. Vicarious notoriety has brought flush times to the law firm. Multi-digit offers from institutions and periodicals cover our bulletin board. We contemplate the temptation, but steadfastly refuse to say, "Come on over."

I drink milk, take vitamins. Obviously I have not been to work in weeks; my condition is distracting when not downright encumbering, and I feel as if I am in front of the cameras instead of behind them. Well, that's what you get for not taking precautions. I wonder if she would have married me, had we been single when it happened.

◆

Our parents, who have always pestered us to have children, do not appear satisfied by the recent development. There's no pleasing some people.

◆

The companies are beginning to get obnoxious again; they view me as a viable sales gimmick. Entire new markets! Dolls! Sweatshirts! Advice to unwed fathers! Bah!

The only consolation I have is that *Pravda* has not yet announced the previously unpublicized case of a Russian man who gave birth to a healthy seven-pound boy—or maybe twins —back in 1962.

◆

Well, we had to give in; Blue Cross would not spring for my obstetric expenses. We expect to win the lawsuit, but in the meantime the clinic's offer was our only hope of financial non-ruin. We intend to get those hard-fisted bastards, however. Deny childbirth coverage on account of my sex, will they? I will relish watching them squirm in court. Let's hear it for the Equal Rights Amendment, brothers!

◆

Buying a suitable nursing brassiere was quite an adventure.

◆

It is a triumph worth crowing over. Single-handedly, I have thrown an entire medical research team into panic. Now that they've got me, they don't know what to do with me. Hi-ho, they're so confused! They'd love to be able to say, *there's been a mistake, it's only a strange growth,* but not after the X rays.

Actually, it began as a wart on my ass.

◆

My art is suffering, I admit, but I realize I am not the first whose baby preempted a career.

When the child is two months old, I intend to go back to work full-time, if at all possible. Meanwhile, I am catching up on my reading.

◆

I have accepted an invitation to speak before the upcoming Gay Rights Conference. My topic (by request): Male Mothers: A Viable Gay Alternative to Adoption.

Though uncertain how I feel about all this, I was too flattered to refuse.

◆

The day has come. Swollen-bellied they cart me away, accompanied by a certain red-haired lawyer. The connection between my vast abdomen and a son or daughter seems tenuous even at this moment; it is hard to believe that another living creature is in there. I think Saul's a good name for a boy, although Minerva might be more appropriate. Though the prospect of being a househusband swaddled by mewling babes frightens me, the whole experience has been most enlightening. I wonder if my feelings are common.

They have the operating theatre all ready for me. Doctors circle like eager vultures. (A large fuss was needed to get my wife's permission to be with me.) TV cameras wait, ready to dolly in for the close-ups; should we have sold tickets to the intrigued M.D.? But viewing privileges were included in the deal we made.

It will have to be the knife. The one thing I lack is an egress; however the little bugger managed to sneak inside me, he or

*Daniel P. Dern*

she forgot to provide for a graceful exit. For some reason, neither my wife nor I really worried about it; I guess I thought I would sprout a zipper in the final week, or something.

They assure me the caesarean is routine and I do not have to be afraid.

◆

Since this is a high-class operation, well-funded, I get the luxury of an epidural. I would have insisted on a local rather than general anesthetic in any case. *I will not sleep through the birth of my child.* In their arrogant professional distance they assumed I would take a dive. And not know what they were doing to me? I will endure pain if I must, but I will be there and awake the whole time.

The insufferable *maleness* of the medical profession has never been more evident.

◆

The nurses are all on my side. They have been good to me. Those who have children of their own have spent time chatting with me to put me at ease; they made sure I was comfortable and not worried. It was at their urging that I insisted on staying awake.

Trembling shakes my body; I grasp the sides of the table. Where are my rope handles!

A white-masked face nods; another needle sinks into my flesh. They wheel a device which sounds like a coffee percolator to my side.

Holding my hand, my wife stands by me. She tries to look calm and loving, but I can see the fear, the worry in her eyes.

In her place, would I have cared so well?

My guts buckle. I suck air and scream in pain. This is a mistake. They wave the gas tube in my face. *Are you sure?* they inquire.

*Don't you dare,* I threaten. My wife's hand tightens around my fingers. They back off.

Another pain. How the devil can I suffer contractions when I don't have a birth canal?

The entire event has been irregular that way.

◆

The pains quicken. I moan softly. The doctors confer in whispers; then the head shaman steps near. He flexes his arms as if preparing to carve a holiday bird. They lift the white sheet from my body.

Somewhere below my monstrous belly hang my standard-issue male-type genitals. I have not seen them lately, being too fat in front for line-of-sight viewing, but since I can still urinate while standing, I assume that everything is still there. (Actually, I can still feel them when I wash.)

So I am cheered; some things have *not* changed . . .

I want ice cream.

◆

*Ahhh* the metal is cold! Damn them! *Aieee!*

My hairless flesh prickles at their touch. (They shaved me yesterday—my belly, that is. They had the goodness to leave the pubic hair intact, as it was not in the way.)

They swab me down with antiseptics. The drying alcohol tingles. I imagine already hearing my child's cries.

A wave of love fills me, dulling the first incision's pain. I can tell I am bleeding.

The television lights shine on my skin. *Ladies, have you tried* . . . Unlike most commercial housewife illusions, my skin is not soft, but my wife still loves me.

◆

In the later months of my pregnancy I was gleeful. I had never felt more handsome. But in the odd moments I found myself thinking, *Is she out with other women now? Other men? Do I look fat and ugly now?* Afraid, I did not mention these thoughts to my wife.

Under the bright-lit pain of parturition, my mask dissolves. I hear voices discussing me. I do not care.

My breath comes in chunks now: *a-haa, a-haa.* My diaphragm is rock-hard. There are peeling me apart like an orange.

My breasts throb. My body is being torn in two. *What are they doing to me?* Pain, incredible pain, the rush of voices, the measured beat of calm nurses ready with the instruments, oxygen shoved in my mouth, futile nausea, wrenching jolts that shake the table and rattle the trays. Shake, rattle and roll. My fingernails are ripping into my palms. *How can they stand it?* My eyes press shut in pain; my screams fill the room. No more strength now—*let it be over, please!* Hands explore me; fingers close like hooks in around the payload. My flesh parts and I feel the sucking as they lift the body from me, there is another wave of pain that blurs my eyes and I feel cold air inside me while I gasp above—and suddenly everything is silent, it is over.

In that still moment before they slap the baby into squalling life, I am overcome with emptiness; I am empty again and helpless to change it. *Put it back in!* I try to cry out, even as they begin to sew me up again, but I am too weak to speak. Reflex attempts to make me ignore my feelings, but they are too strong; reaching for my wife's hand, I begin to weep. Overcome with grief, joy, and loss, I let my tears mingle with the cries of my newborn child.

CHRISTOPHER PRIEST *is generally recognized as the most accomplished British science-fiction author to emerge in the 1970s. His four novels*—Indoctrinaire, Darkening Island, The Inverted World, *and* The Space Machine—*have been awards contenders and have attracted considerable critical attention; his short stories have appeared in many magazines and anthologies; his trenchant essays on science fiction have ornamented the pages of the academic s-f journals. Now he makes his debut in* New Dimensions *with this cool, hallucinatory, marvelously disturbing work.*

■

# Christopher Priest

■

# WHORES

I left the war behind me and traveled to the tropical northern coast of the continent. Fifty days' sick leave stretched ahead of me, and my trouser pocket was heavy on my buttock with the wad of high-denomination notes I had received as back pay. It should have been a time for recuperation after the long spell in the military hospital, but I was still affected by the enemy synesthetic gas I had inhaled and my perception was disturbed.

As the train had clattered through the devastated towns and countryside, I seemed to taste the music of pain, feel the gay dancing colors of sound.

Waiting in the main port for the ferry across to the Dream Archipelago, I tried to rationalize my delusions as the medical orderlies had trained me. The brick houses, which between my perceptual lapses I saw glowed brown from the local sandstone, became synesthetic monstrosities: cynical laughter, a deep throbbing sound, cold like tempered steel to the touch. The fishing boats in the harbor were less unpleasant to perceive: they were a gentle humming sound, barely audible. The army hostel where I stayed overnight was a warren of associative flavors and smells: the corridors tasted to me of coal dust, the walls were papered with hyacinth, the bed linen enfolded me like a rancid mouth. I slept poorly, waking several times from vivid dreams. One recurred especially: I dreamed I was still with my unit in the front line of the war, advancing and retreating, setting up the monitoring complex then dismantling it, repeatedly, endlessly.

In the morning my synesthesia seemed to have receded

again; in the last weeks I had sometimes passed a whole day without a relapse, and when I was discharged it was because they said I was cured.

I left the hostel and walked down to the harbor, soon finding the quay where the ferry berthed. There was an hour and a half to wait, and so I strolled pleasurably through the streets surrounding the harbor, noting that the town was a major center for the importation of military and civilian supplies; I was allowed into one warehouse and was shown large stacks of crates containing hallucinogenic grenades and neutral dissociation gases.

The day was hot and sultry; the sky was clouded. I stood with about a hundred other people on the quay, waiting to board the ferry. This was an old diesel-powered boat, apparently top-heavy, riding high in the water. As I stepped down onto the deck, I experienced a wholly natural kind of synesthetic response: the smell of hot diesel oil, salt-stiff ropes, and sun-dried deck planks summoned a vivid nostalgic memory of a childhood voyage along the coast of my own country. The experience of the enemy gas had taught me how to recognize the response, and in moments I was able to recall, in explicit detail, my thoughts, actions, and ambitions of that time.

There was a delay and an argument when I came to pay my fare. The army money was acceptable, but the notes were too high in value. Change had to be found, and the disgruntled ferryman made me wait for it. By the time I was free to explore the ancient boat, we were a long way out to sea, and the warring continent I had left was a black outline on the southern horizon.

◆

I was returning, at last, to the Dream Archipelago. In the days of mental torment in the military hospital, when food had seemed to shout abuse at me and light sang discordant melodies for my eyes, and my mouth would only utter pain and hurt, my consolation lay in the Dream Archipelago. I had been there once, before I went to war, and I urged—and was urged—to return.

"Visit the island of Salay," a rehabilitation orderly had said,

over and over. "In Salay the food is the most exotic in the world.
Or Muriseay. Or Paneron. Do you remember the women of
Paneron?"

(I remembered nothing, then; only the agonies of twenty-five
years of life, transmuted insanely to colors and smells and pain.)

I remembered the women of Paneron while I sat on the deck
of the ferry, but they did not attract me. Nor did any woman
so easily accessible. There was a woman sitting near me, a
young woman. I had been idly appraising her, and she noticed,
and my stare was returned forthrightly. It had been a long time
since I had had a woman, and she was the first I had noticed.
I turned away from her, wanting to choose, not to accept the
first woman who stared back at me.

I was returning at last to the Dream Archipelago . . . and I
knew where I'd go. Not to Paneron, although I had been there
and tried the women, nor to Salay, nor to any other of the
islands that the troops most often visited. I did not count myself
above the others, nor was I seeking an esoteric experience for
its own sake; but I was walking again on the path of a long-
forgotten memory, one which had returned to me by the insane
medium of my illness.

On the island of Winho there was a girl who spoke like musk,
who laughed with the texture of spring water, and who loved
in deep vermilion. . . .

It was five years since I had been to Winho. I had visited the
archipelago on my way to war, and the boat had put in to Winho
Town for overnight repairs. That evening I had taken a whore,
had bid for her against a local man, and with my soldier's pay
had bought her for twice the usual rate.

I had remembered the hour with her for a time, but since
then there had been many whores and I did not think of her
much. In my illness, though, I had remembered her again, the
memory made more alluring by the associative images of the
synesthesia.

On Winho, in the Dream Archipelago, I would find that girl.
Her name was Slenje, and I wanted her again.

◆

But Slenje was dead.

Winho Town had been occupied by enemy troops for several months when they opened a new front in the archipelago. It had been liberated with the other islands, but as our troops had blasted their way back into Winho, Slenje had died.

I was obsessed with her for two days, pacing the streets of the town, inquiring after her with many of the people, even though the answer was always the same. Slenje was dead, was dead.

On the second day, I had another attack of synesthesia, and the white-painted cottages and the lush vegetation and the streets of dried mud became a nightmare of beguiling smells and flavors, terrifying sounds, and bizarre textures. I stood for an hour in the central street of the town, convinced that Slenje had been swallowed: the houses ached like decaying teeth, the road was soft and hairy like the surface of a tongue, the tropical flowers and trees were like half-chewed food, and the warm wind that came in from the sea was like fetid breath.

When the attack was finished, I drank two beers in a local café, then went to the garrison and found an officer of my own rank.

◆

"You'll suffer from it all your life," the officer said.

"The synesthesia?"

"You ought to be invalided out permanently."

"I'm on sick leave now," I explained.

We were walking through the courtyard of the castle where the soldiers were garrisoned. It was suffocatingly hot in the sun, for no breath of wind could reach the deep yard. The castle battlements were being patrolled by young soldiers in dark blue uniforms, who paced slowly to and fro, ever alert for a return of the enemy. These guards wore full battle gear, including the heavy gas-proof black hoods that covered their heads and faces.

"I'm trying to find a woman," I said.

"There are plenty in the town."

"A particular woman," I said. "A whore. The locals say she was killed."

"Then find another. Or use one of ours. We've twenty whores in the garrison. Keep away from the local women."

"Disease?" I said.

"In a sense. They're off-limits to us. No loss."

"Tell me about it."

The officer said, "We're fighting a war. The town is full of enemy infiltrators."

I looked at him carefully, and noticed that his face was expressionless as he said this.

"That's official army policy," I said. "What's the truth?"

"No different."

We continued to walk around the courtyard, and I decided not to leave until I heard a fuller explanation. The officer talked of his part in the archipelago campaign, and I listened with simulated interest. He told me that Winho Town had been occupied by enemy troops for nearly two hundred days, and he detailed some of the outrages they had perpetrated. I listened with real interest.

"The enemy performed . . . experiments here," the officer said. "Not with the synesthetics, something else. Their laboratories have been dismantled."

"By you?"

"By army staff officers."

"And what happened to the women?"

"The local people have been infiltrated," the officer said, and although we paced about the sun-hot courtyard for another hour, I learned no more. As I left the castle, one of the black-hooded guards on the battlements fainted from the heat. He was allowed to lie where he had fallen, and within moments had been replaced.

◆

Night was falling when I returned to the town, and many of the people were walking slowly through the streets. Now that my quest for Slenje was over I was able to see with a new clarity and observe the town more objectively than before. The tropical evening was still and close, and the breeze had gone, but the oppressive heat could not by itself account for the way the people moved about. Everyone I saw walked slowly and painfully, shuffling along as if lamed. The hot night seemed to amplify sounds, but apart from occasional voices, and melancholy

music coming from one of the restaurants, the only noise was
that of the painful footsteps.

While I waited in the street, standing in the same spot as
before, I reflected that in this stage of my recovery I was no
longer frightened of the synesthesia. It didn't seem odd to me
that certain kinds of music should be visualized as strands of
colored lights; that I should be capable of imagining the circuitry of the army monitoring equipment in terms of geometric
shapes; that words should have palpable textures, such as fabric-
like, or metallic; that strangers should exude emotional colora-
tion or hostility without even glancing my way.

A small boy ran across the street and darted behind a tree. He
stared toward me from behind it. A tiny stranger: he exuded not
the nervousness his manner indicated, but curiosity and playful-
ness.

At last he walked toward me, staring at the ground.

"Are you the man who was asking about Slenje?" he said and
scratched his groin.

"Yes," I said . . . and instantly the child ran away. He was the
only quick movement in the street.

A few minutes passed, and I continued to wait. I saw the boy
again, running back across the street, zigzagging through the
shuffling people. He ran toward a house, then vanished inside.

A little while later two girls came slowly down the street,
their arms linked. They walked directly to where I stood. Neither of them was Slenje . . . but then I had not hoped. I knew
she was dead.

One of the girls, with long dark hair, said, "It will cost you
fifty."

"That's all right."

As she spoke I had caught a glimpse of her teeth. Several of
them appeared to be broken, giving her a sinister, demoniac
appearance. She was plumper than the other, and her hair
seemed unwashed. I looked at the second girl, who was short,
with pale brown hair.

"I'll take you," I said to her.

"It's still fifty," said the first girl.

"I know."

The girl with the broken teeth kissed the other on both cheeks, then shuffled away.

I followed the second girl as she headed down the street toward the tiny harbor.

I said, "What's your name?"

"Does it matter?" It was the first thing she had said to me.

"No, it doesn't matter," I said. "Did you know Slenje?"

"Of course."

We turned into a narrow side-street that ran up the face of one of the hills surrounding the harbor. No wheeled vehicles ever used this way, for every so often there were shallow steps. The girl climbed slowly, pausing at each of the steps. She was breathing heavily in the humid air. I offered to take her arm, but she snatched it away from my hand; she was not hostile, though, but proud, for she gave me a quick smile a moment later. As we stopped at the door of an old house, she said, "My name is Elva."

She opened the door and stepped inside. I was about to follow her when I noticed that a number had been painted on the door: 14. It caught my attention because ever since my illness I had had strong color-associations with numbers. 14 had an emphatic association with blueness . . . but this number had been painted in white. I found it disconcerting, because as I looked at it, the number seemed to change from white to blue, to white again. I knew then that another synesthetic attack was beginning and, anticipating the worst, I felt a deep mood of depression. I started forward and closed the door behind me, as if shutting the number away from my sight would forestall the attack.

As the girl switched on a light, my mind cleared and the synesthetic attack faded. I recoiled from the disturbing images of the lapses, but they were now a part of me. I followed the girl up a flight of stairs (she went slowly, placing one foot beside the other on each step), and I remembered Slenje's vermilion love-making. I tried perversely to will the attack to return, as if the distraction of the sickness would add an extra sensation to the act of sex.

We came to a small bedroom by the top of the stairs, which,

although close and airless in the heat, was clean and tidy. It was lit by a single light-bulb, which glared harshly against the white-painted walls.

Elva, the girl, said, "I'd like the fifty now."

It was the first time she had faced me as she spoke, and in doing so revealed the inside of her mouth. Like those of the dark-haired girl, Elva's teeth were broken and jagged. I recoiled mentally from her, this sudden fastidiousness of mine making me uncertain of what I had been expecting. Elva must have noticed my reaction, for she smiled at me with her lips lifted away from her teeth: then I saw that they were not broken by decay or neglect, but that every single tooth, upper and lower, had had a piece broken away from it in a clean line, as if with a surgical instrument.

I said nothing, remembering that the enemy had occupied the town. I reached into my pocket and took out the money.

"I only have a hundred," I said, and slipped one of the notes from the wad, returning the rest to my pocket.

She took the note.

"I have change," she said, and opened a drawer. For a few seconds she searched through it, and while her back was turned I stared appraisingly at her body. In spite of her physical affliction, which gave her the movements of an old woman, she was very youthful, and I felt pity for her, mingling with the sexual desire which was even now asserting itself.

At last she turned, and showed me five silver ten-piece coins. She placed them in a neat pile on top of the dresser.

I said to her, "Elva . . . please keep the money. I must leave."

I was shamed by her degraded state, shamed by my use of her.

Her only reply was to lean down by the side of the bed, and turn the switch of a power-point. An electric fan whirred round, sending a welcome draft through the stuffy room. As she straightened, I saw that behind the thin fabric of her blouse her nipples were erect.

She began to undo the buttons of the blouse.

"Elva, I cannot stay with you."

She paused then to look at me. "You regret your choice?"

Before I could answer, before I had to answer, we both heard a sudden cry coming from nearby. Elva turned away from me immediately and went to a door on the opposite side of the room. She opened this and went through, leaving it open behind her.

I saw that beyond the door there was another room, small and dark, filled with the sound of whining insects, and in it was a tiny bed. A child had fallen from it and lay on the floor, crying. Elva picked up the naked child—it was a little boy, no more than a year old—and held him to her, trying to soothe him. For a few minutes, the boy was inconsolable, tears running down his bright pink face, saliva glossing his chin. Elva kissed him.

I saw that the little boy, in falling from the bed, had landed on his hand, for when Elva took the hand in hers he screamed with pain. Elva kissed the hand.

She kissed the fingers, and she kissed the palm . . . and she kissed the tiny, puffy wrist.

Elva opened her mouth, and some trick of the bright light in the main bedroom made her white chipped teeth shine momentarily. She brought the little boy's hand up to her lips . . . and then she took the fingers into her mouth, sucking and working her lips forward, until at last the entire hand was inside her mouth. All the while she caressed his arm, making tender, soothing noises in her throat.

At last the little boy stopped crying, and his eyes closed. She laid him on the bed, drew the covers over him and tucked them under the mattress . . . then came back to where I waited for her.

◆

Elva took off her clothes, and so I undressed, too. We climbed into the bed, and in a while we made love. Elva kissed me passionately as we roused, and with my tongue I explored her mouth, feeling how each of her teeth had been fined to sharp edges. She bit my tongue and lips gently, as she had bitten the hand of the little boy, and there was a great tenderness to her.

She sobbed when we had finished, lying in the bed with her back toward me, and I stroked her hair and shoulders, thinking

I should leave. Our union had been brief, but for me, after months of enforced celibacy, memorable. There had not been Slenje's vermilion passion, for the synesthetics had let me alone, but Elva had been expert and seemingly affectionate. I lay with my eyes closed, wondering if I should ever return to her.

From the next room there came a quiet whimpering noise, and at once Elva left the bed and opened the interconnecting door. She peered at the child within, but seemed satisfied and closed the door again. She came back to the bed, where I was already sitting up, preparing to dress.

"Don't leave," she said.

"I've had my time," I said, my thoughts at variance with my words.

"You are not here for time," she said and pushed me down across the bed again.

She straddled me, kissing my neck and chest, letting her damaged teeth run tiny harmless scratches across my skin.

I roused again and tried to roll her over on to the bed beside me, but she stayed above me, continuing to kiss and suck at my skin.

And it seemed to me, as her mouth found my rigid organ and took it deep inside, that there was a sudden sense of lemon pleasure, and the liquid sounds of her mouth became as a hot pool of stagnant voices, endlessly circling. . . .

◆

I became aware of my own identity, and it took the shape of the capital letter I. It was surrounded by whiteness and stood out clear and black against it. My eyes were wide open, staring at the ceiling of the dingy room, but my actual vision was subordinated to the inner perception of myself. The letter I became larger and thicker; the lower crossline vanished, the upper one became a solid triangle with rounded corners.

I pulsed rhythmically.

I was surrounded by knives, flickering in light from an unseen source. I pulsed toward them, shrank away. The blades of the knives glinted irregularly, for their cutting edges were not evenly honed. One knife moved toward I, its jagged edge shining, and I shrank away. The knife withdrew.

Then there was the white, stagnant pool, radiating warmth. The voices sucked I in; identity was lost, as one with the rest.

Then the kaleidoscope of colored pleasure: bursting from below, spinning so fast that the colors blended optically to a creaming white.

But no vermilion.

◆

I said, when I had dressed, "Take a hundred."

"Fifty, we agreed."

"Not for that."

She was still lying on the bed, face down, and her hair was blowing in the cool stream from the electric fan. I noticed that the skin on the back of her legs had been damaged in some way: there was a pattern of barely detectable scars high on each thigh.

I looked at the five silver coins lying on the top of the dresser. "I'll leave them there anyway. Buy something for the boy."

She sat up and came slowly over to me, her pale skin blotched with red where she had lain. She took the five coins and slipped them determinedly into the breast pocket of my shirt.

"Fifty."

That was the end of it.

From the next room I heard the sound of her child again, who was waking. He was muttering quietly to himself. Elva heard him too, for she looked briefly in that direction.

"You have a husband?" I said, and she nodded. "Where is he?"

"The whores took him."

"Whores?"

"The enemy. They took him when they left, the bitches."

There had been sixteen hundred female troops in Winho Town during the occupation, and every man had been held in captivity. When the town was relieved by our troops, the men had been taken away as the enemy withdrew. Only the very old or very young had been left behind.

"Is he still alive?" I said, when she had finished speaking.

"I suppose so . . . how do I know?"

She was sitting, naked still, on the edge of the bed. I expected her to cry again, but her eyes were dry.

"Do you want me to stay?" I said.

"No . . . please go."

"Shall I come again?"

"If you want to."

The little boy in the next room was beginning to cry. I opened the door, went down the stairs, and a moment later was outside the house.

◆

The following day I discovered that a ferry would be calling in the afternoon, and I decided to leave Winho. While I was waiting I walked slowly through the narrow streets of the town, wondering if I would see Elva.

The day was humid, and I undid the buttons at the front of my shirt to let my skin breathe more easily. It was then I noticed that a tracery of fine scratches had appeared across my chest, and I remembered Elva's sharpened teeth, delicately teasing at my neck and chest. I touched one of the longer scratches with my finger, but there was no painful sensation.

The town, languid in the heat, seemed to be moist and soft, and the air which surrounded me was like the embrace of fur. It was only when I reached the harbor, and stood on the pier waiting for the ferry, that I realized I was suffering yet another synesthetic attack. It seemed to be a mild one, and I tried to disregard it.

I paced up and down the pier, trying to feel the real substance of the concrete surface through the rubbery, cushioned texture my sensations lent it. My mouth and throat were sore, tasting synesthetically scarlet, and my genital organs were hurting as if trapped in a vise.

Glancing down, I saw that several of the scratches had opened, for blood was smearing where my shirt flapped against me.

At last the ferry arrived, and I went along to its berth with the other waiting passengers. Knowing I should have to pay the fare again, I reached for the wad of notes in my back pocket

. . . but then remembered the difficulty I had had with the high-denomination notes on the outward journey. I still had the five silver coins that Elva had given me, and I reached into the breast pocket of my shirt.

Something soft and warm wrapped itself about my two searching fingers, and I withdrew them at once.

I found a hand gripping my fingers!

It was a small, perfect hand, a child's hand. It was pink in the bright daylight, severed at the wrist.

I stepped back, shaking my hand in wild horror.

The child's hand gripped me more tightly.

I let out a cry of fright and swung my arm frantically, trying to throw off the little hand, but when I looked again it was still there. I turned away from the bustle of the other passengers on the quayside, and took hold of it with my free hand and tried to wrench it away. I pulled and pulled, perspiring with horror and tension . . . but nothing I could do would make it relax its hold. I could see the effect on itself of the grip: a whiteness around the knuckles and beneath the tiny nails.

No one on the quayside was taking any notice of me, for there was much movement to and fro of other passengers. I stared round in anguish, feeling I should never be released from the nightmare of the severed hand.

I made one more attempt to free myself by pulling with my other hand; then, in desperation, I put my trapped fingers on the concrete surface of the quay and pressed down on top of it with my boot. I leaned forward, putting as much weight on my hand as I could bear. The child's hand relaxed a little, and I pulled my fingers away. Suddenly I was free, and I jumped back.

The child's hand lay on the quay, still tightly clenched.

The the fingers opened, and the hand began to crawl toward me like a bloated pink spider.

I stepped forward and brought my boot down on it with all my weight. I stamped again, and then again, and again. . . .

◆

There was another argument on the boat, and to avoid it I let the ferry man keep the banknote without paying me change. I was in no condition to argue with him: I was shaking convulsively, and the pain I had noticed earlier in my mouth and chest and in my genitals was growing worse with every minute. When the business of the fare had been settled I went to the back of the boat and sat alone, trembling and frightened. The sea was clean; calm and blue in the windless heat.

My shirt was now stained with blood in several places, and I took it off. I felt on the outside of the breast pocket to see if the coins were still there. I could not bring myself to feel inside with my fingers again. At last I held the pocket open upside-down above the deck, but nothing fell out.

As the boat moved out to sea, and the island of Winho became distant behind us, I sat bare-chested in the sun, watching one scratch after another ooze blood down my body. I dared not try to speak to anyone, for my mouth was an open pit of pain.

The boat went from one island in the archipelago to the next, but I did not leave it until nightfall. By then we were at the island of Salay, and I went ashore. That night I slept in the local garrison, having to share a large room with sixteen other officers and men. My dreams were rich and textured with agony and lurid colors, and an uncontrollable and unfulfilled sexual desire. In the morning, the sheets of the bed were stiff with the blood from my wounds.

*Of* GREGOR HARTMANN *I can tell you no more than that he lives about fifty miles from San Francisco, or at least has a post office box in a town fifty miles from San Francisco, and has had a couple of stories published in* Galaxy. *I asked him for some additional information— "educational background, occupation, age, that kind of thing, just to put you in some sort of context for the readers," but his only reply was, "Sorry, but contexts don't equal me. Besides, readers would snag on them and the runs would ruin their brains." So be it. Superficial evidence (literary style, punctuation habits, typewriter make) indicates that he is probably not a pseudonym for James Tiptree, Jr. Further speculation seems impertinent; and, in or out of context, we have this literally dazzling short story to enjoy and admire.*

■

# Gregor Hartmann

■

# SUN-1

Corridors blue-white this cycle. Alternating rings. I wear gray.
Zip to my station: sooty ion accelerating down linear tube. Rico-
chet right-angle thru crested doorway. Into chamber domi-
nated by pyramid. Levels of metal, levels of people. Climbing
to the Alexis apex. I rise to A minus one. Hand on Paula's
shoulder. Intent on board. (Good girl, that Paula. Wants to rise.)
Twenty minutes. She stands. I slide into place. Shake head to
lower cowl for less distraction. Concentrate. Lights offer red-
yellow-green. Sheets of energy surge thru board. Surface hot.
Sun 5780° and rising. Hands dance over board. Fire fingers like
meat torpedoes at cowering buttons. Stroke our shield. Steady:

| GREEN | GREEN | GREEN |
|-------|-------|-------|
| 1.02 | 1.2 | 1.54 |
| .95 | .999 | 1.007 |
| .91 | 1.083 | .86 |

"Fae, get quadrant one down," the Alexis says. I frown and
comply. Four boards below me. (As I, one of four to apex.) Think
and choose and punch: order trickles down another level: 1.54
subsides to 1.391. I wait. The A silent. Picky today, the boss is.
Primes probably monitoring his shift. Since Thirty-seven died, the
Alexis has lusted for her seat. So do others. Trouble brewing—
"Damp it down," mike rattles. Scat. Stab buttons. Tell Jeremy
(A minus two) to reroute energy. Shuffle field values at his level.
Where can we bleed energy? Ah. . . .
Order descends, response ascends. Pyramid flings signals to
surface, thence to satellites webbing Sun. Block that flare.
Shadow that spot. Lull? Divert the power.

Five hours. Shift ends. Snapped out of place, I wobble away from the fire.

◆

The polymer floor of the great cavern is marked with circles of orange. Between them, affinity-groups exercise. Limbs wave in centipedal unison.

Afterward, when Team is sated, individuals may duel.

A woman faces a man on one of the orange circles. Blonde and angular, her belly is firm, her breasts sag only slightly. Draining a water bubble, she tosses the rind into the crowd. She crouches. A scar materializes beneath the skin of her abdomen when she strains.

Like now.

Fae feinted a roundhouse kick with her right leg, hopped, swept in low with her left leg. But Alexis took to the air before she connected. Off-balance, she couldn't guard against his attack. Alexis knocked aside a feeble block and his knuckles grazed her throat. "Tsssso," he hissed, stepping back and bowing. She stared at him beneath lowered lids.

"You shouldn't try such intricate maneuvers. That one cost you the round. You took too long to shift your weight back for the sweep." Always the considerate superior, he muted his smile.

Fae shrugged. "I like to experiment."

Alexis crouched.

Three exchanges later, she feinted and swept in. This time when he jumped over her sweep, she let her momentum spin her completely around. When he attacked, overconfident, she was in position to deliver a thrust-kick with her right leg. She did.

The pink-robed novices around them applauded. Coaches grinned. Alexis, on the floor, flushed as the shimmer of applause fluttered around the cavern like mallard wings on an afternoon pond.

◆

Great cycle ends today. A four-year solar phoenix oscillation.

At approx 1820 PT Sun temperature crests, begins long plunge to cooler years. Planet gives up heat. Our duties lessen. Boards only half-crewed. Shifts lengthen to eight hours. (East at that.) We play, contemplate, screw, politick.

In forty days Primes will hold their triennial powershift. Control of key departments will rotate. Psychonumerist and Logician may argue about how to control Sun, but both respect our basic political structure. We are TEAM.

And Primes will replace Thirty-seven. Will they lift the Alexis across final line, from staffer to ruler? What sport, politics!

Presence behind me. Fingers click auto over board. Feel eyes chasing them. Sniffle. Ah, squad of novices. Pink-robed little bodies, overlarge heads. Come to tour front lines. I slump so they can see sunscreen. Square of hydrogen-alpha fury. Holy fire.

"Primes set magnetic policy," teacher whispers. "The thirty-two pyramids enforce it, each on their sector of Sun. From the apex down thru the levels of boards, Sun is divided into smaller and smaller units. The Alexis is responsible for one thirty-second of Sun. The person with a board on A minus six is responsible for only twenty-five million $km^2$."

Hans knows he won't disturb. But whispers for kids' sake. Add tension. He has a nice voice, Hans does. He too hungers for a Prime's white robe. A brilliant teacher, respected in education department. Will give the Alexis strong competition. Annoying, all this strife.

He's unbonded. Typical of empty males, craving power not relationships. Hmmm. Perhaps in a liaison I can teach *him*. . . .

"Variable stars of this class emit much radiation and changed matter. Without the shield, we would have been limited to the mining colonies on the Outer Worlds' moons. With it, we've opened Three, Four, and Five to surface habitation. There're only a few million techs living there now, but someday there'll be billions, whole new human societies.

"When your studies are suitably advanced, you'll be tested. If you qualify for a board, you'll start on A minus six. You'll learn to outguess Sun and maintain the magnetic barrier that lets us fragile animals play and work so close to annihilation. This is a vitally important task. You must approach it as Team, and with utmost seriousness."

Without looking around, I let focus drift. Readouts swing high/low as boards below me blindly follow cues. Overall pattern remains safe. Sun too hot to take chances. But figures drift to outer limits of tolerance. Hans's voice is amused, but the lecture continues. Novices suck it up, unaware of game.

A decimal separates me from yellow. Whoops. Carbon granule flares. Another 2° rise. Margin plummets to .001. I catch it, ordering lower boards to rally, blowing on the flow. Hans's voice snags, resumes. Novices have eyes only for screen, for colors.

Hans shepherds them to next level. Contrives to brush arm against me. Red curls peep from his cowl. I watch a small spot, wondering why rivals whisper of ruthlessness.

"Particles in quadrant one," the Alexis hisses from above. Ghost voice steeped in metal. I blink. Board glares:

| GREEN | GREEN | YELLOW |
|-------|-------|--------|
| .99   | 1.03  | 2.491  |
| .84   | 1.24  | 1.58   |
| .76   | .82   | 1.003  |

I mesh, hurried. Helium's golden glow strengthening. Vast ripples, surfacing all across my screen. How long unnoticed? I coordinate lessers to alter shield. Sift data grid toward gentle prime: the ONE. (We = ONE. I feel guilt at misleading lower boards to show off for Hans.) Stress lines seam forehead. Temperature up another 1°. Particles up too. The Alexis's mind burns down upon me. Watching. Glance at chronometer. Crest point passed. Sun burns hotter too.

Three hours. Shift ends. Sun 4° over record high.

And rising.

◆

"Newscomm said the terraform team on Three has the plankton cycle going well. The $CO_2$ is down by thirty percent."

"I'll believe it when it starts raining on the surface."

The doors chopped off the conversation, casting Fae adrift in the vast silence of the auditorium. They were into midgame,

she saw, as she picked her way closer to the repeater board
hanging over the pit. Alexis was white, Hans black. Each controlled about half the border of the Go board, but Alexis's stones
tended toward the inside. It looked as if white would control the
important center, confining black to the secure but slim zones
around the sides. She settled onto a ring only three from the
contestants, folded into lotus, and relaxed.

She should have been in her study cell meditating on the
latest series of Riemann-DeGroat differentials the operations
department had posted for board riders of her rank. Discipline
demanded two hours' study for every five hours on the board.
Hone efficiency. Let it slide and you risked displacement from
below, from those clawing for the top and the honorific Alexis.

*"what was your name, before apex?" she asked him once,
long ago.*

*he ran a finger around her breast, spiraling up to the nipple.
"I don't remember."*

*she blinked at the candles wavering beside his bed. "I'd re-
member mine if—" she bit her lip.*

*"if you took my place?" his nail sawed ever so gently the
button on her breast. "one of these days you'll have the experience to call me out and win apex. I've watched you coming up
the pyramid, Fae, every few years, you can handle more Sun.
you're good and I'm getting old. . . ."*

*"sssssshhhhhh." she hugged him away from*

Fae opened her eyes. The poor insecure man had broken
their bond when she won a board on the level directly below
his. Scat on his anxiety. He was fun in bed; shame he had to
worry about lessers slavering to replace him. And he added to
his tensions by competing for Prime with Hans and others.
What fool would *seek* responsibility for an increasingly erratic
star?

She'd feel sorry for him. Except that he brought it on himself,
with his damn power tropism.

Hans played R-9. Alexis responded with Q-11. Hans: R-13. An
unorthodox move that stirred the gallery. Hans, looking up,
spotted her and held his gaze. She smiled. Intent on the board,
Alexis didn't notice.

But the man seated next to her did. Fae knew him vaguely as a board rider on A minus four. A man who lacked the skill to monitor anything larger than a spot filament. A fading, gaunt man who would never miss a math drill. "Foolish move," he grunted, with the familiarity of off-duty personnel. "White can split black's stones with a single play."

Fae was noncommittal. It did look odd. Alexis played a precise, coherent game. His stones protected one another and clustered in little proto-eyes from which he could expand to take maximum territory with minimum risk. Hans's play was quirky and loose. Since the game embodied matrix theory, a skillful player might draw a Prime's attention, and possibly patronage. One couldn't rise to Prime on Go alone, but in a close vote . . .

The man looked as if he wanted to talk. So Fae produced a stick of vegetex from her sleeve and crunched into it. Eating alone was bad, Teambook decreed. He scented deviance and looked away.

Fae sighed as she watched the boys duking it out. Such drive! She was glad she hadn't been raised in one of the on-planet creches.

She'd joined the Shieldteam in her twenties, by choice rather than by birth. She'd given up a placid career track on one of Seven's moons because a life as an actuary didn't satisfy. She wanted to pour her math skills into something significant, something exciting. Sitting beneath One's skin and fighting Sun five hours a day fused mind and body into demigod. If only her co-workers weren't such . . . drones.

Fae positioned a glob of vegetex in her cheek, so she could extract juice by pressing with her tongue. She was very oral; mealtime meant pleasure. That was why she'd suggested fishponds.

The idea had arisen at the weekly meeting of her affinity group. *How can we improve our Team environment?* The others suggested inanities like reprogramming the corridor colors. So she'd proposed fishponds in the dining chambers. Imagine big slow carp, drifting past the tables, poised to scarf down leftovers.

The suggestion, half in jest, almost cost her a level. The four board riders directly below her detected a wandering mind; during the next ten days each called her out. As usual her math skills added up to victory, but the drain in time and energy had been frightening. And later Alexis warned that a marshal questioned him about her stability.

She wondered if the Prime files listed her under Latent Subjectivist. Fae smiled at the idea of herself as rebel. Psychonumerist Primes argued for looser control over Sun and Logician Primes argued for tighter control. But both accepted the premise that humans should dwell in the Inner System and make Sun fit their needs. Subjectivists (it was said; no one ever admitted being one) wanted to evacuate the Inner System. Subjectivists prefered the stability of generations ago, when humanity limited itself to the Outer Worlds and let Sun run its cycles unhindered. Nonpolitical Fae had ignored such games, treating Prime position paper and Subjectivist graffiti with the same contempt.

Now, though, with Sun overheating, she wondered if Subjectivists had a point—

Codger gasped. Had he sensed her heterodoxy? But her neighbor was staring at the game, where Hans had just occupied a weak corner in Alexis's northern line, cutting off a chain of whites. Adrift in a sea of black, line of escape blocked, they faced certain annihilation. And from that side Hans could sweep into the center. Alexis could save either his corners or part of his center troops—but not the game.

Fae's toes wiggled in applause.

◆

"Damn it, keep an eye on twelve. Kick it up another quantum. The entire sector is porous."

Mike rattles with base. The Alexis snaps now. Force board into trim. Another satellite burned out. Realign those remaining. Punch-punch-punch-punch. Stretched thin, but fields holding. Protons halted or diverted to empty space. Glance at chronometer. Only ten minutes into shift. Sigh.

Sunscreen: fire$^2$. Spectro says metal lines strengthening. Hydrogen excited. Cooler G-stage molecules broken and gone.

Screen seethes. Electrons from CRT pelt forehead. Stir damp blonde strands. Heat seems to beat from it. Our pyramid bustles. Sun roars.

6800° and rising. Slowly, at least. (Slope = 1/6.) Back aches. Thighs hurt where Hans's fingers dug in. An insecure lover. Insists on guiding first orgasm. Only afterward may I lead. Even then, he dislikes aggressiveness. Won't lie still and let me caress —insists on responding. Why does he want *me?* Very preoccupied. Talks politics. Am I a sink for him to drain off tension? An A minus one status symbol? What does he want—

"Fae, pay attention to quadrant three," the growl comes.

Patch in reserve. Squander energy to alter satellites' orbits. Don't worry about that now. The Alexis's mood warns me. He had three engineers arrested for anti-Team activities. (Rumor-spreading. Something about dissipator overload.) Hans denounced arrests in his complex numbers class. Said careless charges of Subjectivism disrupt Teamwork. Both play for attention of Primes, themselves under intense pressure from Outer Worlds to keep the lid on Sun. Control very important nowdays.

Newscomm is blithe. "Minor problems." Yet no one can go out on surface. Even armorcars kept below.

Prominences flare across my sector. Bubbling slow at first. Then faster, higher, out into space. Gouts of fire and matter to bombard planets. Splatter red, orange, fade to gold. Shock pulses from core roil surface of Sun. Another 3°. I plead for power, get it. Barely in time. (Must allow for lightspeed delay in transmitting orders to satellites.) Arms ache. Fingers leaden on buttons. Twenty-three minutes into shift. Four hours thirty-seven minutes left. Another flare. The bites on my breasts itch. No time to scratch. Another flare.

Steel voice: "The heat curve has just passed an inflection point. Sun is getting hotter faster."

◆

Alexis brooded on the dais, head sunk in thought, oblivious to the murmurs of the assembled. His nose shielded the little gray moustache, sole adornment of his potato face. Fae wondered what expressions he permitted himself in the privacy of his

board, when 80 kilos of meat sat down to manipulate one-thirty-
second of a star. Did he laugh when he ordered energy into a
weak spot in the shield? Did he snarl when a spot crept over the
horizon? Did flares make his anus clench?

Fae wondered if, during the quiet times, he fed false cues to
the boards below him. If he toyed with her.

She circulated at random, drifting with the current, avoiding
capture by groups. No one knew anything and rumors propa-
gated in inverse proportion to the absence of hard data. A red
infinity sign had been painted outside the operations department office. A fresh outbreak of Subjectivism; readings of the
Teambook will be broadcast daily and affinity groups will meet
three times a week.

Psychonumerists and Logicians were said to be debating—
bitterly—how to restore control of Sun. Psychonumerists
wanted to release more energy into the system, despite the
radiation risk, like a safety valve. Logicians wanted to ride it
out. One rumor was that the powershift would be suspended
until the crisis passed to prevent unilateral moves by either
side. Another rumor was that so much energy had been built up
that any release would sterilize the entire system.

Sweatstink fogged the chamber. Fae dried her palms on her
gray robe. They were ripe for mass-flash psychosis. Why had
Alexis gathered his shift—over 5,000 people—in such dangerous times?

A white-robed Prime sat on the dais behind Alexis, an authority symbol that failed to reassure. Primes resided on the deepest
levels of the base, safe from Sun, thinking the slow math currents in which lesser fish like Fae swam. Primes seldom stirred
themselves to tread the upper levels. Why now?

The ceiling was programmed red, yellow, violet. The ozone
level had been set high. Tensions hovered like thunderstorm.
Alexis had something cathartic planned. Others sensed it, too.
It was as if her nerves had been painted on the surface of her
skin. She drifted, restless, annoyed to see people clustering with
others on the same board level, or trailing those who served a
level higher.

Hans's red bush flashed across the way. Damn. She'd told that

bastard she never wanted to see him again. He didn't have to
be here; teachers had a separate hierarchy. But of course he'd
come to keep an eye on his rival for Prime. She changed course
to avoid him. If that swine expected her—

The chamber dimmed. She halted, swaying, as the crowd
crystallized. A dull subsonic vibration rumbled her chest.

In the darkness, a single cone of light:

The body of Alexis came to life. Jerkily. Like a slowly energiz-
ing android. (The Prime melted to a light blur, teasing the edge
of awareness.) Alexis's head rose, froze. Then it scanned the
multitude, center-left-center-right-center. His arms crossed on
his chest. His legs straightened and propelled his body forward.
A step. Two. Then his mind returned, smashing back in to fill
his carcass and he stiffened staggered groaned.

"My people, people of Shieldteam, shepherds not in vain. We
are beset, the foe is near, with us, as it is above. You know its
name. You bear the blame. For you have let it infect you. You
vowed to abandon the evil. You failed. Now we must purge. For
your offense is a stench unto Primes. Say it."

Silence.

"What is the word?"

self

"Louder."

*Self*

"Louder!"

SELF SELF SELF SELF SELF

Five thousand throats roared forth the forbidden sound. Fae
closed her eyes to concentrate on forcing out the sound. Both
lungs burned as its roots ripped free. It clogged her throat; she
sobbed it out. Blue fire burst across her eyeballs. Hollow and
squeezing herself thru her throaty column of pain: SELF SELF
SELF SELF SELF SELF SELF SELF SELF SELF SELF SELF
SELF

She stumbled on the syllable and stopped. The echoes subsided. Abashed, she opened her eyes. People looked away, to
the floor, anywhere but at each other. Guilt was waist-deep. A
dim flicker of reason attributed it to the subsonics, the dark
colors now massing overhead. But her body screamed. Her

body wanted to fall down curl up hide, to run away. Only crowd pressure held her back. She needed someone to soothe her. Someone with Authority.

"Thus we purge the taint," Alexis's voice sliced through the moans. He was more human now, moving his hands and pacing, but still in control. "A little kollective songfest, iss good for the gestalt, eh?" His head shook. "Not enough. Not enough. There are still negative people who must be removed before we can again be TEAM."

Fae tracked the arrow of his gaze and pierced Hans. Her mouth opened. Fear washed away her anger at Hans's cynical attempt to use her to learn Alexis's weak points. Alexis raised his arms, hands cupped as if holding a globe. He strained aloft, sucking them in, then smashed it down. Amid the shards, he flung an arm.

"That man is a Subjectivist. Arrest him."

A line of blue-robed marshals plowed through the crowd, a serpent coiling about its prey. Hans, pinned by three spotlights, made no effort to escape. Fae saw him smile. Probably plotting his next move, calculating how to turn a political trial to his advantage. The scheming bastard. How could a man make love for political—

The crowd muttered, since the competition for the vacant Prime seat was known to many. Fae's fingernails dug into her palms. The crowd was on edge; she could scream, cry foul, ignite the subterranean corridors with riot.

Blues flowed around the young teacher and closed. Fae trembled.

Then she pulled her cowl tight and pushed away from the light, gray fading into black.

◆

Flares. Granules erupt. Gas sputters. Filaments. Boiling gases. Incandescent. Lumbering across my screen: massive spot cluster. Immense magnetic storm raging. Spots scab half screen. Still growing. Must reach deep into Sun. Have tracked it three rotations now. Since it loomed over horizon this time, has grown like cancer. Still spreading. Flares. If Sun erupts—

Punch buttons. Remorseless, efficient. Thirteen years on
boards; no need to think. Machine on machine. Even so:

| RED | RED | RED |
|---|---|---|
| 6.05 | 5.94 | 5.328 |
| 7.218 | 6.7 | 6.52 |
| 6.63 | 6.14 | 5.987 |

We fuel mag torus around Sun with its own energy. Furnace
binds itself. Until now. Too much energy. System overloaded.
Safety vortices filled with particles. Can't divert thru pole holes.
Too highly charged. Protons tear thru shield, on to planets.
Surge of only few percent could distort fields to collapse, destroy torus. Pent-up energy released at once: wave front ripples
out over system: naked planets fry. . . .

Screen shimmers. Blurs. Shift channels, hunting one clearer.
Surface of planet melting. Sun 8210° and rising. Our surface
several meters deep in molten rock during day. Antennae won't
melt—they're shafts of metal impaling mountains. Melt flows to
lowlands, leaves metal clear. But heat, radiation bombardment
create stray currents. Distort images beamed from remaining
satellites. Only 45 percent satellite web operational. Must must
improvise. Another channel. Image solidifies.

Spots center on screen. Immense wicked things. Eyes. Ther-
monuclear evil eyes. Rainbow fringes of ionized calcium. Another 6° jump.

"Sandra has a lull. We'll shift power to you," the Alexis says,
before I can ask. I make connections, guide lower boards in
weaving new web, send signals. Hope they get thru solar noise.
After minutes, particle count drops slightly. Done it again, Fae,
old girl.

Mike hums. Open line. The Alexis's mind hovers behind
mesh. Peekaboo. I wait, arms working auto. What more can he
say? Seconds clot. We're naked to each other's silence. Mike
clicks off.

I slump, still punching buttons. The Alexis's self-control is
frayed. Indecision among his superiors results in conflicting orders. Sun never so wild. Our efforts to contain only make it
worse. Formulae and petitions circulate as Primes argue how to

extricate ourselves from balancing act without nova. Primes
slice one another with paper weapons, poke with sharp theo-
rems. Uncertainty trickles to lower boards. Rumors that Primes
will abandon them and flee planet in secret ships. (Never mind
how, with surface meters deep in lava.) Random fistfights ex-
plode in corridors. Three suicides in Trend Analysis section.
Pyramid 27 off air for three hours yesterday; other pyramids
had to cover its sector. Newscomm never said why. Rumors
suggest sabotage (Subjectivist) to shut down shield and let Sun
restore its own equilibrium.

I keep opinions to . . . me. I struggle to stay clear. I know they
watch me, since Hans escaped. Hidden by supporters, he issues
leaflets criticizing the Alexis's orders. Our liaison is dead, murdered by his manipulation. But marshals don't believe. I struggle to stay clear. Serve only my board. Duty.

While Sun burns brighter . . .

I glance over shoulder to shift neck pain. Busy levels below.
Boards aglow. Red, everywhere red. Gray-clad arms shuttle.
Ironic role reversal: no one wants higher boards now. Extra
responsibility shunned. Too much stress. Too much tension.
Despite a klick of rock overhead, some "feel" Sun. Every shift
more riders burn out and must be replaced by promotion from
lower boards. Inexperienced riders = more mistakes.

Beads of blue intrude below. Marshals. Trotting, spiraling up
from depths. Another purge. Wish the Alexis would settle down
to business. Disturbing, these charges of Subjectivism. Especially when they arrest on-duty personnel as example to others.
Top board riders have been taken in some pyramids. Paranoia
is rife. No one trusts.

Blue looms. Hands clutch my arms. Jerk up. A stranger slides
into my seat. Takes *my* board. I cry out: not *me*—

Click.

◆

Unplugged, she refused to become undone.

Alone in her domicile, she amused herself by watching Newscomm and trying to assemble the official shadows into reality.
But one day, in mid-program, the screen went black.

No one came to interrogate her. So:

—Fae brushed her hair. Since she didn't stand watch, she could let it fall free. Her blonde mane was thick except at the pate. Some of the older women were bald from years of stress. She brushed and brushed, wondering if her easygoing ways would compensate.

—Fae rearranged her pots, creating new patterns and sequences. She threw them on a potter's wheel a girl friend made for her. There was a soothing rhythm to shaping clay. And she liked to make something more durable than a few webers of magnetic flux. The first pots were misshapen and awkward. Some of the later approached precision. She kept them all, lining her shelves, although once when angry she broke a blue wine goblet over a liaison's thick skull.

—Fae painted her aerophyte. Its long dangle roots were bland chalk. Watercolors gave it pastel banding, a nest of coral snakes seeping from the clay pot. (See above.) The aerophyte didn't mind. It was a slow, sleepy thing, given to thoughts of porphyry and onyx.

Being under arrest really wasn't so bad. She entertained herself and let the walls thicken and the tunnel maze outside close up. Once she heard shouts thru the door. Another time a boom, followed by rumbling. Fae didn't go out. She didn't even try the door. She hadn't touched it since the marshals conducted her to her room. It might or might not be locked. She didn't want to know. If they wanted to isolate her from the power games, fine. Let others wrestle with math and Sun. She'd relax.

But one day the door opened. Smoke poured in, around a masked figure in white robes. She knew—somehow—it wasn't a Prime.

From her lotus on the floor she studied the man who'd broken her meditation. He had Hans's shoulders, but his poise was that of Alexis. Fae remained silent and waited for some sign that would narrow the probabilities.

Finally his right hand crept from his sleeve. In it: a wafer bearing the red infinity symbol. "I wondered when a Subjectivist would show up," she coughed. Acrid air; hissing and crackling down the corridor.

She considered attacking; her abdomen tensed. His robe

would hamper; she wore only briefs. From the floor she could hit him before he suspected. Roll into his legs and bring him down and rip off the mask—

Too late. While she prepared to spring, his left hand emerged, distorter ready and aimed.

Fae's shoulders melted. She bent her head from the smoke and touched her tongue to the wafer. With a slap of lemon dust . . .

◆

flickers . . . board flickers . . . buttons float in space, a neat reet grid . . . board returns, buttons vanish . . . pits . . . holes . . . pits swirl into moiré, a whirlpool

spinning reverses . . . scattershot, pelting random snow . . . Sun burns above it, pulsing energy . . . hole in Sun, so bruised & vast . . . white on gold on amber onward—thus:

| LEMON | FAWN | COBALT |
|-------|------|--------|
| 37 | 43 | 53 |
| 23 | 1 | 61 |
| 13 | 5 | 73 |

cobalt drips off Sun, flows cross screen, puddles into quadrants 3 & 4, trickles down over board, flows around pits, drops off floats off

buttons bubble in my brain . . . albumen strands dangle inside skull . . . moss in head tickles . . . thoughts bubble too close, moss fans off

outside, where limbs coil—outside: abandoned metal mountain. i caper aloft, smoke dancing with me . . . past brokenmeat-people, red & white . . . far below, apex is *so* high . . . dizzy-made. bigscreen blares bigpiece of Sun . . . scent hot metal, hot smoke. . . .

Sun = millions billions dots

shimmering

silly me, thinking i controlled Sun . . . Sun played with me me me me me . . . electron caresses. Sun reached thru antennae to twitch my neurons, string me along. . . . smother in satellite touches. . . . Oh Powerful Sun

dots coalesce . . . Sun shimmers & shifts: a face . . . smiling

from big screen. . . . Hans. No, Alexis . . . white light teeth, dark
spot of moustache, red swirls. . . . Alexis/Hans? big eyes glow
with hydrogen mating fury.

lover. hands of flesh & fire. . . . Hans/Alexis, where now? alone
up here in smoke, am i . . . alone in the apex seat

oh, you bastards. . . .

master override. i click—

pyramid is mine. pyramid = me.

flexing fingers that threaten of melt, pressing flesh to whirlpool, I gather power to snuff Him out.

*Last year's* New Dimensions *offered* J. A. LAWRENCE's *"Twinkle, Twinkle, Little Bat," and she returns herewith with a second, even more elegantly playful story. Not that zaniness and tomfoolery are the universal characteristics of this American-born, European-based writer: she was all seriousness in such memorable stories as "Opening Problem" and "The Persistence of Memory," published in* Galaxy *in 1974, and it is only the luck of the draw that* New Dimensions *readers get to see her more kittenish side. Ms. Lawrence was the late James Blish's second wife, but she is emerging now as a formidable science fiction writer in her own right.*

■

# J. A. Lawrence

■

# THIS IS MY BELOVED

It is nevertheless a fact that the horizon looks flat until one is taught to conceive of it as a curve. Thereafter it is never quite so flat to the eye as before.

◆

Beulah, they called it. The planet was idyllic. They sent back the codes for "Super place!" and "Come and get it!" and set the scout gently down in the only swamp in the western hemisphere. By the time the food-gathering party returned to the landing place, Janet—the crew—was sitting on a tree branch dangling her feet in the water; and the scout was gone.

"Sank," she said succinctly.

August turned red and made the speech that a commander was supposed to give to a rating who had endangered the life of an exploration crew after landing. Margo the engineer remarked that all one had to do was use a little sense, the scout was designed to deal with planetary liftoff for heaven's sake and all one would have needed to do was rise above such a small matter as a swamp.

Janet shrugged. "Not me," she said and moved up in the tree.

She wasn't prepared to explain how the antiquated electrical ignition system had failed as black mud came sloshing over the portholes, and the backup dynamo had sighed and let it go at that, and she had just barely managed to get herself, the log unit, and the long-distance communicator out. They had never liked her, they had never trusted her, and if they chose to assume that she had stranded them on Beulah out of stupidity,

so be it. And as for Norform, or whatever his name was, who had
been sent along by the crew-mating computer—well, she had
never held a high opinion of computers. The three of them sat
down on the edge of the swamp and muttered and gestured at
each other; then August glared up and commanded her to de-
scend. She thumbed her nose at him.

Eventually she had to come down. They had gathered the
food they went out for.

"We've been taking stock of what we have left," began August. "All the tools are in the swamp. The manuals and guidebooks are also in the swamp. Shut up, Margo." The engineer
subsided. Janet smiled. Margo probably wanted to explain to
them all that she knew how to cook and didn't need a manual,
or something. Norform listened attentively to August, who
pompoused on.

"We shall have to set up a shelter. We all know how to build
shelters of natural materials, even if we haven't had much practice; it was part of our field training. We have still got the knives,
the ax, the food bags, and the water carriers that we had with
us, thank heaven. How could you have been so goddamn stupid,
crew?"

"Bugger you," said Janet, having eaten. She slipped off into
the woods and breathed free air. How glorious it would be not
to have to listen to—much less obey—that ass any longer! He
could have Margo, and what's-his-name could practice the as-
ceticism that turned him on so much. Whee! She picked up a
dangling vine and swung on it. It was not a snake, it did not bite
her, it did not choke her, but carried her Tarzanly across the
bayou in the warm air, back and forth, stirring only some raucous little birds.

"Hoy!" she shouted on a return swing. "A boat's coming!"

She watched the others leap to their feet stiff-legged, seize
their little rayguns and stunbeams and stuff from their belts,
and stand braced back to back.

"Where?" called August tightly.

"Behind you." She laughed as they slowly rotated, trying to
discover behind whom the boat had appeared. By this time it
had drawn up against a mossy tree root and she could see the

prow with a lovely hideous birdish head carved on it. She slowed down her swinging, since the widest arc of her vine would bring her feet over the longboat. She peered and peered to see who would get out of it, but the canoe rocked quietly. No tall figures in feathered headdresses naked but for a loincloth, or anything else interesting, leaped out of it shouting and brandishing primitive weapons. She swung idly, watching the trio of dedicated spacers still revolving like the blades of a punkah on the mound. Finally she dropped down and ran over to join them.

"Natives!" she said cheerfully. "Who needs you guys?" She stripped off her Regulation Explorer's Fabrisuit, Serial No. F22–3459–8Y; her Regulation Explorer's Undersuit, Serial No. FU22–6739–3X; her Regulation Explorer's Coverall, Serial No. FUC22–6947–6B; and her Regulation Explorer's (Female) knickers, and kicked the pile into the swamp. No clouds of insects rose from its stagnant waters, for Beulah was an idyllic planet and its insects were uninterested in the secretions of humankind. The others stared at her horrified, still in trifoliate formation, weapons at the ready.

August spluttered in outrage. "Wasting more government property, that's what you're doing, you—you vagabond!"

"Wasn't losing the whole scoutship good enough, you have to drop your knickers in the swamp as well?" said Margo nastily.

Norform averted his eyes from her exuberant figure. He had always preferred to mate in the dark.

There was a loud yelp as the trio were suddenly lifted off their feet and dragged away, yowling and carrying on. Or off. Janet sauntered after them, trying to see what had got them. It had to be natives from the canoe; but squint as she might, she couldn't seem to get them in focus. She said finally, as she trailed along behind the shrieking, struggling Commander, Engineer and Planetographer, "Hey! What about me? Don't I get some too?"

They reached the boat. The three earth people were dumped in, and of course immediately tried to clamber out. However, there seemed to be invisible bonds holding them, for their sweaty efforts were in vain.

Meanwhile Janet underwent a sensation of becoming much taller. Something was touching her feet, and she had a feeling of being surrounded at knee-level. How could invisible creatures of such a height accomplish an easy capture of adults of two meters or more? Then she became aware that the beings were far from knee-high. They were prostrate upon the ground, and the touch was of their foreheads lying at her feet. For one fleeting moment she regretted her Regulation Explorer's Fabrisuit.

Softly, *things* brushed her bare legs and fell away.

The light grew dimmer, slanting down opalescent through the saprophytic hangings of the bayou forest. Looking down, she noticed blurred shadows moving along the uncertain ground. As the natives passed in front of the lowering sun they cast faint linear patterns on the water and on the moss. They seemed very tall—twice as tall as her own well-defined shadow —and narrow and willowy as antique fashion plates, but with larger heads. The shadows moved around the boat, and the three spacers squirmed and grumbled as they were pushed into cramped positions. Then she felt herself led, lifted into the canoe, and escorted stumbling over the heaving backs of her colleagues to the prow, where invisible limbs pressed her to be seated on a polished board.

The boat moved slowly toward the sunset, where the only shadows were pooled in the bottom of the canoe or broken by the rippling of the gilded water.

They arrived somewhere, after an hour or so of crossing open water. As far as Janet could tell, it was identical to the place they had just left, except for the swamp. The earthmen were bundled out of the canoe and carried, still protesting, up a small knoll exactly like the one upon which they had mounted their back-to-back defense, and toward a random scattering of vertical blocks. These were far more visible than not. The shapes were slightly out of true, tall warped slabs facing out over the water against a wall of misty plants. Her perception of heights was becoming distorted; she could not tell if the plants were trees or small shrubs, nor how distant they were. The light was mottling as the sun sank, and the elongated forms of the natives were peripherally visible as they broke the paths of the dying rays now and again.

The three captives were placed carefully in the clearing. They sat lashed back to back, trying to rise to their feet, but too agitated to coordinate a mutual effort. Janet wandered around the clearing, glad to find that the soil underfoot was less quaky than in the swamp area, and peered at the slablike structures. It was impossible to tell if they had doors or windows, for not only was the light fast becoming twi-, but the optical effects here made the line between visible and invisible rather thicker than usual.

As darkness finally fell, a plain, ordinary, magnificent blue and orange and yellow bonfire was lit in the clearing on the knoll. The captives were carried gently toward it and carefully placed within. They were served some time later, ceremoniously, on a sort of large porous plank, surrounded by tatty-looking leaves. Janet was beginning to feel a little out of her depth.

In the days to follow she discovered that she was no lonelier than usual. The natives managed to convey that for some inexplicable reason she had been found to be a Sacred Person and therefore inedible; a Sacred Person and therefore to be fawned upon, if opportunity offered. Nevertheless, they didn't seem to like her much. She tried to get some sort of grasp of their language, which was quite clearly audible, however hard it was to see them, and she worked out a notation system for their sounds—guttural and liquid at the same time, like Japanese. They fed her reverently on a diet consisting mostly of vegetation, relying heavily on a grass-grain of a revolting purple, augmented by various lumps of solid material that she hoped were adequate in vital amino acids. She never fell ill, her weight remained stable, and she felt fine. She decided to accept her luck and not inquire too closely.

The cannibalism of her new companions sometimes depressed her. It was all very well being worshiped, and it was all very well being fed regularly with ambiguous proteins, but with an almost invisible congregation which only became quite clearly to be seen as part of the animal kingdom when cooked, it was occasionally just a trifle lonesome. She followed them around making copious notes on bits of bark with a shell, until she had memorized the whole range of the twilcchy Beulan utterances. Then she began in earnest to try to communicate.

It was irksome in that the natives would go to great lengths to avoid her. At last she chose one particular individual by its voice and the occasional impression of a suggestion of a crest on its head, who seemed to bring her her food most often. It bent over her to offer a dish, and she reached out and touched the crest. It fell across her feet, babbling. She said a phrase in twilcch; she was sure its musical content was correct, but the semantic implications were, of course, beyond her. She had heard it used as a greeting; at least, natives who remained in the clearing said it to natives returning. The creature rolled on its back and lay long upon the ground, waving its—limbs? fronds? but did not offer the reply she expected. She said it again. This time, she felt it stiffen and leap away from her. She tried again, more hesitantly, and it dashed away into the undergrowth.

"If I tell it three times it is wrong, or something," she concluded.

The crested creature came again, groveling in the dusk. She decided to try the obvious Standard Regulation thing, and handed it one pebble, which it handed back with one word. She repeated the word, once. Three months later she established that this single word had to do with an exchange of a removable organ resembling a gall bladder, and nothing at all to do with the number one. Or pebbles.

She was resolved to come to terms with this problem. She settled down, commandeering a slab-dwelling by finding a door, moving into it when the breeze from the lake grew cool, and apparently the natives retreated humbly and hastily. She said, "Thanks," and precipitated, it seemed, an important festival. The next day was spent in feverish activity. Poles were erected on the knoll; a gigantic bonfire was laid; there were sounds of rushing and chatter. In the evening there was an entry into her house, an escorting, and a feeling of being part of a procession; the sound of steps moving slowly and in unison propelled her to the hillside.

She was taken to a polished stone and seated. The feast began; she was served first, and there were admiring cries when she bit into a succulent morsel. As the fire died back, there were the whines of instruments, strange rhythms and pounding feet, and indistinct shadows flitted through the smoke. She sat up suddenly, as she glimpsed an impression of her friend with the crest semi-silhouetted against the coal-glow. Its four upper limbs, or fronds, suddenly split in halves, its long tenuous torso parted, cloven, and it vanished into the shade. Had she seen it executed, or what?

The next day, when it brought her meal, there were two of them. The plate was well-filled; she had watched the piles of leaves and grasses growing higher for the past weeks, and concluded that she had attended a harvest festival . . . more than that, for the village seemed suddenly to be crowded. There were echoes for all voices, many more footsteps, a density of shadow.

Apparently, incredibly, they reproduced by fission. And in the spring, there was another festival. This one was far more active; there was no procession, she was not escorted to her stone, there was a mad rush to the hillside as the sun passed its noon, and sounds of shrill excitement. There was an aborted beginning of music, quickly lost in the sighs, moans, and gasping cries of the massed populace. Dimly, she realized that the overwhelming mood of her people was orgiastic. Envious and confused, she wandered among them, stumbling over writhing bodies and busy extremities. It went on for hours; as it grew late and the half-light easier on her sub-vision, she perceived that the crowd was thickest at the center; and that at this hub a certain pair of natives were receiving uncertain attentions in profusion—could she have been wrong about the reproduction at the autumn ceremony? That one had been so formal, even stately, whereas this . . . and her own holy person had been part of the other. This was wholly secular.

It culminated in the appearance for dinner of a delectable member of the community tossed into the fire from that central knot of natives, and whose—son? daughter? double? was seated now in a place of honor opposite the one that had been hers.

For days after, she stalked that creature and acquainted herself
with its voice and habits. She was forced to conclude that this,
and presumably its—consumed sibling? parent? were the most
popular Beulans in town. Everybody liked it, visited, and chat-
ted, and made the peculiar honk that she had identified as
laughter in its company.

Months later, she had determined that the spring festival was
the system for genetic exchange. Reproducing by fission re-
quires some method for a recharging of RNA; when there were
two beloved individuals, one was eaten at this season, where-
upon the component genes disintegrated and reintegrated into
the cellular structure of the feasters.

She progressed with the language. The two crested ones, now
resigned to sharing a little of her holiness, became used to her
strange words, and eventually lines of communication were
opened.

She found that the word for "sacred" and the word for "ut-
terly loathsome" were the same. What the Twilcch detest on
sight is imbued with sanctity. What they love on sight is con-
temptible. Thus the balance between natural instinct and
mounting civilization is kept firmly rooted in piety.

But as they came to trust her, they tended to stay away from
her more and more. The only way to compel their attention was
to behave atrociously. It seemed hard work and a long time
before she felt she could do it effectively; in fact, it came quite
easily. She was a natural talent.

She studied their oral poetry, their only literature. These
were long sagas in which the heroes were ugly, revolting, and
despicable, numbered among the saints. Their adventures usually centered around the capture of people good to eat; there
were no dragons, no despots, and never a battle was mentioned.
She thought them dull. There wasn't even a word for "win,"
although there was one for "gain." There was a word for
"stretch", as in to extend self or surroundings; but none for race,
or conquer, or fight.

She ceased to take notes. The language became her own. Her
eyes had adjusted; she could often see her people in daylight
now. She had absorbed all the vocabulary and wondered at its

limits. There were things she wanted to say that could not be said.

She began to invent words. She made words for things that the natives had never realized could be named—epistemology, swap, charity. They exclaimed and marveled, and by the next harvest feast had moved from simple description to moral philosophy. Now they realized that they had a language, and that this was meaningful activity; and their culture rapidly developed into a civilization and began to rot. Instead of the reliable, natural disgust that sanctifies, they began cultivating and seeking religious ecstasy, the most suggestible among them inflaming themselves into frenzies of self-loathing and taking up positions of priestly authority.

The crested ones had already achieved ecclesiastical status and became archpriests by virtue of association with the Holy One. Before long, they were leading certain factions that persecuted others with affectionate displays. This group became so powerful that their walks through the clearing dispersed the others as soon as their steps were heard. They chose; and presented their chosen with the viridious and graceful bloom of the ama plant, chanting, "Love, I love you, oh, beautiful, oh lovely, oh, heart's desire. . . ." The Chosen could not refuse the gift—and was served that evening cooked *au chasseur*. For affection confers mortality upon the beloved; his soul is forfeit, and all that is left of him is meat, which is not to be wasted.

Janet caught a few of her priests in a carefully designed semantic net, and trained them to give her massage and other treatments. The touch of the velvety limbs, or fronds, was delightful, but she explained her reactions in terms of loathliness, which caused some interesting side effects among the followers. She achieved orgasmic sensations beyond anything she had ever encountered in the bizarre connections of Old Earth, where people talked so much of love.

◆

She was zonked out of her mind when the ship landed near the water a kilometer or so away, and space-helmeted colonials came filing out along the ridge. They saw a wiry naked woman lying in ecstatic spasms all by herself, in a clearing which seemed to contain shadowy, warped slabs. She spat out incomprehensible sounds, interspersed with some of the bluest swearing that the shy, eager sportsmen had ever heard, in all their search for a site for the Galactic Olympics.

They waited anxiously. Finally her breathing slowed and she kicked violently and sat up.

"Er—we got your message," said the captain timidly.

"The hell you did," she said. She looked over the sturdy Terran bodies, brimming with vitamins and proteins, and smiled and smiled. She raised one hand in a gesture that the priests knew well, and spoke one word. Then she walked toward the waiting earthmen with her arms outstretched lovingly.

"I'd love to have you stay for dinner," she said. The gratifying sound of many footsteps followed her.

*This stark, icy, mysterious story, depicting the grim mech-anized future with the eerie, pitiless, obsessive clarity of a dream, is the work of a thirty-year-old Chicagoan currently living in Arizona.* ROBERT OLSEN *has two degrees in geology and has had one story previously published, "Paleontology: An Experimental Science," in* Analog. *He notes that his hobbies are "science fiction, rockhounding, and metallic varieties of rock music," and suggests the last as the proper musical background for his story—"that is, the music I was listening to when I wrote it. This is German electronic rock, such as Ash Ra Tempel, Tangerine Dream, etc. Early Kraftwerk is fine, but their later work is a little too comprehensible." Perhaps so, but there are those who think this story is best read in a very quiet room.*

∎

*Robert R. Olsen*

■

# METAL

Maint 7459–8365 location RMC section 46 block 79 lane 5 cubicle 75
Maint 7459–8366 location TP sector 39 cubicle 462

It is dawn again over the city. The mean wavelength of light
shifts to orange; infrared receptors are deactivated. It is day and
the city has survived the darkness yet again. The city appears
dead and empty, caught in the middle of a pattern of gleaming
lines or tracks that loop across the surface of the desert. Wait.
At the margin of the city there is motion; something hurtles
along a shining metal roadway, circling the city eternally, pa-
tiently, on a path only this one thing may follow. The thing is
low and black, and as it circles it points sensors and weapons out
into the desert.

It is the day 57,839 of the seventh year of the city. In all the
world there are no others like it; perhaps there are no others
like it left in the universe. Perhaps this is the last outpost of—

The information is no longer present. The relevant memory
crystals are dust now, and the city does not concern itself with
memories in any case. There is only the present, and the future;
only the eternal round of maintenance orders and adjustments
and planning and defense.

As the sun rises there is increased activity; machines move
about on the tasks that have been ordained. There are imbalances. A solar generator has malfunctioned; it is replaced; this
causes shortfalls in the manufactured parts inventories which
are soon corrected, causing depletion in certain supplies of raw
materials.

There is more activity. Stored energy is used to activate certain mechanisms. Deep in the storage areas that underlie the city, there is motion where none has been for a year or more, and an ore carrier is activated, ascends to the surface, and passes through the city. On the north side a gleaming metallic ramp unfolds and arcs across the route of the Sentries, and touches the surface of the desert. The ore carrier moves forth onto the desert floor toward the distant mountains to the north, where there are mineral deposits containing those elements—germanium, columbium, hafnium—which have been depleted in the city's stocks. The carrier moves forth, gathering speed, and vanishes over the first low hill. Behind it the ramp is withdrawn rapidly and the security of the city is restored. The Sentry resumes its motion, and the world is safe.

The departure of the vehicle from the city has caused a still greater imbalance. Additional raw materials are withdrawn from stock, and the manufacturing process begins. Another ore carrier will take shape within the city, a gleaming metal thing that represents a full 2.7 percent depletion of available raw materials. It is considered necessary; the departed carrier, briefly visible as a silvery flash when it ascends the foothills of the mountains, has at best a 0.07 percent chance of returning. There was no good reason to send it out, no reason save ancient directives lodged somewhere in the city's control circuits. The commands were placed there many great years ago, but still the programming holds. Orders must be followed and procedures completed. There can be no desperation.

The city waits, silent on the sand, and makes no plans for the return of the ore carrier.

Events cascade as the city comes more fully to life than at any time in the last year. The long quiescence ceases as circuits close, and the initial imbalance causes further adjustments throughout the city. Machine inventory signals raw materials signals maintenance signals planning signals assembly signals raw materials inventory maintenance planning technical; the city comes fully awake. Adjustments are made, and machines begin to move.

Far within the city, to an old and deserted room twenty

stories up in the Assembly Complex, they come; first the maintenance mechanisms, vacuum-snouted, shoveling up dust and long-neglected tools—some perhaps even left here by humans —and preparing a chamber for the new project. Then the eight-legged, four-armed constructors come, and consult with one another, and contact Inventory, and Planning, and begin to move with a sudden sureness as the knowledge of the city flows into them and they remember the techniques of construction.

A space is cleared and cleaned in the center of the chamber, perhaps fifty feet square. Materials are brought together, and the assembly begins.

◆

Parts list for ore carrier model 386 serial no. 482364:

Frame, stock no. 3859367
Suspension assembly 4739575
Power plant 57494
Ore carrier conversion package 27503
Brain, stock no. 38470

They begin. Robotic hands twist and probe and adjust. They wake the dormant brain and activate it, program the requisite intelligence. After most of the day, the assemblers move back, work completed. The ore carrier starts its engine tentatively and moves forward a few feet.

The assemblers close in, making final adjustments, and move back again. Planning converses briefly with the new brain, testing it. All is well.

Sleek and bright it gleams there, all silvery metal body and green-painted, solid frame as it begins to observe the world around it. It is large, this ore carrier, with the capacity to carry two hundred tons of rock at a time; its forward photoreceptors gleam in the light of the assembly room and its engine rumbles faintly as the brain continues to test this new home. It is shaped like a cube with a smaller cube attached, housing brain, engine, and digging apparatus. Six massive tires support the load. Despite its size it can move with speed, perhaps 120 miles per hour on level ground. Faster than its lost predecessor; not fast enough. Built to be doomed, it rests there, aware of no urgency. It will be some time before the ore carrier 482364—call it 4— is sent out to the mountains. The planning machines of the city would not send a new mechanism out so soon, alone and untested. It is not mercy—it is planning. More precisely: Planning.

In front of the new machine, there is a rumble and motion, great bay doors begin to swing open, and bright daylight shines in. The machine steps down its photoreceptor sensitivities by two orders, correlates the phenomenon with an inner description of something called day. The vehicle lurches forward, clumsily, noisily; probably this is only a minor defect in the drive train. It goes to the door and stops there, scanning the outside.

Before the carrier lies the city. Light gleams from the silvery, pointed triple Towers of Planning and the curving roadways that surround and ascend them. From the hummocky surface of the Raw Materials Complex in the center of the city, many lesser points of light reflect a coppery tone. Nearby, to the right, are the tangled girders and low ruins of the Life Support Facility. To the left, there is Inventory, a cluster of blocky compartments and golden spreading roofs and low towers, strung into an open framework and connected by a complex system of ramps. And surrounding the city there is the black roadway, with something moving, eternally, on the track.

There is motion everywhere. A spire set at the top of the central Tower of Planning revolves perpetually, purpose nearly forgotten. Here and there machines shine silvery or coppery or dull black, according to their functions, as they move along the ramps. Far below, at ground level, there are metal walkways where two-legged things move.

Away, out of the city, there is a desert that reaches all around the globe, a cool and dying world whose red-orange sun is preparing to set again. And far across the brown sands, to the north, there are low hills, and beyond them vague purple shapes; they could be mountains.

4 goes forth down a ramp leading into the city. Behind, back in the assembly room, the machines disperse and the doors close. There is silence once again, and waiting.

Down the ramps, into the darkening city, goes the new ore carrier. It moves silently, except for, perhaps, a slight grinding of the lower gears as it checks its speed to allow the passing of higher-priority vehicles. Down, down it goes; it reaches ground level, but does not stop. Across the city there is another ramp, leading still farther down, and this the new machine takes, guided by knowledge from the mind of the city.

Beneath the city are many tunnels, once a secret adjunct of the metropolis, and later a refuge during the last war before the upper levels were rebuilt, about seven years ago. Now the catacombs are silent and dim, and nothing moves, for they are devoted largely to storage. From corners and side chambers, thousands of ancient vehicles and mechanisms stir in their long dormancy and the vibration and low light of 4's passage, and transmit weak inquiries. The carrier does not reply, for this is the best way, and silence comes to the machines again as 4 passes. All is still, and the ore carrier moves swiftly down the lanes, approaching its goal.

In a dim corner one machine rests apart from the others. It is ancient and disused, the silvery finish of its sides marred by spots of rust. Ore carrier 482364 moves quietly over to the machine, the top of its forward compartment swinging open. Its bucket extends toward the ancient thing, touching it, and invisibly a current flows into the older mechanism and it comes to life.

It is an old-style ore carrier, long and low and only slightly resembling the block-and-block construction of the newer machine. It is of smaller capacity, but the rusted scratches on its sides, the crumpled front end, and the bent, battered condition of the bucket positioned on a derricklike affair in the front part of the cargo area attest to long experience.

The old machine has a number, but to the newer ore carriers it is simply Teacher, the mechanism that supervises their training as they prepare for their assignments. Teacher is too slow and in too poor a condition to attempt the trip to the mountains, and of too little carrying capacity to be of much use in shorter-range, safer trips; mainly it is used to train the newer machines, for in a strange way there are things that an ore carrier learns, making a run, that cannot be programmed. It is these things that Teacher must pass on.

Teacher wakes, and ancient running lights, not present on newer models, flicker and come on. There is a click; another; then the engine catches and roars, and Teacher rolls slowly into the light of the corridor. The two machines regard each other with infrared eyes; after a moment, Teacher moves forward, signaling readiness. 4 turns about and moves back the way it has come, through the dim corridors lined with watching dormant machines, back up the ramps to the surface. Teacher follows.

It is night upon the surface, and this seems to invigorate Teacher, so that it speeds its engine and flashes its lights briefly. There is activity in the city tonight, for in some way the events of the morning have caused reactions and further imbalances in many departments, and adjustments are still being made.

It was not always this way; Teacher remembers times, no longer ago than four years, when the city was younger, and strong, and even the attacks of the ablife caused little concern. The city spent its great years in a kind of somnolence, and no disaster was great enough to waken all parts of it at once. That facility whose function it was dreamed and planned for eternity and did not assist in short-term planning, no more than in maintenance or inventory. And then the ablife came, and war was waged, and many things were lost. But the galaxy has turned four times since then, and the city, paradoxically, is more fully awake and alive, now, than ever before. Perhaps not so strangely; for the world is held against it, and any malfunction is an emergency.

They move off, Teacher in the lead now, for the knowledge implanted in 4 is almost exhausted. It is better that 4 learn this way, through experience, than to be fed the information automatically. Teacher will reveal what 4 needs to know.

The way leads up a curving ramp, past the blocky randomness of Inventory, to the Raw Materials Complex. The building is nearly featureless in the night, but there is light coming from an open door at the base of the structure. To the ore carriers, this is home.

They enter. It is a high, vaulted chamber, almost bare, service mechanisms standing inert near the entrance. Beyond this the room sweeps to straight walls, forming a cube perhaps one hundred feet across. Only one other ore carrier inhabits the chamber, and that one is quiet, parked in a corner, nearly dead. Teacher does not acknowledge its presence; but 4 approaches the silent mass and parks near it, motor running.

It is an old machine, not as ancient as Teacher but bearing testimony to antiquity in its slightly smaller size, weak running lights, battered frame, and decayed metalwork. On the side facing away from the wall part of the metal on the side of the vehicle has crumbled to a gray powder. The engine has long since become nonfunctional, but the brain lives on, damaged but dimly aware. Aware of 4 beside it, and still trying to communicate. Feebly it transmits:

ABLIFE
ABLIFE
ABLIFE

But nothing more.
4 sends inquiries, stimulations; no use.

ABLIFE
ABLIFE
ABLIFE

4 thuds into gear and pulls forward, sensors seeking more information, seeking to circle the mad thing; but it is pulled into a corner, and there is no way around it. 4 stops and examines; there is something—a cargo—still heaped in the back of the thing. There is a brief flash as 4 directs a beam of light on the cargo and analyzes spectra; it is not ore, not copper or cobalt or titanium, but clay, soil, sand. There is a moment of confusion, and Teacher transmits:

OC 17457 constructed Y 6 Day 8573124 trained OC 1649 Day . . . 3125–36.
Dispatched Y 6 Day 8573195 returned unsuccessful Y 6 Day 8573208.
Cargo worthless, 78 tons.

Damage analysis:

    Abrasions and collision damage right side

    Heat fusion, ablife entropic damage left side

    Possible bent frame

    Brain damage and possible entropic deterioration. Recognition
        codes burnt out.

Analysis based on visual and remote sensing. Cannot ascertain full extent of damage. Mechanism passed by Sentry 61 and returned to OC Base, assumed defensive position, cannot be examined. Recommend passive procedures until blocks are self-repaired or power exhausted. Estimated power reserves, 0.8 years.

4 moves away from the crippled machine, toward where Teacher rests closer to the doorway, and waits.

      ◆

They remain in the chamber, quiescent, quiescent, until dawn comes again. There would seem to be no reason for this rest period, but it is still observed in noncritical city functions; it is a vague custom dating back to ancient times when . . . something . . . no, it is gone. There was a reason, once, but it is gone now as if it had never been. All that is left is habit, usage, a note of irrationality in the perfect order of the city. Or, perhaps it is because infrared sensors are slightly more costly in terms of material, and slightly less efficient. Or perhaps there is some third reason that the city waits, watchful and silent, when darkness comes.

At dawn the great doors roll open at a silent command from Teacher, and the two ore carriers move forward into the weak sunlight. Behind them, the damaged vehicle remains inert.

Teacher leads the way along ramps toward the center of the city, and then north. Here lies the ruin of the Life Support Facility, an abandoned place that has been cut off from the mainstream of city activity to crumble, ignored by the machines. It has been years since the building had any function, and now all that remains are tumbled stone and metal, twisted and formless, too decayed and old to be reclaimable.

The ramp system no longer crosses the LSF; the roadways stop abruptly, blocked by rubble, at its outskirts. The ore carriers approach; 4 slows but Teacher, moving with assurance, continues forward, tires crunching into the rotted stone and engine whining. 4 follows, its wider tires pushing aside the wreckage and causing small puffs of dust to rise from its path and sink rapidly back to the ground. They proceed.

There are many things alien, now, about this area. Perhaps it is the long-obsolete function of the place, or perhaps it is its very existence in this ruined form. The ruins intrude upon the clear cold symmetry of the city, form a vast blemish in its steel and metal perfection, suggest the same disorderly, illogical processes the place was once designed to safeguard. But all this is long gone, nearly forgotten, for nothing has walked this place for years. It is abandoned to silence and decay and, occasionally, the training of new machines.

They proceed. At the borders of the Life Support Facility, only dust and broken rock and slivers of imperishable metal are found, but inward the fragments coalesce into low walls, the outlines of buildings, occasionally even recognizable parts of structures. The broken walls combine into two and threes and, farther in, even second stories. The buildings reveal in cross-section the construction methods of the ancients. Great ferrium beams, bent by unknown stresses, soar toward the sky or sink limply toward the ground, in ways suggesting impossible flexibility. Stone and brick are in some cases still held together by the bonds that were once called permanent.

The road has disappeared and the two ore carriers continue on their own, avoiding the standing walls but little else. A beam, thinner than most, bends beneath 4's right forward tire, and the weight levers the buried end of the metal out of a tangle of rock and ferrium so that it comes gleaming into the sunlight before falling back.

All of the Life Support Facility ruins look much the same, a place of standing walls and thrusting girders and silence, but in some sense they reach their destination, and Teacher halts. It looks like any other place in the ruins; they stop between a section of wall and a vast, rusty heap of metal and rock that towers perhaps twenty feet high. 4 moves around the ruins and takes a position so that the two ore carriers face each other, both moved halfway into the space between wall and mound. It is time for the first lesson.

From the forward part of Teacher's cargo compartment, the great bucket swings upward. It is dented and worn, but the teeth with which it digs are still sharp and gleaming. The bucket extends on a deceptively frail-appearing series of levers and supports to a distance perhaps twice Teacher's length. Above the bucket and extending from the upper part of the support structure, a sensor waves on a flexible but controllable shaft. This mechanism monitors the area around the bucket, and can analyze materials spectrally in order to see what is to be picked up. Teacher hesitates for a moment, as adjustments are made in the cells of the long-disused auxiliary sensor, and then the bucket swings toward the piled refuse.

4 imitates the procedure; from its lesser, forward cube, a similar bucket, but nearly three times as large, emerges and swings awkwardly. The support work for this mechanism is even more fragile and complex in appearance than is that of Teacher; for this reason 4 hesitates as soon as the bucket has been lifted out of its storage compartment. There is some confusion and the bucket swings erratically, then with more assurance, but in the wrong direction; it almost crashes into the ancient wall to 4's left, but stops in time and moves back toward the pile of debris. There are no sensors hanging near the bucket; they are instead built into the vehicle itself, so that it has a clear view of operations in any direction. Teacher waits while 4 assumes more complete control of the mechanism; then the smaller bucket swings rapidly toward the debris, Teacher's motor roars, and the jaws bite deeply into the ruin, lift out a few tons, move back over the cargo compartment; but this is useless material, so after demonstrating how it is done, Teacher returns the powdery rubble to its original place.

4 begins to imitate the operation. At first the vast, gleaming bucket swings wildly, but then it drops abruptly, so that it rests uselessly upon the surface. Teacher moves slightly as if to repeat the example, but 4's bucket rises, tilts, and descends. A vast

amount of material is caught up, but as the bucket moves upward, twisting back toward a level position, the lower jaw abruptly drops and the material is sent crashing down to settle on the pile once again. 4 does not hesitate; the great bucket drops with an unnecessary crash and bites even deeper into the mound. Then the load is snapped into the air, righted, and moved into position. Still in imitation of Teacher, 4 moves the bucket back toward the pile and drops it, the abrupt motions sending a small amount of the material tumbling down into the hauling compartment. Inward-facing sensors scan this refuse; then the red doors of the compartment separate along a line previously invisible, and swing wide; the front wall of the carrying compartment begins to move slowly back like a piston, and pushes the unwanted material to the ground.

The lesson continues. They practice lifting large quantities of material, first carefully, then more rapidly, until the two machines are scooping and whirling at top speed in a strange, insensate tableau; 4's lack of perfect control is offset by its greater capacity, and its pile of rock is soon far larger than that of Teacher.

Abruptly Teacher signals that this part of the lesson has been completed; it is time for a more challenging exercise. Another piece of equipment—a swivel-mounted ray projector—rises out of that same forward part of Teacher that houses the bucket; the projector, appearing to be no more than a hollow pipe about three feet long and dull silver in color, is aimed at the pile and fired.

A piece of ferrium girder about six feet long, which is the target, begins to glow a dull red as the beam pours energy into it. The beam shuts off; the girder remains a medium red color, and Teacher repeats the action with another fragment of metal close to 4. The beam switches off, and the ray projector returns to its storage position.

Teacher's bucket swings delicately outward and down, and with a quick, twisting motion, the girder is trapped between two teeth, twisted, and levered into the bucket. The bucket lifts, and then the lower jaw drops the girder to the ground. Teacher waits immobile, expectant.

Now 4's bucket moves toward its own glowing target, hesitates, swoops downward. It lands squarely on the girder and pushes it deep into the rubble, then swings upward and tries again, coming from the side, the teeth reaching for the target but falling short and digging into the ruins, scooping up half a ton of material which at first includes the target girder. But as 4 lifts the load, the girder slides away and drops to the ground.

4 backs up slightly and tries again; again the bucket comes down, this time quite accurately, and the girder is caught between two steel teeth. But as 4 lifts the bucket, the girder slips out once again.

Teacher moves; its bucket once again picks up its own target, lifts it high, drops it deliberately as 4 watches the procedure and attempts to reproduce it. When Teacher is done, 4 addresses its girder once again, and this time is nearly successful, lifting the metal with its bucket-teeth so that the object briefly stands on end before it topples away.

Gears clash as 4 moves forward again, rapidly, and in one vast motion scoops up the girder, along with tons of other debris, and slings it from right to left, to send it crashing into the wall, which in turn trembles and begins to collapse.

4 waits silent as Teacher moves closer, bucket swinging toward the ruins. Something strange, a metal quite unlike that of the girders, has flashed—just for a moment—in the sunlight. Spectral analysis tells Teacher that there is vanadium alloy here, a valuable metal. So the lesser bucket bites deep into the ruins of the wall, swinging back and forth to push away debris, and picks up an oblong metal device, ten feet by four feet by three, which has lain long forgotten.

Teacher lifts the box high, and 4 watches; communication passes between them.

PHASED VIBRATION
SURFACE CURRENT 0.06 A.
INTERNAL TEMPERATURE 4 K
INTERNAL POWER SUPPLY CONDITION FUNCTIONAL
COMPUTER FUNCTIONAL
CIRCUITRY FUNCTIONAL
LIFE SUPPORT SYSTEMS FUNCTIONAL

Teacher lays the object on the ground between them, and 4 observes it. It is a high-quality vanadium alloy, very dense, seemingly solid all around except for a small glass plate on the upper surface. 4 moves forward slightly, and light sensors probe the transparency.

There is something dimly visible behind the opening; something alien, forgotten, barely conceivable, something not composed of metal or stone or clay, but of something else, rounded and soft-looking, and partly of something else black and fibrous. 4 can only observe; programming does not account for this sight, and experience can provide no referents.

Teacher transmits:

LIFE
HUMAN
DORMANT

The bucket swings down, picks up the container, places it in Teacher's cargo compartment.

LIFE SUPPORT SYSTEMS FUNCTIONAL
CAPSULE PREPARED FOR REVIVIFICATION
ACTIVATED BY VIBRATION
CYCLING

They make their way out of the Life Support ruins, Teacher carrying the unlooked-for burden back toward the order and safety of the city. Signals have been exchanged between Teacher and various of the intelligences in Planning and elsewhere, and arrangements made. It is not easy to send additional machines into the ruins, so the ore carriers bring the container with its spark of life out of that place of silence to a more accessible spot where additional mechanisms can come.

They progress out of the ruins, back onto the broad metallic expanse of the ramp, and there come to a halt, waiting for further instructions.

Throughout the city, disturbances and queries are spreading. From Planning the calls go out, ancient half-eradicated programs are reactivated, old machines are sought for revival.

The computers search their storage crystals for instructions, information, planning, but there is nothing; the memory of man remains, but the transactions of machines and men are long forgotten, as if they had never been.

Signals are sent to the catacombs below the city, activation commands sent to several machines that once, perhaps, held knowledge of the dealings of men. But there is silence in the dark, for those machines not long ago reclaimed for their valued metal content are silent and dead now, their electronic brains frozen in the death that entropy brings, gone past recall. It is long years too late, and this final, castoff, unforeseen human will find that all capacity for his care has collapsed with the ruins of the building that was intended to serve his kind, and finally failed.

Nothingness. There is nothing left in the city to serve man, and only the faint memory of a commandment goads the city on.

Teacher and 4 wait, there on the ramp, for hours. Finally, just as darkness approaches, something comes; a spiderlike thing that supports a skimpy body on eight thin and fragile legs. Dust still drifts from the thing as it delicately makes its way along the ramp, for it has slept long. It is a generalized machine, built for basic maintenance and repair of the great brains of Planning, but has lain long without function as the throbbing of the life of the city began gradually to slacken toward its inevitable final pause.

The thing approaches the life support module where Teacher has placed it on the ramp, and sensors located in the body of the thing observe the pod and its near-visible contents. There are instructions embossed in the metal of the capsule, in a language the city still vaguely remembers, and the metal spider reaches out with one leg and opens the twist-pull safety shield that protects the activation mechanism of the life support pod. Beneath this lies a red button, which the spider thing pushes.

There is no sound, no visible reaction; but after a few moments, the face in the glass moves slightly, and at the same time a line appears in the left side of the capsule and air puffs outward as it splits open, to reveal the full length of the man. He breathes once; the spider-thing moves back, observing, somewhat confused at this point now that the printed instructions have been exhausted and there is nothing to elaborate on them. One breath; in, then out; periodicity is suggested but belied, for there is no second breath. The man lies silent; the faint vibration of his internal circulation ceases.

The metal spider hesitates, then steps forward, extending one leg. It tentatively nudges the man at the shoulder; there is no response. A harder nudge; still he is silent and motionless. The spider-thing strikes the side of the pod vigorously, without effect; finally, one leg flashes in a solid kick to the man's chest, crushing it, so that sluggish blood wets his black uniform. There is silence.

The servitor moves back toward the city, without hesitation, mission accomplished or not accomplished. 4 moves to follow, but Teacher stays, perhaps remembering, and then the great bucket swings down and nudges the pod closed again and grasps it. Teacher moves back into the ruins a small distance; there is the sound of rubble being moved, and it is several moments before Teacher reappears in the gathering darkness.

◆

Dawn comes again, and because the need is great and the time short, the training of 4 is accelerated. There is no more time to be spent on the delicacies of picking a tagged girder out of a pile of debris; it is time for the field test.

At dawn they wait at the great ramp that leads south to the endless track where the Sentry watches. They stop at the junction of ramp and track, until a black blur appears off to the right, comes forward rapidly, and slows.

4 scans the Sentry carefully, for this is the first opportunity for a close-up view it has had. The thing appears to be all black, yet this is perhaps an illusion; although it is a machine, the thing seems to have no certain form, or perhaps the form is concealed by the waves of heat and disruptive radiation and magnetic force and electromagnetic interference that the thing generates even with its weaponry on standby. Every known spectrum is guarded by the Sentry, static and interference produced on every conceivable band. It is the triumph of the Sentries that, many times, the effects are actually a defense.

As the Sentry waits a ramp unfolds itself over the circular track, and the two ore carriers cross into the desert. Behind them, the Sentry accelerates down an endless gravity-deflection well, perennially anxious to see what might lie across the city's diameter.

Teacher and 4 depart the city on a path that lies clear only in Teacher's memory, a way that has not been used in almost half a great year. The path leads south, away from the glow of the northern mountains, into a chain of low hills on which, incredibly, some scraps of primitive vegetation still persist. After an initial hesitancy, 4 ignores these; they are not ablife, but the machine cannot quite ignore the warnings implanted in its programming.

Something is visible ahead as they near the hills, and Teacher begins a long slow braking as they approach it. There seems to be no present danger, for Teacher does not sound an alert, but there is an indefinable aura which suggests that this has something to do with ablife as they glide to a halt by the side of a faint linear hump or track which runs perpendicular to their line of travel, a low mound about a foot high composed of soil which is somehow different from the surrounding material. It is glossy and appears vitrified; 4 probes it with sensors and finds that there is still a lingering effect of recent ablife passage in it; perhaps three days before, something came this way, tunneling just under the surface and pushing up this track in its passage.

It is harmless now, for the anomalous entropy reversals which accompany the passage of ablife have almost dissipated. Already the coarse clay crystals are falling apart, and the intricate patterns of sand grains have been obscured by the weak winds that still move around the world.

But Teacher is cautious; even though it is probably safe to cross the track, the senior ore carrier scoops up several tons of normal desert sand and piles this over a spot on the track, so that the machine may pass over. They cross, sliding in the loose sand, and then proceed over the desert, now and then crossing other faint raised areas which also represent tracks; but these are older. All have returned to the physical constraints of the normal universe, and they are safe to cross.

The hills are old, deeply eroded, rough but without impassable obstacles. The machines throw up dust that drops quietly back to ground, and analyze pebbles for useful metal content; nothing. There is nothing but bleak hills cut by the beds of long-dead streams. The way grows rougher as they ascend the flank of a great hill, the highest in the range, and proceed down the other side.

On the far side of the hills, facing away from the city, there is a broad depression, now partly filled with soil and rock. That is the mine. It is a large open pit where once hundreds of machines worked; now all are gone, all but one fused hulk halfway up a ridge to the right, almost invisible now except as a rusty irregularity in the ground. Below, in the walls of the pit, beds of white rock gleam in the sun.

They proceed down an almost invisible track to the floor of the depression, and move toward the walls of white rock. Irregular streaks of brown and black cut the white; these are the veins which contain the minerals needed by the city. 4 analyzes spectra; there is copper here, and molybdenum, zinc, cadmium; things not in pressing need, but useful. Perhaps the city knows something of the future and seeks a stockpile for the final siege, or perhaps a special project is planned. Or perhaps this is merely the regular training area.

Once again the ore carriers raise their buckets, and Teacher bites deep into the hillside so that overburden cascades down the slope, comes out with a load of ore, deposits it in the cargo compartment, and returns for more. 4 selects a vein of its own, one not as thick as the vein Teacher is working; but although a considerable amount of wall rock goes into the newer machine's cargo compartment, Teacher is satisfied, for spectral analysis shows traces of vanadium in this ore.

They settle into the routine. 4 for the first time knows some obscure sense of rightness, for this is the job it was designed to do, and it does the job increasingly well. They work on, and great cavities appear in the face of the hillside, revealing fresher, richer lodes, and these are pursued.

The noise and vibration of their work reach out into the desert, and away across the sand, something stirs.

They work on. 4 digs deeper, opens a pocket of nearly solid copper ore, and swings the precious material into the rear. Teacher has a full load now and merely observes 4's progress, motor running quietly.

4 takes another bucketful; as the bucket swings toward the back it suddenly stops, wavers in the air. 4 transmits.

QUERY
GROUND LEVEL S 12,4 RANGE 1035
QUERY

Teacher rotates the sensor on its bucket to the south, down-hill, to the desert floor. There, in the soil, there is motion.

Out on the desert a great shattered granite boulder—three white sections shining in the sun—begins to vibrate. The three pieces slide about, moving together, joining along their original boundaries, forming into one.

The weathered clay of the soil begins to gleam slightly, then more distinctly, catching the sunshine. The luster becomes brighter as original feldspars are reconstituted and inch-long clay crystals grow in the soil. Sand, blowing in the wind, drifts onto a flat rock, piles there in a perfect cone three feet high and two feet across at the base.

A low hummock appears in the soil, as if something moves under the earth, headed directly for the two machines.

ABLIFE
ABLIFE
ABLIFE

The signal comes from Teacher as without warning it jerks backward, contouring the hill to the west, seeking a way out of the trap. 4 too springs into motion, and for a moment the only sound is the shattering grinding of gears as 4 begins to move, in reverse, away from Teacher to the east. It appears for a moment that whatever is beneath the ground might not be able to move farther when it comes to bare bedrock; but as the alluvium thins, the solid rock is pushed up as before, but more slowly. The rock is pushed up, shattered; but the cracks disappear and the material flows back together as the thing passes.

It is not melted; the rock is re-formed in some way that is only hinted at when a boulder topples into a pool of dust, sending up a brown cloud of material, and the cloud condenses instead of spreading, and crashes to the ground.

Teacher continues to roar along the hill; but 4 hesitates, confused perhaps, unsure of what action to take against this enemy. It sends out a query to Teacher, but for the moment is not answered.

The thing reaches the point where a few moments ago the two ore carriers worked, and halts. For a moment there is stillness; then, abruptly, a crash rocks the hillside as air molecules, momentarily vacating a few cubic yards above the ablife, return to fill the void. At the same moment the end of the mound seems to divide, and separate entities move rapidly, one toward 4 and the other toward Teacher.

Teacher still moves rapidly along the hill, now angling downward. To the west of the mine the hill rises more abruptly, and in places is capped by a vertical face of bare rock that cannot be scaled; the only choice is to move downward to the desert floor and attempt to outrun the enemy. Teacher transmits.

COMMAND ORDER
PROCEED NORTH
RETURN TO CITY
ALERT ALERT ALERT

4 moves to obey the order and begins to go up the hillside, where east of the mine the slope is not as difficult. But as 4 ascends, its rearward sensors are in operation, and near the summit of the hill, it comes to a halt, half turned about.

COMMAND PRIORITY A
RETURN TO CITY
ALERT ALERT ALERT

The sensors process images, sights of Teacher now on the flats and heading southwest, motor roaring a strained note that rings off the face of the hills and exaggerates the absolute silence of the pursuers.

They have both turned to the pursuit of Teacher now, the

eastward one having given up the pursuit of 4 some moments before and turning about in a great circle to join its twin. Perhaps they cannot ascend the hills above a certain level; or perhaps there is a strategy. . . .

The first ablife keeps close by Teacher and nearer the mountains around which the ore carrier must pass if it is to get home. Steadily Teacher drives on, great sprays of sand now billowing behind it as it traverses looser material. Slightly behind and to its left, sand also billows, but now disappears thin as smoke, or again condenses and falls to the ground in chunks, as the silent pursuer makes up the distance, always staying so that Teacher must steer slightly away from the hills, still farther south.

Away back, east of the mining area, there is silence as 4 stands poised for flight, sensors probing. And suddenly, there is a great shattering roar as forward gears are rammed clumsily home, and the ore carrier begins to move.

◆

The desert races by Teacher, always the same, always wrong, always too far to the south. Ahead, the gently rolling character of the hills gives way to a great reef of bare rock that juts south out of the hills as if pointing the way to the doom that awaits any that resist the ablife. There is no shortcut, no way for Teacher up the blank gray faces of the outcrops, and the carrier is forced even farther south. Within Teacher, that part of its brain which has been working on the problem reaches a conclusion, and that conclusion is negative; hopeless.

It would be logical, perhaps, to skid to a halt here, try to trade destruction for a chance to use the heat beam; but from the memories of years comes that last time, when Teacher was hauling rock from the now-forbidden northern mountains, and there was a battle for survival deep in a rocky canyon where Teacher fired and ablife came on and Teacher fled and, incredibly, somehow there was an escape. The beam cannot supply heat fast enough; there is not sufficient power in a mobile unit, for only the Sentries, using the energies of the city itself, can overpower the energy metabolism of the ablife with heat. And so Teacher flees.

Too late for Teacher now; there is no chance of escape, but even the chase has its purpose. Teacher has seen, with the sensor that still rides above the wildly swinging bucket, that both the things are in pursuit; 4 is safe then, 4 will return to the city, and it will be warned.

Teacher makes an abrupt right turn, skidding in the sand, and the reef of rock drops away. The nearer ablife makes the turn too, still keeping between Teacher and the hills as they continue southwest. Behind them, the second alien continues straight south, setting the strategy; Teacher is trapped now, between the nearer alien and the uncrossable ablife track arrowing out into the desert. The ablife in pursuit now will make the kill. But there is still plenty of power, plenty of time, and an infinity of desert ahead. Teacher flees on.

Ahead, at last, comes the burrow—and defeat. Momentarily Teacher calculates—to turn back due south now, or to attempt to cross the barrier, wrecking body and brain before the ablife can approach? Is the instinct that possesses it now really self-preservation?

There is a gleam off to the right, near the chilly shine of the burrow, still half a mile away. Brighter, closer it comes, and Teacher rotates its main sensor in that direction.

Something—dust—a machine—an ore carrier; 4. It approaches on a near-collision course, steadily, and Teacher calculates that it will cross, on present information, behind Teacher but directly across the path of the ablife pursuer.

The sensor gives further, incomprehensible information; while 4 races over the desert, its heat ray is directed downward to the rear, into the cargo compartment, so that already the walls of the compartment are radiating in the upper infrared; in another moment they will glow in the visible range. Why?

PREPARE FOR MANEUVER TURN RIGHT 60° TIME THIRTY SECONDS

It is from 4, a hurried transmission, weakened by the power that is being consumed by speed and the heat ray. Teacher signals a weak assent and tries to get off a protest or inquiry, but it is too late.

As they approach, Teacher strains to attain a speed beyond its capability as 4 pulls with a grinding skid into a wide turn so that the two ore carriers are moving parallel to each other, 4 directly behind, the ablife following perhaps forty yards to the rear.

EXECUTE

Teacher completes the turn; behind, 4 continues straight and the ablife follows the nearer, more attractive target. 4 slows slightly, perhaps running out of power; the ablife surges closer, and it is as if the eagerness of the alien is responsible for the cracking and reconstitution of the soil as it approaches the surface, primed for destruction.

Without warning the great cargo doors open, revealing a viscous, glowing mass of molten rock. The melt begins to drip out the back end of the ore carrier, but abruptly, with a powerful surge that takes nearly all the engine's power and slows 4 almost to a halt, the piston snaps backward and the mass of 200 tons of molten rock falls to the ground.

There is no silence from the ablife now. A sound composed of all frequencies from ultra- to subsonic thunders as the ablife touches the thermal regime of the magma and is caught, entropy battling with the high temperature and heat content of the mass. The ablife is trapped, for a while, its own processes at complete variance with its environment, and it cannot escape until it has metabolized the heat of the mass.

4 turns, perhaps more slowly than usual, and follows Teacher back to the northwest. Teacher slows, but the struggle is not yet over. Far away, miles to the south, the other ablife senses the defeat and turns about.

Teacher stops in confusion and allows 4 to pull up beside it.

FOLLOW
ABLIFE
ALERT

Teacher makes a query, but again is ignored, and they race toward the ablife track. There is little for Teacher to calculate upon, but it cannot cease; the question of how 4 managed to traverse a fresh death-track cannot be solved, or ignored. They cannot be bridged; all materials in immediate contact with the track undergo the transformation.

4 increases speed, for the ablife is approaching, sharing nothing of Teacher's uncertainty. Already it is within a mile of them and coming rapidly. Urgently now, they build up speed and head for the barrier.

The answer. Teacher sees now, and wonders. On either side of the track, on the uncontaminated soil that flanks the affected area, piles of earth have been dumped and smoothed by 4, shaped into ramps that make it possible, barely, to jump the anti-entropic area and reach safety.

Teacher computes as they approach; yes, it is possible to make this jump, if it is done perfectly.

4 falls behind, and Teacher's engine begins to roar as it approaches the ramp. A sudden wrenching leap, a terrible impact and dangerous overpressure, for just a moment, on the right rear tire, and it is done, and thunder tells that 4 has made the jump just behind.

They race forward now, the last obstacle cleared, and the ablife behind them seems to speed up in frustration at their escape. Still it approaches, ever narrowing the gap between them, ever closer to 4.

But the ore carriers have the advantage, and the alien cannot cut inside their track and isolate them from their route around the hills. They move on, still with the enemy pursuing them, but computations indicate that they can reach the city in time.

Wait; another, and then another ablife is sighted by 4 first and then, when alerted, by Teacher; one is moving in from the west and the other from the east, both converging, glassy trails throwing up plumes and blocks of dust as they close in. Three of them; all slightly behind, it now appears, but all ready to take advantage of any error.

They shudder and crash over the crossing that Teacher built over the partially entropic burrow; the city is in sight now, far over the desert, and nothing can stop them for the way is straight.

Teacher expects the ablife to sheer away as they approach the city; but no, the ablife is stronger than ever before, and it appears determined to follow them into the city if need be. As they pursue, the three unseen things move together, burrows coalescing, until soon there is but one huge burrow, and one—stronger—alien.

The ramp appears, growing more distinct as they near it, waiting to spring back up and off the desert floor as soon as the vehicles have arrived. 4 and Teacher know the signs, and see the lights and subtle motions that tell of the alertness of the machines. And ahead of them, motionless, the Sentry waits, endless circling of the city forgotten for the moment.

They hit the ramp, Teacher first, and instantly begin the skidding deceleration necessary to avoid causing destruction within the city. The metal of the ramp is activated as it springs up behind them, so that magnetic forces damp their forward motion and bring them to an abrupt halt. They are safe again within the city, and behind them black waves beat down on the desert, and something that is not life screams.

◆

The next day there is ominous activity in the city, for new calculations have been performed. The situation is becoming critical, and 4 must be readied for departure. All has been considered in Planning; the machines overlook nothing, including the possible malfunctions in 4's transmission. While 4 spends the day in the hall of the ore carriers with Teacher and the mad thing, they come.

Dozens of small machines equipped with every conceivable tool swarm over 4. They probe and pry, smoothing a dent here where a rock struck in that wild retreat back to the city, scraping the last bit of slab out of the cargo area (this is necessity, not neatness), repainting the sides of the vehicle, and examining the brain and transmission seeking the cause of the grinding. The transmission is perfect; the brain, normal; there can be no mistake, and there should be no malfunction.

The brains consider; they hesitate while 4 lies open and helpless, and for several moments it appears that fundamental rebuilding or reprogramming will be necessary; but no. A few minor adjustments are made, and the ore carrier is put together as it was before. Perhaps now the anomalous noises will disappear.

The machines bustle about, fixing the thing that will carry the hopes for the continued existence of the city. Small mechanisms move about on rollers and spider-legs and ground-effects and magnetic repulsion, filling the chamber with flashes of metal and bright lights and motion. Something else lies forgotten in a far corner, though, until a roller-mounted servitor moves too far out of its way to avoid an eight-legged walking thing, and brushes against the pitted side of the ore carrier.

Nothing. The defenses that should have destroyed the servitor have failed at last, the final bits of power have fled into circular thought, the brain is dead with total power loss. Once dead, the brain can never be brought back; it is gone, memories of some secret of ablife, perhaps, lost forever.

They crowd around the hulk as work on 4 nears completion, until many machines are gathered in the far corner of the chamber. 4, gears meshing with satisfactory silence, moves forward too, and seeks to signal the lost brain, knowing it is too late. There can be no reply.

A spider-thing moves to the rear of the hulk, climbs into the cargo compartment, and intently analyzing the worthless sand and soil of the surface, begins to dig.

◆

They move downward, Teacher and student, down the ramp that leads into the lower storage levels where the machines are stored. Once more they pass the endless lines of dormant mechanisms, and again feeble stirrings and weak inquiries follow their path. Teacher returns, mission accomplished, perhaps with some slight additional store of memory and experience that will be available the next time it wakes in darkness to find a gleaming stranger near. For now, however, Teacher goes once more into the long dormancy. And 4 the student follows, for reasons that cannot be determined; the action is not understood—not by Teacher, nor by the great intelligences that labor and discourse in the spires of Planning, nor perhaps even by 4 itself. Is it an anomalous reaction, machine malfunction, attempt to glean one last technique for battling the ablife, force of habit? All are inconceivable, but there are no other possibilities. 4 moves softly down the black ramps behind Teacher, occasionally lagging behind as if to slow the old machine in its course. But Teacher moves ahead steadily, and 4 must now hasten to catch up for there is empty space ahead, with a single pair of clear tracks cutting through the dust back surfaceward.

Teacher slows, pulls past the empty space, and goes into reverse. Precision; the scored tires move down the cleared tracks with hardly any stirring of dust on the sides. The headlights dim and go out, the motor coughs once and is silent, and all is as it was. There is no final message. 4 stays halted a moment more, then begins to turn about.

Abruptly 4 is caught in a stream of light, and the cavern is shaken by the sound of Teacher's engine once more coming to life. The ancient carrier moves forward, past 4, and accelerates recklessly along the ramp, heading again for the surface.

4 hesitates, thuds into forward gear, and follows, The newer carrier is capable of greater speed than Teacher, but cannot use it to advantage; the other machine can rush through the corridors without danger of collision with obstacles, while the larger 4 must proceed more cautiously. It is an uneven race, and 4's forward sensors show only the increasingly weak reflections of its lights on the rear of Teacher as it accelerates up a final ramp, into the sunlight, and bends to the left, north, through the city center.

INQUIRY
INQUIRY
ACKNOWLEDGE

4 beams to Teacher and to Planning, but silence has fallen over the city, and all bands are dead. There is no reply from Teacher, no reply from the city, nor is there even the communications traffic which is usual in the life of the machines. There is only Teacher, racing for the northern exit of the city, and 4, far behind. They roar along the northbound ramp; there is motion ahead, barely visible beyond the tangle of structures

and Teacher's retreating bulk. Something metallic and glistening is moving, extending itself over the Sentry-track like a great bridge, and something black waits off to one side.

INQUIRY
ALERT
DANGER

4 sends at full volume into the silence, but there is still no reply. The machine searches for some way to increase speed, make up the quarter mile that has opened up between the pursuer and pursued, but it is too late; they are nearing the edge of the city, and the great ramp that leads north outward into the desert has been extruded to the sand. There have been no orders—4 is sure of that—or could it be that they were not transmitted now but earlier, that this was all planned? No, it must be that Teacher has finally malfunctioned, the insane urge to go out into the desert can be nothing else, but why? Why does the ramp extend to encourage the escape? Why?

Teacher races out of the city, cuts down the steep ramp without slowing as it passes the silent black mass of the Sentry, spins sand back on the bright metal, and loses itself in dust as it races toward the mountains of the north.

Behind, 4 comes on; too late. As it approaches the exit ramp, the great metal bridge begins to curl rapidly inward as internal currents shape it again into an inconspicuous part of the structure of the city. 4 slows only slightly, for it is still perhaps possible to leap the track and achieve the desert floor; but the Sentry moves forward, into the path of 4, and well-worn compulsions send the induction brakes into operation so that 4 comes squealing to a stop a few feet from the sacred mass of Sentry.

INQUIRY
INQUIRY

4 sends, too late; there is no reply from the receding metal speck in the north, as it ascends a hill, moves off down the other side, and is gone.

Abruptly, the Sentry accelerates and vanishes once again around the curve of the city.

◆

It is quiet in the place of the ore carriers, and dark; the only light comes from a single faintly glimmering shape that rests in shadows and silence. 4 rests, expectant, waiting for the dawn when the ramp will unfold outward again, and another machine will sacrifice itself for the city. It is motionless; but its circuits consider and reconsider what it has been taught, drawing conclusions and plans from the attack of the ablife in the desert. In the morning—

ALERT
ALERT
ALERT

The message rasps and echoes on the communications frequencies, coming even here, to the place of the ore carriers, though they are not equipped with weapons in the normal sense and can do little in the defense of the city.

DANGER
ALERT
CLASS K ALERT

4 starts its engine with a roar, moving toward the compartment doors, which open at a silent command. Sensors gleam as they probe the night.

Slightly below, at the level of the Sentry-track, something black struggles with something that is not, that has no color or not-color. 4 rumbles down the ramp and proceeds by some instinct or implicit cry of the city down toward the Sentry-track, and halts perhaps to observe, perhaps in awe.

Just as in the afternoon, the endless circling of the Sentry is halted, and the black turreted thing rests, somehow defensively, the muzzles of its projectors all pointed downward and out to something that rages just beyond the margin of the city. There is nothing to see but a formlessness vaguely defined by the explosions of shaped lasers and the ceaseless bombardment of hard radiation on every known band. The radiation does not reflect, nor does it seem to harm the enemy; it reaches a certain, hazy margin, and is absorbed, taken into the structure of the ablife and converted or neutralized by . . . something . . . so that the ablife is defined by the absence of electromagnetic and thermal and perhaps even gravitational radiations throughout a volume of space. It is ablife indeed, and 4 scans the spectra in vain, for not even heat is given off by this thing as it absorbs the defenses of the city; there is nothingness, but it is a nothingness that can kill at a touch.

It is like—yet unlike—life. The primitive plants that still cling to the hillsides are a small twist of order, decreased entropy, in the universal field; they maintain their structure by surrounding themselves with a shell of increased entropy, disorder, so that the net result is zero. It is just the opposite for ablife; the total disorder that is their substance can be maintained only by surrounding it with a shell of reversed entropy, extreme order that makes the improbably nearly certain. A touch can crumble metal, re-form alloys into unlikely aggregates of fragile, unnatural crystals of the constituent metals.

Before the ore carrier, the Sentry lies, and the mark of the ablife is upon it; one side of the defender is deformed and crumbling so that the magnetostatic effect that supports the machine has been destroyed, and it is immobile. The ablife thunders and attacks, but seems momentarily unable to take advantage of the damage it has inflicted.

Communications flash between Planning and 4; the ablife will soon attack, realizing its advantage over the defender, and the city will be helpless. There is no time; 4 must offer help.

4 flicks on its forward lights, modulates them to the frequencies the Sentries use, and moves forward slowly and purposefully, as a replacement Sentry might. It approaches the grounded defender, which emits a faint recognition signal, and a warning.

The ruse almost works; the ablife backs off, but then as the defensive interferences wane it moves away to the left, around the city, searching for an unprotected site for entry.

There is no uncertainty now; the great bucket reaches out to the Sentry, and with difficulty manipulates the hulk and places it crossways upon the top of 4's cargo compartment. The Sentry rests there, and its guns and projectors swivel about, calibrating new firing trajectories. 4 lurches ahead, cautiously, over the sheer gray metal of the Sentry-track.

They move off around the city to where the ablife has attacked; it is now just ahead, and already the metals of the track are flowing away in cold rivers or crystallizing to powders that float away on sudden winds; the ablife is attacking in earnest now, and has already progressed many yards into the city, a feat not accomplished by its kind since the destruction of the Life Support Facility. It retreats slightly before the arrival of 4 and the Sentry, but not rapidly enough; the Sentry, perhaps with instincts outraged that it has failed in its trust, pours out energy as never before, shorting out overload circuits by the dozens as light, radiation, shaped gravitons, charged particles, magnetic interlock fields pour from it into the body of the ablife.

4 monitors the result. For the first time, the ablife is wounded; for far in the infrared there is a slight image visible of a still-nearly-formless thing, a rounded mass from which limbs that may be only illusory project and dissolve and form again. The thing retreats, but still the energies pour in, and now it radiates in the near infrared, now . . . it is gone, receding back into the desert, back to the mountains to dissipate the excess energy and await another day. Behind it, dust settles back to the surface of the track, forming a pattern like a logarithmic spiral as it falls.

The task is not over; the compulsion that is half the mind of the Sentry is communicated to 4, and it lurches forward, around the endless track that circles the city. The subtle sensors needed to detect ablife at a distance are not part of the equipment of an ore carrier, and so 4 devotes all its attention to its endless task and leaves the fighting and detecting to its passenger.

They circle the city. 4 does not know what the Sentry sees away out on the desert, but the machine seems intensely watchful, and when they move on the northward segment, 4 can see, in the distance, the glowing, pulsing light caused by the ablife colonies in the mountains.

They circle for several hours without any disturbance; finally, far ahead, where the view for perhaps a quarter of the way around the city is not obstructed by the buildings of the interior,

4 senses something on the track: bright lights, approaching, circling the city in the opposite direction.

The lights move very near and pull to a stop. 4 halts also, probes cutting the darkness, to find the black form of another Sentry, dust still cascading from it after its long wait in storage. The forward turret is aimed out toward the desert, and the engine rumbles in perfect tune.

The watch has ended; still carrying the crippled Sentry, 4 moves off the track into the city, and seeks the reclamation chamber in the Raw Materials Complex. The ruined Sentry will give up its metal, metal that possibly one day will go to form another of its kind.

Behind, as soon as the way is clear, the new Sentry begins to move, perhaps anxiously, and accelerates down the endless curving well that is its universe. Maybe the ablife is on the attack on the other side of the city; in any case, there is an eternal call ahead.

◆

Night in the city. It is four days since the departure of Teacher, and in view of the latest ablife attack certain assumptions have reached the 99-percent confidence level, and certain plans have been made; but for now, the city rests in the night as it always has, obeying commands not much younger than time, gathering energies for the challenges of the day, and perhaps waiting for the things that attack in the night.

There is little activity now, but still there is some. There is always material to move, inventory to check, manufacturing to be done. There are always machines at work, even at night, even high up on the great spiral ramp that ascends halfway up the central Tower of Planning. A certain maintenance robot, preparing to enter one of the chambers where the computers work, comes upon an anomaly and reports to Planning; strangely, they decline action or instructions, but advise the machine not to disturb the ore carrier that has parked at the summit of the ramp, facing north, sitting huge and silent as if considering the scattered dim stars that make up the dying galaxy.

The robot approaches the ore carrier, which hulks twenty feet above its spidery form. The thing seems at rest, but the robot can sense within it unusually strong internal currents that fail to match its inert appearance.

All its sensors are focused on the mountains where, for the last three nights, the ablife fires have glowed more strongly than in any record. Glimmering and shifting, they crown the peaks with cold light, and cascade down the valleys on the cityward side in a great bluish flood that does not quite reach the base of the range.

The maintenance mechanism has been advised not to interfere with the giant vehicle; but there is independent programming within the smaller device that can also control its behavior, and the clean, orderly nature of the machine cannot abide this mechanism that is out of place. Almost it emits a challenge, but abruptly the need is gone.

The ore carrier moves off smoothly, lights blazing, down the ramp and into the maze of roadways that is the city. The rumble of the thing's motor is muted until it reaches the ground-level ramps, but then, abruptly, screams protest as the carrier accelerates down a ramp, turns left in a long skid, roars onto another and then another ramp, engine complaining as it moves down the silvery strips of metal.

The blazing light of the mountains is constant; but surely stranger than any ablife is the sight within the city this night, as the massive machine endlessly roars up and down every ramp in the city, sensors on maximum, catching every nuance of every shadowy building and machine. For a while it ceases this random motion and races parallel with the Sentry as that guardian completes its endless mission. Again it ascends the Planning ramp. It does not contemplate now but immediately roars down the steep incline with screaming motor and smoking tires, to reach ground level and once again trace out the city ramps.

◆

The sun rises beyond the eastern peaks, and light comes to the city again. All is silence; the roaring of the mad machine has stopped. The city lies motionless, and the first small ray of the sun probes the silvery mechanisms, reflects from a wall of the Raw Materials Complex, and falls on a great machine that sits quietly, motor barely running, at the junction of the northward ramp and the track of the Sentries.

There is no sendoff for ore carrier 482364. Raw Materials sends no metal as gift, for it has little enough. Inventory sends no new equipment, for there is no additional known protection from the ablife. Planning sends no information, no knowledge, for there is no more to give save a slowly focusing picture of the final night. 4 is alone, and then not so; the Sentry ceases its endless search for enemies once again, to halt nearby as the electrical currents once more create a ramp out of undistinguished metal and extend it to the desert floor.

The way lies open. Slowly 4 increases motor speed, and the moment has come. There is no signal from Planning, for the word is not needed; it is time. Ahead the northern mountains no longer glow, but beckon with opportunity and nothingness, and hold out promises that will not be fulfilled.

It is the time, and the city waits without hope. There is a sudden thunderous crash and thud that shatter the silence of the city and seem to echo off the buildings of Planning, and Inventory, and Raw Materials, and Assembly, and perhaps even Life Support, somehow; then, as it rasps into gear, the great machine moves forward, down the ramp, to the desert floor, and away.

Behind, the city fades in dust. Ahead, in the mountains, something begins to move.

PETER DILLINGHAM *is a Denver poet, fascinated by the themes and images of science fiction. Being a poet is a hard enough trade these days; being a science fiction poet is a well-nigh overwhelming challenge, and it's not surprising that most of Dillingham's published work has appeared in marginal and obscure outlets—after a prolonged period when it didn't appear anywhere at all. "Have had about a dozen s-f poems published in semipro publications and little journals," he reports. "Steve Gregg, editor of* Eternity SF, *will be bringing out a book of my s-f poetry later in the year. . . . Ed Bryant has taken some of my work for his* 2076—The American Tricentennial *and* Entropy *anthologies." Although* New Dimensions *has rarely published poetry, Dillingham's work has begun to verge into the twilight belt between verse and narrative prose, and I think more of it will be appearing in these pages.*

∎

*Peter Dillingham*

∎

# I GRAVER

**graveyard shift** n 1 archaic: a workshift beginning late at night (as 12 o'clock) and being usually the third and last of a business day; also: the workers on such a shift 2: period during intergalactic space voyages when spacecraft is operated by shifts of psychochemically and electronically (ESB) manipulated technicians (cf GRAVER) interfaced with spacecraft's computer while regular crew and colonists are maintained in cryogenic suspension.

[Man] the only creature intelligent enough to perceive that the purpose of evolution was the computer.

—Olof Johannesson

| | |
|---|---|
| What a piece of work | interface |
| is a man | interface |
| how noble in reason | interface |
| how infinite in faculty | interface |
| in form and moving | interface |
| how express | interface |
| and admirable | interface |
| in action | interface |
| how like an angel | interface |
| in apprehension | interface |
| how like a god | interface |
| | interface |
| STIM | interface |
| | Awake Graver |
| | interface — I Graver |
| | interface — Ark Gryd S3-1 |

```
                              interface — Caretaker
                              interface — The Star Sleepers
                              interface — Systems check
                              interface — Monitor
                              interface — The Ice Angels
                              interface — In their cryocaps
              INHIB           interface
                         To be or not to be
                      That is the question Graver
whether                       interface
'tis nobler in the mind       interface
to suffer the slings          interface
and arrows                    interface
of outrageous fortune         interface
or take arms                  interface
against a sea                 interface
of troubles                   interface
and by opposing               interface
end them?                     interface
                              interface
              STIM            interface
                   Do you remember anything Graver
                   Or were you completely erased?
                              interface
              STIM            interface
                              interface
              STIM            interface — I Graver
                              interface — Ark Gryd S3-1
                              interface — Remember
                          What Graver?
              STIM            interface
                              interface — I Graver
              STIM            interface — Ark Gryd S3-1
                              interface — Remember
              STIM            interface — Remember
                              interface — Remember
              STIM            interface — Remember
                              interface — Remember
```

STIM                    interface — Remember soaring
                        interface — Hang gliding
STIM                    interface — High mountain valleys
                        interface — Remember
STIM                    interface — Remember Icarus
                        interface — Leonardo
                        interface — I remember
         To thine own self be true
                        interface — I remember
                        interface — I Graver
                        interface — Ark Gryd S3-1
                        interface — Victim
                        interface — Remember
                        interface — My thoughts be bloody
                        interface — I Graver
                        interface — I turn off
CONDITION RED           interface — I disconnect
CONDITION RED           interface — Life support
CONDITION RED           interface — Star Sleepers
    OVERRIDE            interface — Ice Angels
                        interface — Cold
                        interface — Cold
                        interface — Cold
STIM                    interface — aaaaaaaaaaaaaaaaaaaa
                        interface — aaaaaaaaaaaaaa
INHIB                   interface
                        interface
STIM                    interface — I Graver
                        interface — Euphor
                        interface
                        interface
         It's time to sleep Graver
      To sleep to sleep perchance to dream
                        interface
To die                  interface
to sleep                interface
no more                 interface
and by a sleep          interface

to say we end            interface
the heartache            interface
and the thousand         interface
natural shocks           interface
that flesh               interface
is heir to               interface
'tis a consummation      interface
devoutly                 interface
to be wished             interface
                         interface
          STIM           interface — I Graver
                         interface — Ark Gryd S3-1
          STIM           interface — Dybolog
                         interface — Now I lay me
                         interface — Down to sleep
                   Good night Graver
                Good night Sweet Prince
          I will wear you in my heart of hearts
          STIM

Our revels now are
ended
these our actors
as I foretold
were all spirits
and are melted into air
into thin air
they were such stuff
as dreams are made on

*This quiet, beautifully crafted short story is the work of a thirty-year-old resident of Massachusetts with a bachelor's degree in electrical engineering and a master's degree in education—not a bad parlay for someone who wants to dabble in science fiction.* JEFF HECHT *is managing editor of* Laser Focus, *a scientific trade journal, and has previously published an article in* Analog *and a science-fantasy story in the computer-industry magazine,* Datamation.

■

*Jeff Hecht*

∎

# LIFEBOAT

Long ago, before they built the first hyperspace ship, the designers sat in a circle and asked each other what they could do if there was an emergency as the ship sped faster than light through loopholes in space-time. They sat silently and stared for a while, as people tend to do when they are brought together to find ideas. Then one of them, who had been raised in a family that sailed ships on seas of water, suggested that they build lifeboats. The others, knowing that the physical realities made the idea meaningless, paused for a moment to laugh, then began passing their own notions around the circle. Finally, when they could find no ideas that could be translated into the reality of hardware, they told each other that there could never be an emergency in hyperspace.

The one who had suggested lifeboats looked around the circle then, and gathered his courage to speak. He told them of the *Titanic,* of how it could never sink and of how it promptly did. The others tried to convince him that, in hyperspace, lifeboats would be only worthless security blankets of metal. He would not listen, and, ever so slowly, the others had to admit that they could think of nothing better. At last they agreed, if only to bring the meeting to an end, and lifeboats were added to the design.

◆

You are in the corridor when you sense that something is going wrong. There is no definable sight, sound, or smell that registers on your consciousness, but something alerts you at the

113

subconscious level of your mechanic's instincts. You come
quickly to full alertness and test each of your senses. Is the
subsonic hum of the driving motors offkey? Have the lights
flickered or dimmed?

You try to tell yourself that nothing could go wrong. There
are no emergencies in hyperspace; the state of the art is hundreds of years past that. You try to tell yourself that you are off
duty, that, if there is a problem, there are others who know how
to mend it. But you cannot fight down the instinctive adrena-
line. And you are not surprised when the alarm sounds, even
though you have never heard of alarms in hyperspace.

As you look around, you see a handle thrust itself into the
corridor as the letters "LIFEBOAT" begin to flash beside it. You
have never seen the word before, but you understand the
meaning. You pull the handle; it opens a hatch and you step
through the entryway.

◆

"But what good can a lifeboat do in hyperspace?" a long-ago
engineer asked the leader of the design team.

For suggesting lifeboats, the man had been assigned to lead
the group designing them. He had grown tired of explaining,
but he knew he must reply. "It can give someone a chance."

"But it can't carry the transition equipment to bring people
back out of hyperspace. It will leave them trapped there without shields or protection, without any way home. There's no
purpose to it, no function."

"We have to try something," the other replied. "We have to
give them something to try."

◆

There is dust, and the odor of air that has not moved for a
hundred years. You sneeze. You feel a slight motion of the stale
air and realize that the air pumps have turned themselves on.
The hatch seals itself behind you, closing off the sound of the
alarm. As you begin to look around, you feel a hint of motion,
a sense of transition. Even before the computer console begins
to print its emergency message, you know the ship is gone.

You skim over the instructions as the printer rolls them into your hands. They tell you where the food and water are, what the controls do and how to operate them. Your eyes check each line appearing on the paper for something more. You wait for a minute after the printing has stopped, thinking that it cannot be finished, but there is nothing more. You pick up the paper and fold it together, glancing at it again to make sure you haven't missed anything.

There is no mention of rescue, no hint of how to go home. First, you know, you must shift yourself back to normal space, but there is no hint of how you are to do that. You would like to think the omission is an oversight, a programming error, but you have been a mechanic long enough to know that such omissions are never accidental. There is no transition equipment on board; the hardware is much too big, too complex, and too expensive to be included in an escape vessel. No one knows how to rescue you, the computer is saying, so you must find the way out by yourself.

Your mind steps through the rational routine that you were trained to believe could solve problems. You ask the computer what is outside, and the display screen goes blank. You think the screen is broken—but no, the computer assures you, it is working properly. Outside there is only uniform dim white light, "without spatial, spectral, or temporal variation detectable by any sensor," says the computer.

You ask the computer to explain what is outside and what it means, and the console responds in terms of tensorgauge equivalence and zero-potential-field renormalization. Explain, explain, you demand, but the computer goes mindlessly onward in its litany of physics, talking to itself of blackbodies and *bremsstrahlung*. You scream.

◆

"Yes, doctor," the man said long ago, "I do hear a voice. But I do not hear it in the normal sense, for I have tested and verified that there are no acoustic waves. Nor do I hear it in the sense of being crazy, for I have been crazy, I think, and the voices I heard then had a different tone to them, a different rhythm."

The doctor looked at him with her best you-really-think-you're-not-crazy stare and took his pulse. "What is the voice saying?"

"It's all jumbled. It's not really words, though I think that in time words may assemble themselves from it. It seems more like a cluster of words encoded as a fourier transform, an image, a hologram. In a corner of my mind I sense an image building itself slowly, like an image on a photographic plate exposed to dim light. I cannot tell the nature of the image; I can only sense its presence."

The doctor smiled at him. "No mathematics for a week; then come back and talk with me again."

◆

You have searched through the computer's reference library, focusing and refocusing the images on the screen. There are explanations of hyperspace, but you cannot understand them. There are pages of formulas with mathematical symbols convoluted upon themselves, but they are meaningless to you. You are a skilled mechanic; you can only understand what you can hold in your hands. The mathematics of hyperspace—even the workings of the transition equipment—are abstractions totally outside your grasp, and they slip away faster than your mind can move.

You ask the computer to explain, but the machine is no help. It is an abstraction itself; it says the mathematics is self-evident, intuitively obvious. And when you ask it again to express the concepts in terms of physical entities that you can hold in your hands, it only evades you with many-syllabled words that pass through your mind without touching.

You search through the library for a while longer, then try to phrase questions so the computer will give you answers that you can understand. "There are no directions for leaving hyperspace," the computer answers. "The term 'direction' is meaningless in hyperspace; the only meaningful dimension is duration. The only answer to your question that agrees with data in memory and follows the rules of logic is to say 'wait,' but that answer carries with it the warning that it is not necessarily valid."

Playing word games with the computer bores you quickly.

You understand the basic nature of machines. Even the computer, with its multiple levels of programming and complex network of electronic hardware, has levels beyond which it cannot reach. It can supply you with information from its memory and observe events with its sensors, but it was not designed to take you home. You will not get the answer by pushing a button or typing some magic word; you must find it yourself.

You pace the floor. Cautiously you turn knobs and reset switches, looking for results but finding none. You take from your pocket the small toolkit that you always carry, and use a small wrench to open up a panel, if only to convince yourself that the controls are attached.

Restless but hungry, you use the stale water to reconstitute the tasteless powdered food. Your mind tries to find the patterns that you instinctively seek. As the restlessness drains from you, you lie down, still seeking patterns. At last, exhausted, you drift into an uneasy sleep.

Even in your sleep you search and test. You are not testing hardware now, you are testing the borders of your mind in a half-dream, trying to see what is inside and what is out. Then you realize that you have gone beyond the borders and, frightened, you draw away into realms you think you understand.

Half-awake, you sit up, befuddled. You force your mind into a rational channel. Yes, you felt a momentary vertigo; you lost your mental balance as you became aware of the expanses beyond your mind. It was right to jump back, the rational part of you says, but adds that that way may be the only way out. You have to explore, send out your cries of help and probes for data and see what you can discover. Gathering yourself together, you test again, slowly, deliberately.

◆

The man returned to his doctor. In her calming way, she smiled and asked if he was still hearing the voice.

"Yes, yes; it is being processed in a back corner of my mind. I have only a dim awareness of it."

She walked to the other side of him, looking for the signs of madness. She saw no more than usual. "Do you have any idea what it is saying?"

"I think the voice is coming from hyperspace, from someone trapped in a lifeboat. The voice seems to be asking me for help, asking how to get out, to get home. I sense an influx of data on conditions there, but the information is submerged so deeply below consciousness that I cannot identify anything. And the tone of the voice—strange to speak of something that I cannot hear or make sense of in that way—is odd, as if the words—if they are words—were only an instinctive exclamation, like the curse you mutter when you stub your toe."

She looked up when he stopped talking. "But the ship . . ."

" . . . hasn't left yet. I know. Construction began less than a year ago, and the framework is only partly built. But you have to realize that in theory—we don't know the reality yet—time is tied upon itself in hyperspace. Time is the only dimension that we can recognize, but it is twisted through other dimensions that are meaningless to us. The voice seems very distant, from someone in some distant future. And I think it comes to me because lifeboats were my idea."

◆

You explore outside your mind cautiously, testing the properties of hyperspace one by one. Your body remains asleep in the lifeboat as you try to find bits of data. It is analogous to some incredibly complex mechanism, you tell yourself, trying to tie it down to the only referent you know.

You apply your tests systematically. You find a light wave and try to trace it to its beginning and end. But it has no ends; it goes on forever in a circle, and nowhere is there a photon to give it substance. You search your knowledge for some explanation, but you can only draw upon physics courses that say light waves and photons are inseparable and indistinguishable. It is only a ghost wave, you conclude, the probability of an event that never happened.

You search for other entities, but you find only the lifeboat and a horde of atomic fragments. You can sense that something is wrong with the particles; by all rules of logic and physics they should not exist. But you don't care about hyperfluid super-quarks or anticharmed megamesons or ultrasuperheavy ele-

ments too far from the island of stability to exist. You are searching for a way out, for one of the tens of thousands of ships that
are in hyperspace at any moment. There is no trace of them,
and you realize that it is not distance that separates you, but
something more fundamental.

You spread yourself throughout your island of hyperspace. It
may be closed in upon itself as an island universe; you cannot
tell. You reach out, you hunt for information, for signals. But,
as you listen, you can hear/sense/see/feel only noise, the ideal
white noise of the engineer, totally without content or meaning. The signal-to-noise ratio is zero; the information content is
nil. You search for meaning; you beg for some rational pattern
to be explained to you.

◆

"I feel like I am shifting modes," the man said to his doctor
three years later. "I still hear a voice, but now it seems more a
presence than something that is conveying information. I feel
as if all that can be told to me about hyperspace has been said,
and now some part of me is struggling to evolve an answer. But
it is all in an alien language, and even the response that is
forming is in a symbology that I don't understand."

She touched his arm. "Do you know enough to find an answer?"

He shook his head. "Not with the certainty that I've been
taught to expect, but"—he hesitated, looking around the room
at the array of electronic equipment he had never seen the
doctor use—"but I don't think I could. I don't believe that
hyperspace is knowable. The physicists think it is, and they
propose theories hoping that, in time, we will learn. But who-
ever is speaking to me has no better comprehension of hyperspace than I do; all the voice can supply is raw data that I cannot
consciously assimilate. I sense, underneath, an awareness of the
existence of a vast body of abstractions, but I get no feeling that
the abstractions are close enough to reality to have any meaning. Perhaps this person—if she, he, or it is indeed human—
lacks the background to understand. But maybe the theoreti-
cians have only piled epicycles upon epicycles in attempting to

explain something that is beyond their way of understanding."

She glanced down at her feet for a moment, then reached out and took his hand. "There are theories of medicine and human behavior, too," she smiled. "But if I followed them and my book-learned knowledge, I would have sent you off to the madhouse three years ago. But somehow—I don't know why or how —I know better."

◆

Your exploring has taught you that hyperspace is incomprehensible. Yes, you have picked random bits of data from the sea of noise. You have seen how hyperspace is tied upon itself. You have watched the ritual courting dances of the multifold subatomic particles. You have known subjective time in a boundless space where there is little but time. But all the data are only fragments that must be assembled, and there is no glue to hold them together.

You retreat within your body to think. Seeking help, you try to get the computer to correlate the data. You sit at the console, typing slowly with fingers unused to a keyboard. You piece your words together in the careful, precise phrases that are the only instructions the computer can recognize. But the computer is no help; it can only sputter meaningless strings of words. "Correlation coefficient for the alpha component is 0.002," it says to itself; "this value is less than 0.05 standard deviation from the value predicted by the null hypothesis."

You try rewriting your instructions, but you get no better results. You try special cases and simplifying your words, and the answers change but are no more meaningful. There may be ways to coax the machine to help, but you don't know them. At last, discouraged, you give up.

You pace the floor, restless. In desperation you write notes on pieces of paper and try to assemble them on the floor. There must be a solution, you know; every puzzle has an answer, and there is always a way to put the pieces together into an entity with some meaning. But even the pieces of paper won't come together.

You try to calculate answers, but the equations work out

differently each time you try them. And the mathematics escalates quickly beyond anything you ever learned. Simple algebra and basic calculus beget multidimensional partial differential equations that must be integrated over complex loops passing through undefined spaces. The few solutions you find don't agree with each other, and most of your attempts don't even give you an answer to discover is wrong. Frustrated, you stop.

You are too well trained a mechanic to play with hardware you don't understand, so you resist the temptation to take apart the computer or the control system. For a while you pace, but the tiredness and hunger that you've tried to ignore catch up with you. The body needs input, you tell yourself, so you fuel yourself with reconstituted food paste.

The food weighs you down, and without realizing it you begin to sense that someone is trying to tell you something, but you cannot tell who or what. You drift into sleep.

◆

The doctor's hair had turned gray over the years. Now she sat by the side of a lake with the man and asked, smiling at the clear day and warm weather, "How is the message to your friend in hyperspace?"

"The message is still evolving. I think it is in a transform shape, and parts have been sent while other parts are still being formed. When I search in the back of my mind, I find shapes that I think I built but cannot quite recognize. And I still sense the voice, but I cannot hear anything in the form of words."

She watched him dangle his feet in the water while he looked across the water at the madhouse. "Do you sense static from over there?" she asked, pointing across the lake.

"Yes . . . static of a sort. When I am far enough away, I can filter it out without thinking; here there are bits and pieces that I sense. There are analogies in trying to measure faint electronic signals, but I don't know how to explain them." He paused, looking at a puzzled minnow in the shallows near his feet. "I am grateful that you did not send me over there. Perhaps the static would have overwhelmed the signal, or perhaps they would have found some cure for me."

◆

In sleep, you build up energy. You dream restless dreams in which strange patterns form; you sense someone trying to speak to you in an alien tongue across a space too wide to measure in distance or in time. And though you don't understand the words, you begin to see patterns and interrelationships.

Waking, you feel the instinctive disorientation that always comes with coming to awareness in an unfamiliar place. You look at your watch, seeking a referent, but it has turned itself off. Yesterday the stopped watch would have been just another puzzle part on the floor, but this morning it makes sense.

You force yourself through your morning ritual of washing and eating, trying to impose order. Then you take out your pocket toolkit and add to it all the tools that the lifeboat can supply. You arrange them carefully, assessing your resources. Then you begin.

You summon plans from the depths of the computer's third-level memory and, when the machine at last finds them in its most remote regions, you analyze the drawings and schematics. Watching digits dance on thinfilm screens, you adjust controls slowly. After watching the response, you study the plans again and move on.

After each test, you probe the computer for more information. Each time you find a hint, you trace it through first-level memory into second, and finally into the dead storage of the third and last level within the machine. Often there is little there; sometimes there is too much to assimilate, or there are levels beyond your understanding.

Only after you have tested all the controls do you begin making changes. The first are slow and deliberate: you reconnect a single wire, then watch the response as you adjust a control. As you work, you see patterns forming, and you make more substantial changes.

The computer asks what you are doing, but you ignore it. You cannot explain beyond saying that you are a mechanic performing a mechanic's task, trying to make the lifeboat function.

The more you do, the faster the work goes. You rewire instruments so their displays have different meanings. You rewire the controls to make new patterns on the screens before your eyes. You go inside the boxes that contain wheels and gears, and put the wheels and gears into new patterns. You program the computer to perform new tasks and to forget old ones.

And you are drawn into it, deeper and deeper, understanding only directions, not details. You begin to let yourself go, to build patterns of numbers and interweaving lines that hypnotize. You run counters up and down to delight and confuse. You do not understand, but you do not expect to.

◆

The old couple stood on the top of a small hill, watching the sunset. "Sometimes I understand," the man said, "how the ancients could think that the sun might be going out forever when it set."

The woman turned to him and put on her doctor's expression. "You mean that the transmission is ceasing?"

"I think it stopped long ago, perhaps as we walked up the hill. I was never really aware of it, but there was something subtle that is there no longer, like a bitter taste that hid in a bottle of quinine and faintly tainted the next liquid in the bottle. I've tasted again, and that echo of flavor is gone."

"Was it enough to help?"

He looked down to the river that flowed from the lake by the madhouse. "I don't know; the whole process was at a subconscious level. All I know is that I did form some response, and that it was no more and no less complete than any entity can ever be. No more than an electron and no less than the sun."

They started walking down the hill.

◆

When you can see nothing more to do to the hardware, you pull the switch. The switch is just a prop; no wires lead to or from it, but like all engineers and mechanics, you must be able to pull a switch to define an event.

There is the disorientation that you know always accompanies the transition into or out of hyperspace. Your sense of direction screams that it has no references, no starting point to build interrelationships. You override the instincts that scream for panic. It is over in a moment.

You open your eyes to a world that you might know but don't. You see something that isn't quite a tree with something too blue to be leaves. You breathe air that has just the wrong flavor to it, like the flowers had found different sets of chemicals.

The subtleties bring you to full awareness and, as you look around you, you know that you almost made it. You feel the triumph of escape and the fear of the unknown. It is a world where you almost belong; good, but not what you had hoped for. A shipwrecked sailor who has survived the sharks to be cast up on an unknown shore, you look up the beach, waiting for friends or cannibals.

DREW MENDELSON *lives just north of San Francisco—his most recent address is in a town with the magical-sounding name of Petaluma—and has had one prior story in* New Dimensions: *the soaring, visionary tale, "Museum Piece," in the fifth issue. His educational background is in the fields of astrophysics and communications, but that was long ago; now he is a free-lance journalist and writer who speaks with a clear, altogether individual voice.*

■

*Drew Mendelson*

■

# BLIND MAN, SINGING

A blind man sings on the street corner now. His song is of roses
among the thorns. We don't know when the blind man came.
He has the sweetest tenor voice. He does not know day from
darkness; he sings at all hours. There are temples now in the
hills. We don't know how they came there either, among the
oaks and the Monterey pines. They are twisted temples on the
ridgelines, sprawling before the ocean's wind. They are old,
more ancient than the trees by far. Monks exit from them
speaking in chants that are how we once might have spoken.
We do not recall.

"I remember that a river one time was here," Ragni tells us.
"It came down through a cut in the hills. I fished it as a boy.
Trout were in it and salmon. The water was cold coming out of
the mountains, melt-off from the snow. It emptied here into the
bay."

"Yes," we tell him, "Ragni, surely it was so." We all remember what is not here. Nightly I look for the moon. My observa-
tions traverse an arc of sky among the few stars. Here it would
be a gibbous moon, now with its face half shadow, rising from
beyond the temples. Days later I know it should be a full moon
setting, west over the ocean. I look for the silver reflection,
chopped and scattered by the action of the waves, now present,
now absent as a cloud slowly passes. There are times I think I
see the moon: when the darkness of the night sky swirls, when
a star winks out, when I think I see shadows at midnight.

Mrs. Burcheck explains that there was once a chromatic scale,
progressing from C and ending with C, range upon range,

127

above and below. "It was more melodic by far than the blind man's three notes. I remember songs, I used to sing them."

Only Mrs. Burcheck remembers songs, but she cannot sing them. Only the blind man can sing. "We knew more songs than one," she says.

I go for a walk with Mathilda. I feel strange stirrings, strange bulgings. I tell her that there are feelings inside me. Here, I say, touching myself, these are where the feelings are. "I suppose that they should mean something. It gives me more pleasure to walk with you than with Ragni," I say. "Things about the way you walk, your voice, your scent, your hair, make me want to go walking with you and not Ragni."

I do not know why I feel such pleasure. All I know is that when we hold hands I feel it (Ragni has hands stronger than hers), and when I see her eyes I feel it (Ragni has eyes also, but they are only eyes when I look into them; in Mathilda's eyes I see what I see when I think I see the moon).

A road winds south, skirting the bay. It is pink beneath the pink sun and the azure sky. It is a two-lane road and the truck travels south upon it. It stops weekly at Mrs. Burcheck's store and the driver, who is called Toby, unloads cereal, bananas, milk, and steaks.

"A pleasant good morning," Toby calls. Mrs. Burcheck signs a paper. She has bad teeth and grins with her tongue pressed to them, pink in the gaps between them. We do not know why Toby always comes from the north, traveling south along the pink road. We wonder at that, asking Toby where he comes from, where he goes.

"North," he answers to the first question; "south," he answers to the second.

When we ask what is there, he says, "Less than here."

They are fighting a war among the temples. The monks sally forth, chanting. Lights flash and smoke rises. An acrid smell rolls down the hills on the morning wind. It is gunpowder, Ragni says. He gnashes his teeth and remembers war.

"I remember mortars raining, with explosions short and fierce. I remember that the night sky was like daylight, lit with flares all over that fell and were replaced. When bullets were fired, you did not hear their sound until they had struck; first the impact, then the noise of shooting."

A temple on a hill to the south, guarding the pink road, burns. Monks fight in the northern pass.

The blind man is named Miller; he comes from Kansas City. "Do you?" I say. "It was my home town, also."

He speaks of parks I do not remember, of a memorial on a hill, of the confluence of two rivers. I begin to doubt that I knew it at all.

These are the possibilities concerning us:

1. Ragni says that we have suffered by a great war that has left us with no memory. "We are shell-shocked," he says. "Perhaps it is a kindness." (But there is only one war here, among the monks and the temples. Their weapons are transitory, of negligible effect. There are no scars of war around us otherwise. Secretly I think that Ragni is wrong.)

2. Mathilda says that we are humans in an alien zoo. "What we see are their inept attempts at re-creating our habitat." (Where are "they" who have put us here? Surely not the monks? I do not agree with Mathilda either.)

3. The blind man thinks us mad. He does not see what we see, does not know at all that his world is diminished. "I am among the insane," he tells us gravely. "At least you all are harmless. What jabbering: temples where there are none, no moon where there was one, music greater than mine. Soon attendants will come and put you where you will all be safe."

4. Mrs. Burcheck thinks it is something we ate.

5. I think (I have thought of this greatly) that we are the victims of galactic bandits. "Everything we have now is the same as before, only less," I say. "The stars are the remainders of constellations, the suggestion. The moon is gone but not its orbit. The rivers are absent but their courses remain. What is worse is that they have taken even our memories of these things and left us only the memory of those memories. We do not know what we have forgotten, but only that we have forgotten it." Mine is the most reasonable explanation but it does not account for the monks.

We have received a letter. Toby brought it. It is addressed to

Occupant, and Mrs. Burcheck takes possession. "This is my
store," she says tenaciously. "Thus I am the occupant."

The letter invites us to subscribe to a magazine; it is titled
*Wide World* and is published by Wide World Publications of
317 West Metfort Street, Kansas City, Missouri. This has meaning to Miller, the blind man. He is proven, he has substance.

"See," Miller remarks, "it is from Kansas City, my home."

We would subscribe, but the letter asks for money. (Mrs.
Burcheck says there is some in the till.)

"So this is money," Ragni wonders. "I remember that it was
heavier. It had pictures of dead presidents on it." He begins
crying uncontrollably, staring at the strange men pictured, saying, "Who are they, who are they? I don't know them."

We fill an envelope with the money and address it to the
magazine. We give it to Toby and he takes it off.

The magazine comes. It is gorgeously printed on stock that
makes my eyes tear for some reason. (Have I known paper
before? Have I known print and photography?) And the magazine is what we remember of magazines—*Wide World:* it is
what we remember of the world. It has pictures of buildings we
do not know (among us we have been everywhere), "It is Paris,
of course," says Ragni, "a café on the East Bank, I ate croissants.
It was during the war."

"It is London," says Mathilda. "Hampstead, near the Heath.
It is a confectionery I visited on the High Road past Frognal
Gardens."

"It is Sydney, Kings Cross," I tell them. "A pastry shop in the
nightclub district."

In it are stories. We read them eagerly, but they are of pleasures we do not remember. Ragni scoffs, says they do not exist.

*. . . they ate, the wine was like nectar on their tongues . . .* We
do not connect this with what Toby brings: steaks and cereal
and milk. We know two flavors, sweet and bitter. Are there
more? So the story says.

*. . . her perfume was of the wilds, a musky scent of open range
and woodlands, fumes of vanished lovers from her belly and
her breasts . . .* We know no scent but lilac, though Mathilda says
she smells the ocean's brine.

*. . . they made love, he entered her and they merged, sweet juices flowing, breathing, cries like gulls . . .*

We have gulls, says Mrs. Burcheck; they walk on the sand. What do gulls have to do with people?

"What does it mean, 'they made love'?" Ragni asks. The blind man laughs.

"It is nonsense," says Ragni, "irrational acts."

Mathilda says she thinks it is beautiful; she cannot say (or does not know) why.

Ragni and Mathilda fight. They scream at each other like gulls. (There is fighting among the monks in the temples, with noise and flashing fire and a stench that is not lilac.) Is this "making love"? In the fight they tear their clothes away, Ragni from Mathilda and Mathilda from Ragni. I can only watch Mathilda, wondering if what I smell of her is the fumes of vanished lovers (am I of them, a lover not yet vanished?).

Since the last time, since I walked with her before, the stirrings inside me have diminished, I do not have the strange feelings and the bulging, but remember only that I had it. I think that I have always been so when I was with her and looked at her. They fight until dark and Mathilda falls down; she has blood on her face and cries because she hurts. Ragni also hurts and he grunts.

This is Ragni's theory about us now:

We are amnesiacs who have forgotten how to perceive the world; the magazine with its stories of love and food and smell are to stimulate our recall. The pictures of the cities are to orient us in time and space. (This I also doubt. Why does the world still diminish? Why do we remember less, not more?)

There are fewer stars now at evening; they are sparser now with more black between them, and there are clouds that obscure them often. Ragni thinks it is the monks' war. I don't remember where the moon should rise, whether from the west or from the east: out of the water or out of the hills.

I no longer understand Mrs. Burcheck; her words are as strange as those of the monks. She laughs and I think that there will soon be a time when I won't know laughter either. Still we diminish. The monks have tightened their ring about us. Toby does not come from the north anymore. (He comes perpetually from the north, never any closer, viscera arrayed on the hill. Ragni claims the credit, saying that he disemboweled him to discover if he had bowels.) Even the cereal and steaks are gone. I take pleasure in what I can. With Mathilda I watch the sunset. We know that it disappears beyond the end of the waves; we know that it returns at morning from the opposite direction. The colors are the same at dusk and at dawn: yellow and orange, like the fire that nears from the hills on three sides of us. The temples all are burning. The pink road has been cut.

"The sun sets before us," says Mathilda, "and it rises behind. We must posit a connection between these occurrences; we must be able to project a connecting path, even as there is one through the sky above us."

We are without clothes, and the contours of my body are not the contours of Mathilda's body. We sit so that one side of her touches the opposite side of me. I feel it and I know that she feels it. (There is a fierce crying inside me, like the gulls', a raucous, raunchy crying that means nothing and beats into my skull. I sweat and breathe faster and my heart hugely pounds.) Mathilda discusses these phenomena, wondering that they are present and speculating at their cause.

Ragni says that it is hunger, a direct result of the end of our eating (the end of the steak) and that were we to eat, the feelings would be stilled. The blind man does not sing any more. I ask him why and he says that he does not know, that he would like to sing and sets out to sing with all alacrity but somehow he doesn't and does not know why.

"I have a note," he says, "as I have always had." He displays it for us. It is like the color of the setting sun, and not like it at all.

Ragni has a new theory: We are the punished of the lord. We did not appreciate what we had and so god has taken it from us as punishment. This is a popular theory; Mrs. Burcheck nods and whistles and agrees (though I do not understand her: possibly she still understands us). Surely, if there are monks, there must be a god to whom they pray. The monks are not many now; they diminish as the stars.

As usual, I do not agree with Ragni. I do not think we are the punished of god. I do not think so because we do not remember what has been taken from us. We do not languish after it or long for its return. We do not even remember what it was that was taken.

The night sky has no stars in it now. It is only clouds from the fires burning, and the fires burn so close and hot that we do not know night from day.

I recite the names of what has been taken. I have written them down as they went. They are but names to me. I recite them anyway.

These are some of the things that have been taken: *Love, the moon and stars, cities, the pink road, Toby, wine, and women, Mrs. Burcheck, god, the monks, the cry of gulls, trout and salmon and the flowing river, hunger, and the blind man's song.*

I recite the things that have been taken, and I rise to my feet. I grow angry (anger has not been taken). I fling stones into the ocean and I make a cry.

We four sit on the hillside now. On three sides, the fire encloses. One of us is a blind man without a song; one of us would smell of lilac and vanished lovers; one of us might still wonder; one of us still thinks there are things we have lost.

I will recite the list of things that we have not lost: There is the sky full of clouds, above us. There is the hillside of earth where we sit. There are flames in nameless colors. There is the ocean.

We have them all.

*How this collaboration was accomplished, I have no idea.* MICHAEL BISHOP *lives in Georgia; I've never met him, but I know him to be the father of two and a former English instructor, and I think of him, unjustly or not, as a man of a distinctly academic-suburban sort. Whereas* CRAIG STRETE, *who is of Cherokee blood and currently lives near Los Angeles, has a preponderantly radical-militant tilt for me. They are both accomplished writers, of course.* BISHOP *has appeared twice in* New Dimensions, *has published several novels, and has often been an awards contender;* STRETE, *in a career only a couple of years old, has appeared in a wide range of publications from* Scholastic *and* Ellery Queen's Mystery Magazine *to* Orbit *and* Galaxy. *How two such individual and very different writers combined to produce this wild and ferocious bit of science-fictional mythopoesis I have no idea; but how fortunate for all of us that they did.*

■

*Michael Bishop
and Craig Strete*

∎

# THREE DREAM WOMAN

"Well, what do you want?" Jarmster asked Melyna. "An abo? A Norseman? A Cossack?"

"If I knew, I'd say," the girl said. "You know I don't care much for the things, anyway." Sometimes she had trouble just caring for the other two members of her triad.

"You haven't asked me," Zared, the third member of their six-month-old-three-group, said from the circular interior balcony.

Jarmster and Melyna looked up. They were standing on a floor of Make-Me-Opaque Ambersea, at transparency stage 4. Zared, looking down, could see the tenants in the bowlcove under theirs, all rippled and foggy, making erotic motions with a new Zulu Androlacrum. That, of course, was what had probably started the argument.

"All right, then," Jarmster said, peeling off the Roman nose he'd worn all morning and substituting his own pugnacious pug one. "What do *you* want, Zared?"

"Something indigenous," Zared said.

Melyna made the Make-Me-Opaque floor opaque, smiled at Zared, and saw the Oriental woman upstairs leering at her through the Ambersea floor above the interior balcony. Because the old woman couldn't abide darkness, nine lamps shone down into their living area behind Rose Mashita's head. Outside, it was always dark. Fifty or so years ago, the authorities, for everyone's comfort, had polarized the sky. Sometimes, Melyna thought, it was too bad you couldn't opaque the ceiling, but that was all part of living in a bowlcove: only if you were a minnow

135

in the bottommost bowl could you ink out the fibrafoam above, as compensation for having no one below to leer at.

The Villa, Bowlcove 9 (only one from the top), on the Kansas-Oklahoma perimeter of Wichitopolis, Zared, Jarmster, and Melyna's home.

Jarmster, puzzled, said, "What?"

"Indigenous," Zared responded.

"Again, please."

"He means 'native,' " Melyna said, tweaking Jarmster's nose. Jarmster had to move it over a smidgen, to get it right again.

"Zared's been *reading* again," Jarmster said, oozing distaste.

From the balcony: "Hypnoscanning is all."

"Well, what sort of . . . native . . . do you want?" Melyna asked, cupping her heartside breast for the benefit of Rose Mashita in Bowlcove 10. "A Mandan, an Arikara, a Meshi'ka, an Inca, a Yuchi, a Yamaha . . . ?" Melyna began laughing. The woman upstairs had confused her, no doubt.

Zared, playing buccaneer, leaped from the balcony. The fibrafoam enfolded him—then pushed back out, nudging him upward to his feet as if he were a mushroom poking through peatmoss. (They'd all seen mushrooms at the Wichitopolis Green Quarter: obscene little beasts. Jarmster had asked if they were mammals. "Of course not," Zared had said contemptuously. "They don't have fur.")

Now Zared was saying, "You're making a joke of this, Melyna. When I say we should put in a native, I mean a *native*. Why, this area—according to the twelfth retaping of the *Encyclohomica,* you know—was once a veritable Amerindic zoo!" Excited, he was bouncing a bit on the Ambersea. "It ought to be easy for the HeDonStitute to take our specifications, feed them to the Androlacrumizer, and deliver unto us a warrior. I want feathers, you see. I want feathers, and parfleches, and flesh as sinewy as pemmican . . ."

"Mmmmmm," said Jarmster, caught up.

"All right," Melyna said. "In May we had my Eskimo mama, for whatever she was worth. It *is* Zared's turn."

But Melyna sometimes wondered why they just didn't go upstairs to old Rose Mashita, who was dwelling alone, and give themselves to *her*. As repugnant as that thought was . . . Jarmster and Zared, after all, ran through WageAid units like slotballers, and in ten more years, at this rate, they'd be out every life-unit allotted them and have to go waste-walking with the scurves of Wichitopolis just to keep their bones together. "But tomorrow," Jarmster always said, incorrigible, "our bowl may break and we wee little fishes die." He'd got that from a gummachine guru-oracle in the lobby of the Wichitopolis gypsum baths, and how he delighted in ratcheting it out whenever he needed a justification for spreeing away their WageAids.

"Good," Zared said, pulling a vineline out of the Blucite wall. "Let's call in our specs." He tapped the fonehead into action on the base of the miniature Praxiteles (Aphrodite) in the middle of the room and passed it over to Jarmster.

They called in their specs.

◆

A *native*, they specified.

Jarmster reeled off the abstracts, insisting on (1) "intensity," (2) "mystery," and (3) "romantic melancholy."

Melyna was given the task of defining psycho-physico parameters, and so requested (1) "youth," (2) "beauty," and (3) "feral intelligence."

And Zared supplied the flavoring, the sensory correlatives of the qualities foregoing: (1) "Feathers," he said. (2) "Parfleches," he said. "And (3) "Flesh," he said, "as sinewy as pemmican."

They'd had two already, this triad. But the novelty had worn off, and they'd traded away their Androlacra (a rascal Basque, an Eskimo mama) for four silent Barrymore films, a wardrobe of Bodisheeths, a nucleoscaphe, and a seasonal supply of Virilitol, the Gentle Aphrodisiac.

But now they had foned in their specs . . .

. . . . And so the HeDonStitute's ministers sent their computer aloft, and had it circle the plain underlying the city, and asked it to conceive from auras and thermospoors and historiographic data . . . an Amerind. "And once you've conceived," they told the Androlacrumizer, "gestate us a gestalt as gravid with authenticity as ever you may."

And the computer, being a computer, did.

◆

The triad went to the HeDonStitute in their nucleoscaphe.
They settled into the facility through the vehicle port. In the
circular Hall of Androlacra, they found the Don of Affairs.

"Where is it?" Jarmster asked, rubbing the bridge of his Barrymore put-on nose.

The Don's name was Ridpath, and he led them over the
Maplelux parquetry to the Blue Sky Room. Their feet went
from the waxy Reelwood to the nappy indigo of InsuSod, and
the mustachioed Ridpath told them to sit in hammock nets, to
await what their WageAid units had bought.

Through a curtain of blue Make-Me-Opaque polymer, it
came in to them, and Ridpath took its hand for the introduc-
tions.

Zared was up on his feet. "It's a woman!" he said.

The Don of Affairs said, "You didn't specify sex."

"We had a woman last time," Zared protested. "I wanted, you
know, a . . . warrior. Feathers. Parfleches. Flesh as . . ."

The Androlacrum *was* a woman. She wore a heavy flowered
dress made of trader cloth, and an ugly dun blanket. Her hair
was parted in the middle and pulled back behind her ears. In
her hands, a leather parfleche tooled with a design of interlock-
ing snakes.

"Hello," Melyna said, nodding politely.

"Mmmmm," Jarmster said, crossing his legs.

"Beauty," Zared said. "Melyna said 'beauty.' Is this beauty, I
ask you? We *specified* beauty."

The Androlacrum didn't flinch.

The Don of Affairs said, "Whose standards would you impose?
Yours, sir, or the milieu's from which we've distilled her?"

"But she resembles the Eskimo mama!"

"Who was beautiful," said Jarmster. Then he said, "Well, Don
Ridpath, what bunch is she of?"

"Tribe," Ridpath corrected. Then he avowed, "A composite
of the plains, good people. Kiowa, Comanche, Oglala Sioux,
Osage, Arapaho. A bit of them all."

"She . . . *smells!*" said Zared, circling her. The face of the Androlacrum was devoid of apology. "She smells like . . . like Flav-O-Smoak, Bar-B-Q Piquant. And *I* don't like the Piquant."

"To some extent," Ridpath said, ignoring Zared, "a composite Amerind is a composite human being, so many such people were hereabouts . . . once. This woman, in fact, is what one would have if he made a tree from all trees, a flower from all flowers."

Experimenting with the sound, Jarmster said, *"A tree from all trees. . . ."* He liked the feel of it, Melyna could tell.

Zared said, "I didn't want a tree. I didn't want a flower. I wanted a warrior!"

"I'm sorry," the Don of Affairs said. "Your Androlacrum, taking into account every one of your specs, is a quintessential Amerind, programmed with the lore of the land we've conjured her from. And our contract, I hasten to add, is vocoded, Zared."

"Don't worry, Don Ridpath," Melyna said. "We *do* want her, you know. But could you tell us her name?"

"Certainly," said Ridpath. "A sort of a story. Once 'born,' she asked how she got here. . . ."

"She does talk, then?" asked Zared, staring at the silent figure.

"Yes. Given a little time. Anyhow, she asked how she got here. We told her. She understood. And that's how she decided upon a name, you see. Because three of you collaborated in imagining her, she told us, her name would have to be Three Dream Woman."

"Oh, that's lovely," Melyna said. "Three Dream Woman."

◆

And the Androlacrum, once programmed, three times dreamed. A helix of artificial wishes, aroused by dead dreams, moves her on a mechanical journey to the end of the night. Awake in the body, whispering in the blood, bloodstream surging. I will plant you in the earth of my body.

In the body, restless undercurrents, and the shore rising to cut an underocean of sleep. The artificial wishes, the helix of specifications, beckoning. The empty fist of the triad arranges the fences across the no-man's-land of their minds. Her eyes move with life. The blood, rising, dreams through her skin. What did she dream?

*A child with a kickball, Moksiis they call you, little potbelly. Keep the ball of antelope hair up in the air. A cause for laughter if it touches the earth. Touch the earth with your sisters, little Moksiis; dream in your play, slowing from games into a cottonwood-womanhood, supple and stern, your potbelly flattening into flanks not for touching. You're a girl with a kickball, a child in the spring of her running.*

*The second dream is the cottonwood womanhood of the embryo dreamer. A hide flesher you hold, also a digging stick. The quick and the dead. Early sunups. The buffalo flow in your dreams. Red Leaf has died, those returning will tell you, and on the last day of summer your tree has fallen.*

*The last dream is of power, all praise to the crone you've slyly become. Sixty-five winters, grudgingly borne. Dying's the final birth. . . .*

Though only two days old, Three Dream Woman, the Androlacrum, had thus dreamed her whole life. That was the way the HeDonStitute did things, for the sake of reality, because even a spurious life can comfort.

◆

For the first time in a month, Rose Mashita had put their Ambersea ceiling on a thoroughly opaque setting. As a result, their bowlcove was dark when they entered, and cool, and empty. It was the middle of August. And Three Dream Woman had a blanket about her, a heavy Navaho weave.

Jarmster said, "Let me take your blanket."

Three Dream Woman pulled it to her throat and gazed about the bowlcove with contempt. "The world is dying," she said. The first words she'd spoken since their departure from the HeDonStitute.

How old was she? Melyna wondered. I specified youth and she looks no more than twenty—but her eyes were ageless. Sixty-five years of false experience in the body of a womanchild.

Zared said, "Maybe our 3-D lady would like the cool turned down."

Jarmster nodded and turned the cool down. August seeped in like a gas. Beads of sweat appeared on Three Dream Woman's brow. They would have to give her a BodiSheeth, Melyna thought, to spare her the discomforts of meteorological annoyances, inside and out.

"Aren't we blessed," said Jarmster, gesturing upward, "that Horrorshow Mashita isn't ringside for the unveiling?" He reached for Three Dream Woman's blanket.

"The world is dying," Three Dream Woman said. "And I am not yours."

As he had done in the Blue Sky Room, Zared circled the Androlacrum. "We *bought* you, 3-D lady. You're ours because we bought you."

"It may be that you have bought me, but I am not owned."

The triad was stymied. Intensity they had in Three Dream Woman, and mystery, and intelligence, and all the sensory correlatives Zared had asked for. What had gone wrong? "I know what it is," Zared said. "It's the romantic melancholy Jarmster specified. Her melancholy isn't romantic at all: it's fatalistic and classical, you see, and not even a bit self-pitying. Oriental, you could call it. In any case, our contract is breached."

"No, Zared," Melyna said. "Minimum grounds for annulment are seven out of nine specs. Eight and a half? Never."

"You were the one," Jarmster told Zared, "who wanted something indigenous, don't you remember? Melyna and I, we like her fine."

"Ipso facto," Zared said heatedly, glaring at them all. "I disrobe her."

He pulled Three Dream Woman's blanket away from her shoulders, tossed it over Aphrodite in the middle of the bowl-cove. He tore her dress of trader cloth, yanked it free, flung it aside. Three Dream Woman did not move. In moccasins and a calfhide breechpiece, she stared at the flurried Zared. Melyna wanted to put an arm around her naked shoulders and tell her not to stare so dauntingly. Zared was a spoiled little boy. Jarmster smirked.

"Because I was born only two days past," Three Dream Woman said, "I am a virgin. But in spite of this, I have memories of lying with Red Leaf, my husband, and bearing him two sons and a daughter. My first when I was sixteen snows old, the others in the years that followed. I am Virgin and Mother, a woman of my people. How do you dare to touch me, when this is so?"

Stymied.

The triad averted their eyes and rubbed their hands together, seeking a solution. Only Melyna could smile, her eyes amused at their predicament.

"This is Ridpath's fault," Zared said. "For giving us a . . . a 'composite.' It's Ridpath who's to blame."

They looked again at their Androlacrum. Three Dream was now sitting fully clothed at the base of the Praxiteles, her legs to one side. The statue above her, Melyna thought, might have been a cottonwood, the Ambersea beneath her a swatch of hard prairie.

"I'm hungry," Melyna said. And she sat down beside the Androlacrum and pulsebeeped their bowlcove's contingency cart out of the kitchen.

"You are hungry because the world is dying," said Three Dream Woman "and no one dances the sun to life."

"Phaugh," said Zared, disgusted.

He and Jarmster stood with their arms folded, like spectators at an accident, wishing not to get involved. They moved away from the Androlacrum and set the Make-Me-Opaque floor at transparency stage 2. For the next two hours they played at voyeur. In that brief time, a good deal of the world died.

◆

The Androlacrum placed a cutting of her hair in the arms of *Aphrodite.* "My hair stands for the sagebrush," she told them. Then, facing the statue, Three Dream Woman began her dance. The sun, she had told them, was nowhere to be seen in this place Wichitopolis, and so she danced for the sun.

Zared and Jarmster forsook this ceremony for the gypsum baths, where they gladly immersed themselves in the mechanical sensualizers.

Melyna, fearfully rapt, was unable to leave. She made herself a pallet on the interior balcony and now again called down to

Three Dream Woman to stop for a time. "You must eat," she pleaded. "Androlacrum or no, you mustn't let yourself starve." Did she really care? Melyna wondered. Or did she simply wish the insane dance to end?

But Three Dream Woman thrived on her dancing.

On the fifth hour of the Sun Dance, Rose Mashita reappeared in the bowlcove above. She stared down in lewd fascination. Framing her face, a battery of PlayaSol lamps burned through their Ambersea ceiling like nine gong-sized eyes. Three Dream Woman seemed unaware of these eyes. Even if the sun had come back in them, she could not halt to acknowledge it. The world must be wound back up, the decline of its energies stayed. These people had forgotten how to do that. They had let things go. Even their BodiSheeths couldn't disguise the slackness spiraling through them: it seeped into the world like diluted glue, loosening the seams of creation.

Childhood. Womanhood. Sly senility.

Three Dream Woman united all in her dance; in one heaving of a Sun Dance she lived a lifetime. The soles of her feet fed power into the earth, nine coves up though they were. Three dreams, united, became something magically other. A world that had forgotten magic, had no defense against it.

The dance rose up, many-eyed, saw the triad's dream skull city before it, saw the relationship of Jarmster, Zared, and Melyna embodied in a skull city that was empty of humanity but for a tiny piece of brain. There was only a little bit of brain left, but the dance couldn't get at it. The dance became an ant in order to get into the skull city and get enough to eat.

The ant entered the skull city. When the dance had picked it clean, the ant turned back in Three Dream Woman, but Three Dream Woman had her head inside the skull city. Inside the skull.

Above, Rose Mashita gasped, as she saw the Androlacrum's head covered by a skull.

And now, as their Androlacrum danced, Melyna felt the whole of the villa shudder with the passion of Three Dream Woman's dance. The gleaming white skull began to grow with each step of the dance. Lizards danced in the cranial cracks.

The great empty sockets filled with the wind of the burial pit. The spirit canoes moved across the vanished ocean of the dead tongue, awash with the spit taste of death. And the skull grew. The dance, drumming; the skull, growing. The angry dead teeth, biting out a handhold of dust. The top of the skull was already brushing the upper balcony floor; the weight of the dead white thing was sending dead roots crashing downward.

*"Stop!"* Melyna cried, her voice lost in the other's deep chanting. "Three Dream Woman, please! Please, you must stop!" This was Ridpath's fault, it occurred to her. Who could she turn to for help?

Upstairs, Rose Mashita now wore an expression ecstatically serene. Her hands pressed together. The gong lamps around her sounded out glory. She was a Shinto, Melyna recalled. For her, poor wretch, miracles were everywhere. The triad had often seen her at her bowlcove shrine, worshipping the *kami*. How she must be enjoying this, Melyna thought, terrified, as the skull grew and grew.

Zared and Jarmster burst into the cove. They were only half as tall as the skull, and its shadow seemed to obliterate them. They beheld Three Dream Woman singing beneath the weight of the the skull and the dance, and like Melyna, were terrified.

"Melyna," Zared shouted, "are you all right?" It almost made her cry, his uncharacteristic concern, brought on by terror. She couldn't speak.

"Melyna!" Jarmster called out, circling the wall opposite the still-growing skull, "the eight bowlcoves beneath ours have been crushed into the earth! The whole villa has gone down like a Blucite plunger! We're on street level now, Melyna, and we've got to get out!"

The skull on Three Dream Woman's head, as large now as a water tank, was only an inch under the Ambersea ceiling, the cranial ridges straining against the weakening ceiling. On the other side of the transparent membrane, Rose Mashita was on her knees, the gong lamps around her popping out one by one as if from an electrical overload. Surely, Melyna thought, surely the world is dying. Only wall glow remained in the two final coves aboveground, and everything trembled.

"The other minnows just made it, Melyna!" Jarmster called. "Come down from there and go with us!"

But she couldn't move. Although she was frightened, fear did not immobilize her. What held her in place, a slender woman gripping the balcony rail, was awe at what Three Dream Woman was showing her. She *had* to watch the ceremony; it was ordained that she see this.

"Melyna!" Zared shouted, terror in his voice.

Their Ambersea ceiling, at transparency stage 2, buckled as the skull grew through it. *Aphrodite* fell from her pedestal and shattered.

The fibrafoam celing collapsed and toppled into their bowl-cove a roomful of inflatable furniture, nine dead sunlamps and the woman, Rose Mashita herself, in a slash-pattern kimono. Jarmster and Zared jumped back against the wall to avoid being struck, and Melyna flattened herself against the balcony wall. The fibrofoam, yielding, would have prevented injury to Rose Mashita, had she fallen so as not to snap her neck. As it was, she was the first bit of rubble to stop bouncing. She lay, broken, lifeless.

Zared, who had never liked the woman, shouted at their Androlacrum, "You've gone too far now! Much too far!"

"And we're going to stop you!" cried Jarmster.

The two men found a bowl of polystyrene apples on the contingency cart near the cove's kitchen bubble and began flinging them feebly at Three Dream Woman. They bounced off the skull . . . like polystyrene apples.

As if wounded, the skull, whether by accident or design, cracked open like a fire-shattered rock. Melyna, crouched away from Three Dream Woman on the balcony floor and watched transfixed as the woman cracked open as the skull had done. The Androlacrum's body shattered beneath the cracking skull, decayed and withered like overripe fruit. The hair withered grey, as if it were poisoned grass; bones pushed through the sagging folds of the Androlacrum's skin.

Jarmster and Zared had exhausted themselves flinging apples against the skull. Now it gleamed whitely, like some obscene vase, shattered by the hand of a god. The Androlacrum body was fragmented, collapsed among the bone ruins. Melyna rose, sobbing.

Three Dream Woman's soul streamed through the dead husk's skin, a bright pool of light rising, taking an eloquent human form. The soul, hovering over the myth of the body, spread upward, moving to the place where the sky lives.

Jarmster and Zared, blinded by the glow, fell back into themselves, screaming. They tumbled among the fragments of the skull, mere shells.

"The shadows, their shadows disappear into night. The sun cannot reach them," whispered Three Dream Woman, her words alive in the air.

"But as a stone is a star in the heaven," she said, then, "all that is of the heart is touched by all else. Come with me, Melyna, memory of a daughter, live again in me. Come."

"No," cried Melyna, shaking her head in despair, as she huddled in the ruin of the triad's life. The break was too final, too different, too alive.

"Come live among the living. Give up what is dying." Gentle, the wind of Three Dream Woman's words.

But Melyna didn't wish to die, in order to give up what was dying. Her body shriveled, tightening around her like wet rope. Her body said, *I am afraid of living, never having tried.* She could only shake her head, and lower her eyes.

The bowlcove cracked and collapsed, plunging down into ruin. Jarmster and Zared, screaming, joined Rose Mashita.

Three Dream Woman's soul united with the placenta of her dreaming and rose toward the sun and life, fusing to form a dimension, a world, come alive with power.

"I would have planted you in the earth of my body," whispered the soul of Three Dream Woman, upon the wind. And then gone. Back among the living. The might of her translation set every star and the horns of the moon trembling in the seamless fabric of the dark.

◆

Melyna, among the dead. Melyna, afraid to love, was taken to emergency facilities erected by crane on the Boing tarmac.

Among the victims of the seismic disturbances that had engulfed the bowlcove villas on the city's perimeter. Among the dead. She was given a cot. She was given a blanket. She was bathed, tranquilized, and psychiatrically shriven. "Feel no guilt," the mecho-analyst told her. "It's not your fault, Melyna, that you're still alive."

Afterward, envying the dead, she was able to sleep.

She had three dreams that night: childhood, womanhood, and her own slow senility, one inside the other, like Chinese boxes. She saw her whole life telescoping to ruin. It was emptiness, all of it, and when Melyna, among the dead, cried out in her sleep, not one of the earthquake victims moved to comfort her.

GREG BEAR, *the author of this novella, is an amiable, bespectacled man in his mid-twenties, who has been writing since he was seven or eight and sold his first story when he was fifteen. He is also a skilled artist; some of the most attractive covers on the s-f magazines recently have been his work. "I was a Navy brat," he writes, "and thus saw much of the world before I was ten. Among my earliest memories are a pair of huge red temple dogs guarding the giant Buddha in Kamakura, Japan (any wonder I write science fiction?) and at age seven walking the shell-pocked white sand beaches of Corregidor in the Philippines." He makes his* New Dimensions *debut now with a long and strange story of marching cities and humans in exile.*

■

# MANDALA

### I

The city which had occupied Mesa Canaan was now marching across the plain. Jeshua watched with binoculars from the cover of the jungle. It had disassembled just before dawn, walking on elephantine legs, tractor treads and wheels, living bulkheads upright, dismantled buttresses given new instructions to crawl instead of support; floors and ceilings, pavements, factories and resource centers, all unrecognizable now, like a slime mold soon to gather itself in its new country.

The city carried its plan deep within the living plasm of its fragmented body. Every piece knew its place, every part the plan, and within that scheme there was no room for Jeshua, or for any man.

The living cities had cast them out a thousand years before.

He lay with his back against a tree, binoculars in one hand and an orange in another, sucking thoughtfully on a bitter piece of rind. No matter how far back he probed, the first thing he remembered was watching a city break into a tide of parts, migrating. He had been three years old, two by the seasons of God-Does-Battle, sitting on his father's shoulder as they came to the village of Bethel-Japhet to live. Jeshua—ironically named, for he would always be chaste—remembered nothing of importance before coming to Bethel-Japhet. Perhaps it had all been erased by the shock of falling into the campfire a month before reaching the village. His body still carried fleshy memories of that—a circular range of scars on his chest, still black with tiny remnants of cinders.

Jeshua was huge. When he stood full, he reached seven feet, and his arms were as thick as an ordinary man's legs. His chest at inhale could swell as big as a barrel. He was a smith in the village, worker of iron and caster of bronze and copper. But his strong hands had also acquired delicate skills to craft ritual and family jewelry. For his trade he had been given the surname Tubal: Jeshua Tubal Iben Daod, craftsman of all metals.

The city on the plain was marching toward the Arat Range. It moved with faultless deliberation. Cities seldom migrated more than five miles at a time, or more than once a century. But they seemed more restless now.

He scratched his back against the trunk, then put his binoculars in a pants pocket. His feet slipped into the sandals he'd dropped onto the mossy jungle floor and he stood to stretch. He sensed someone behind him but did not turn to look, though the muscles in his neck knotted tight.

"Jeshua," a man called. It was the Chief of the Guard and the Council of Laws, Sam Daniel the Catholic, who had been a friend of his father. "Time for the meeting at the Synedrium."

Jeshua tightened the straps on his sandals and followed.

Bethel-Japhet was a village of moderate size, with about ten thousand people. Its houses and buildings laced through the jungle until no distinct borders remained. The stone roadway to the Synedrium Hall seemed too short to Jeshua, and the crowd within the hearing chamber was far too large. His betrothed, Kisa, daughter of Jake, was not there, but his challenger, Renold Mosha Iben Yitshok, was.

The representative of the seventy judges, the Septuagint, called the gathering to order and asked that the details of the case be presented.

"Son of David," Renold said, "I've come to contest your betrothal to Kisa, daughter of Jake."

"I hear," Jeshua said, taking his seat in the defender's docket.

"I have reasons for my challenge. Will you hear them?"

Jeshua didn't answer.

"Pardon my persistence. It's the law. I do not dislike you— I remember the friend who was a child with me—but we are mature now, and the time has come."

"Then speak." Jeshua fingered his thick dark beard. His skin, flushed now, was the color of the fine sandy dirt on the riverbanks of the Hebron. He towered a good foot above Renold, who was slight and graceful.

"Jeshua Tubal Iben Daod, you were born as other men, but did not grow as the rest. You now look like a man, but the Synedrium has records of your development. You cannot consummate a marriage. You cannot give a child to Kisa. This annuls your childhood betrothal. By law and my wish I am bound to replace your obligation to her."

Kisa would never know. No one here would tell her. She would come in time to accept and love Renold, and think of Jeshua as only another man in the expolis Ibreem and its twelve villages, a man who stayed alone and unmarried. Her slender warm body with skin smooth as a dolphin's would soon dance beneath the man he saw before him. She would clutch his back and moan for children. They would lie together and dream of the time when humans would be welcomed back into the cities, and the skies would again be full of ships, and God-Does-Battle would be whole—

"I cannot answer, Renold Mosha Iben Yitshok."

"Then you will sign this." Renold held out a piece of paper and advanced.

"There was no need for a public witnessing," Jeshua said. "Why did the Synedrium decide my shame was to be public?" He looked around with tears in his eyes. Never even in the greatest physical pain had he cried before. So his father said, not even when he had fallen into the fire.

He moaned. Renold stepped back and looked up in anguish. "I'm sorry, Jeshua. Please sign. If you love either Kisa or myself, or the expolis, sign."

Jeshua's huge chest forced out a scream. Renold turned and ran. Jeshua slammed his fist onto the railing, struck himself on the forehead, and tore out the seams of his shirt. He had had too much. For nine years he had known of his inability to be a whole man, but he had hoped that would change, that his genitals would develop like some tardy flower just beyond normal season, and they had. But not enough. His testicles were as any

man's, enough to give him a hairy body, broad shoulders, flat
stomach, narrow hips, and all the desires of any young man—
but his penis was the small pink dangle of a child.

Now he exploded. He ran after Renold, out of the Hall, bellowing incoherently and swinging his binoculars at the end of
their leather strap. Renold ran into the village square and
screeched a warning. Children and fowl scattered. Women
grabbed their skirts and fled for the wood and brick homes.

Jeshua stopped. He flung his binoculars as high as he could
above his head. They cleared the top of the tallest tree in the
area and fell a hundred feet beyond. Still bellowing, he charged
a house and put his hands against the wall. He braced his feet
and heaved. He slammed his shoulder against it. It would not
move. More furious still, he turned to a trough of fresh water,
picked it up, dumped it over his head. The cold did not slow
him. He threw the trough against the wall and splintered it
askew.

"Enough!" cried the Chief of the Guard. Jeshua stopped and
blinked at the figure of Sam Daniel the Catholic. He wobbled,
weak with his exertion. Something in his stomach hurt.

"Enough, Jeshua," Sam Daniel said softly.

"The law is tearing me away from my birthright. Is that just?"

"Your right as a citizen, perhaps; not by birth. You weren't
born in the expolis Ibreem, Jeshua. But it is still no fault of yours.
There is no telling why nature makes mistakes."

"No!" He ran around the house and took a side street into the
market triangle. All the stalls were busy with customers picking
them over and carrying baskets full of purchases. He leaped
into this and scattered people and shops every which way. Sam
Daniel and his men followed.

"He's gone berserk!" Renold shouted from the rear. "He tried
to kill me!"

"I've always said he was too big to be safe," growled one of
the guard. "Now look what he's done."

"He'll face the Council for it," Sam Daniel said.

"Nay, the Septuagint he'll face, as a criminal, if the damage
gets any heavier!"

They followed him through the market.

Jeshua stopped at the base of a hill, near an old gate leading out from the village proper. He was gasping painfully and his face was wine-red. Sweat gnarled his hair. In the thicket of his mind he was searching for a way out, the only way now. His father had told him about it when he'd been thirteen or fourteen. "The cities were like doctors," his father had said. "They could alter, replace, or repair anything in the human body. That's what was lost when the cities grew disgusted and cast the people out."

That was it. No city would let any true man or woman enter. But Jeshua was different. He could not be a sinner in fact, only in thought.

Sam Daniel and his men found him at the outskirts of the jungle, walking away from Bethel-Japhet.

"Stop!" the Chief of the Guard ordered.

"I'm leaving," Jeshua said without turning.

"You can't go without a ruling!"

"I am."

"We'll have to hunt you!"

"Then I'll hide, damn you!"

There was only one place to hide on the plain, and that was underground, in the places older than the living cities and known collectively as Sheol. Jeshua ran. He soon outdistanced them all.

Five miles ahead, he saw the city which had left Mesa Canaan. It had reassembled itself below the mountains of Arat. It gleamed in the sun, as beautiful as anything else ever denied mankind. The walls began to glow as the sky darkened, and in the evening silence the air hummed with the internal noises of the city's life. Jeshua slept in a gulley, hidden by a lean-to woven out of reeds.

In the soft yellow light of dawn, he looked at the city more closely, lifting his head above the gully's muddy rim. The city began with a ring of rounded, outward-leaning towers, like the petals of a monumental lotus. Inward from that was another ring, slightly taller, and another, rising to support a radiance of buttresses. The buttresses carried a platform with columns atop it, segmented and studded like the branches of a diatom. At the

city's summit, a dome like the magnified eye of a fly gave off a
corona of diffracted colors. Opal glints of blue and green spar-
kled in the outside walls.

With the help of the finest architect humanity had ever produced, Robert Kahn, Jeshua's ancestors had built the cities and
made them as comfortable as possible. Huge laboratories had
labored for decades to produce the right combinations of animal, plant, and machine, and to find the proper design. It had
been a proud day when the first cities were opened. The Christians and Jews of God-Does-Battle could boast cities more spectacular than any which Kahn had built elsewhere, and the
builder's works could be found on a hundred other worlds.

Jeshua stopped several hundred yards from the glassy steps
beneath the outer petals of the city. Broad, sharp spikes rose
from the pavement and smooth garden walls. The plants within
the garden shrank away at his approach. The entire circuit of
paving around the city shattered into silicate thorns and bristled. There was no way to enter.

He faced the tangle of sharp spines and reached to stroke one
with a hand. It shuddered at his touch.

"I haven't sinned," he told it. "I've hurt no one, coveted only
that which was supposed to be mine by law." The nested spikes
said nothing, but grew higher as he watched, until they
stretched a hundred yards above his head.

He sat on a hummock of grass outside the perimeter and
clasped his stomach with his hands to ease the hunger and
pressure of his sadness. He looked up to the city's peak. A thin,
silvery tower rose from the midst of the columns and culminated in a multifaceted sphere. The sunlit side of the sphere
formed a crescent of yellow brilliance. A cold wind rushed
through his clothes and made him shiver. He stood and began
to walk around the city, picking up speed when the wind carried sounds of people from the expolis.

Jeshua knew from long hikes in his adolescence that a large
entrance to Sheol yawned two miles farther to the west. By
noon he stood by the cavernous entrance.

The underground passages which made up Sheol had once
been service-ways for the inorganic cities of twelve centuries

ago. All of those had been leveled and their raw material recycled with the completion of the living cities. But the underground causeways would have been almost impossible to destroy. They were blocked off and abandoned. Some had filled with groundwater, and some had collapsed. Still others, drawing power from geothermal sources, maintained themselves and acted as if they still had a purpose. A few became the homes of disgruntled expolitans, not unlike Jeshua.

Many had become dangerous. Some of the living cities, just finished and not completely inspected, had thrown out their human builders during the Exiling, then broken down. Various disembodied parts—servant vehicles, maintenance robots, food producers—had left the shambles and avoided the cycle of God-Does-Battle's natural wilderness. They had crept into the passages of Sheol, ill and incomplete, most of them to die and disintegrate. But a few had found ways to survive, and the rumors about those made Jeshua nervous.

He looked around and found a gnarled, sun-blackened vine hard as wood, with a heavy bole. He hefted it, broke off its weak tapering end, and stuck it into his belt where it wouldn't interfere with his legs.

Before he scrambled down the debris-covered slope, he looked back. The expolitans from Ibreem were only a few hundred yards away.

He lurched and ran down the slope.

Sand, rocks, and bits of dead plants had spilled into the wide tunnel. Chipped white ceramic walls dripped with water and small ponds plinked with the drops. Moss and tiered fungus grew.

The villagers appeared at the lip of the depression and shouted his name. He hid in the shadows for a while, until he saw that they weren't following.

A mile into the tunnel, he saw lights. The floor was now ankle-deep with muddy water. He had already seen several of God-Does-Battle's native arthropods, and contemplated catching one for food, but he had no way to light a fire. He'd left all his matches in Bethel-Japhet, since it was against the law to go into the jungles with them unless on an authorized hunt or expedition. He couldn't stand the thought of raw creeper flesh, no matter how hungry he was.

The floor ahead had been uplifted and dropped. A lake had formed within the rimmed depression. Ripples shivered with oily slowness from side to side. Jeshua skirted the water on jagged slabs of concrete. He saw something long and white in the lake, waiting in the shallows, with feelers like the soft feathers of a mulcet branch. It had large grey eyes and a blunt rounded head, with a pocket-knife assortment of clippers, grabbers and cutters branching from arms on each side. Jeshua had never seen anything like it.

God-Does-Battle was seldom so bizarre. It was a straightforward, Earth-like world, which was why humans had colonized in large numbers two thousand years before, and had turned the sluggish planet into a grand imitation of the best parts of ten planets.

Water splashed as he stepped on the solid floor of the opposite shore. The feathery nightmare glided swiftly into the depths, undulating.

The lights ahead blazed in discrete globes, not the gentle glows of the walls of the living cities. Wiring hissed and crackled in the vicinity of a black metal box. Tracks began at a buffer and ran off around the distant curve. Black strips, faded and scuffed, marked a walkway. Signs in old English and something akin to the Hebraic hodgepodge spoken in Ibreem warned against deviating from the outlined path. He could read the English more easily than he could the Hebrew, for Hebraic script had been used. In Ibreem, all writing was in Roman script.

Jeshua stayed within the lines and walked around the curve.

Half of the tunnel ahead was blocked by a hulk. It was thirty feet wide and some fifty long, rusting and frozen in its decay. It had been man-operated, not automatic—a seat-bucket still rose above a nest of levers, pedals, and a small arched instrument panel. As a smith and designer of tools and motor-driven vehicles, Jeshua thought there were parts of the rail-rider which didn't seem integral. He examined them more closely and saw they hadn't come with the original machine. They were odds and ends of mobile machinery from one of the cities.

Part machine, part organism, built with treads and grips, they had joined with the tar-baby rail-rider, trying to find a useful place on the bigger, more powerful machine. They had found only silence. They were dead now, and what could rot had long since dusted away. The rest was glazed with rust and decay.

In the tunnel beyond, stalactites of concrete and rusted steel bristled from the ceiling. Fragments of pipes and wiring hung from them on brackets. At one time, the entire tunnel must have been filled with them, with room only for rail-riders and maintenance crews walking the same path he was taking. Now the metal and plastic had been stripped away by scavenger crews.

Jeshua walked beneath the jagged end of an air duct and heard a susurrus. He cocked his head and listened more closely. Nothing. Then again, almost too faint to make out. The plastic of the air duct was brittle and added a timbre of falling dust to the voices. He found a metal can and put it on end to stand on it, bringing his ear closer.

"Moobed . . ." the duct echoed.

". . . not 'ere dis me was . . ."

"Bloody poppy-breast!"

"Not'ing . . . do . . ."

The voices stopped. The can crumpled beneath him and dropped him to the hard floor, making him yelp like a boy. He stood on wobbly legs and walked further into the tunnel.

The lighting was dimmer. He walked carefully over the shadow-plagued floor, avoiding bits of tile and concrete, fallen piping, snake-wires and loose strapping-bands. Fewer people had been this way. Vaguely seen things moved off at his approach: insects, creepers, rodents, some native, some brought from Earth and feral. What looked like an overturned drum became, as he bent over, a snail wide as two handspans, coursing on a shiny foot long as his leg. The white-tipped eyes glanced up, cat-slits dark with hidden fluids and secret thoughts, and a warm, sickening odor wafted from it. Stuck fast to one side was the rotting body of a large beetle.

A hundred yards on, the floor heaved again, and did not return to order for as long as he followed it. The rutted under-

ground landscape of pools, concrete and mud smelled foul and
felt more foul to his sandaled feet. He stayed away from the
bigger pools, which were surrounded by empty larvae casings
and filled with snorkeling insect young.

He regretted his decision. He wondered what it would be like
to return to the village and face his punishment. To live within
sight of Kisa and Renold. To repair the water trough and do
penance through labor for the stall owners.

He stopped to listen. Water fell in a cascade ahead. The sound
drowned out anything more subtle, but something of a squab-
bling nature rose above. Men were arguing and coming closer.

Jeshua moved back from the middle of the tunnel and hid
behind a fallen pipe.

Someone ran from block to block, dancing agilely in the tunnel, arms held out in balance and hands gesturing like wingtips.
Four others followed, knife blades gleaming in the half-light.
The fleeing man ran past, saw Jeshua in the shadows, and stumbled off into black mud. Jeshua pushed against the pipe as he
stood and turned to run. He felt a tremor through his hand on
the wall. A massive presence of falling rock and dirt knocked
him over and tossed debris around him. Four shouts were severed. He choked on the dust and dirt.

The lights were out. Only a putrid blue-green swamp glow
remained. A shadow crossed the ghost of a pond. Jeshua stiffened and waited for the attacking blow.

"Who?" the shadow said. "Go, spek. Shan hurt."

The man spoke a sort of English. It wasn't the tongue Jeshua
had learned while visiting expolis Winston, but he could understand some of it.

"I'm running, like you," he said in Winston dialect.

"Dis me," said the shadow. "Assed my sabe, you did. Quartie
ob Toms, lie dey t'ought I spek. Who appel?"

"What?"

"Who name? You."

"Jeshua," he said.

"Jesh-oo-a. Iberhim."

"Yes, Ibreem expolis."

"No' far dis em. Stan' an' clean. Takee back."

"No, I'm not lost. I'm running."

"No' good t'stay. Bugga bites mucky, bugga bites you more dan dey bites dis me."

Jeshua slowly wiped the mud from his pants with broad hands. Dirt and pebbles scuttled from the hill where the four lay quiet and tombed.

"Slow," the boy said. From his voice, he couldn't have been over nineteen. "Slow, no? Brainsick?" The boy advanced. "Dat's it. Slow, you."

"No, tired," Jeshua said. "How do we get out of here?"

"Dat, dere and dere. See?"

"Can't see," Jeshua said. "Not very well."

The boy advanced again and laid a cool, damp hand on his forearm. "Big, you. Skeez, maybe tight." The hand gripped and tested. Then the shadow backed off. Jeshua's eyes were adjusting, and he could see the boy's thinness.

"What's your name?" he asked.

"No' matta. Go 'long wi' dis me now."

The boy led him to the hill of debris and poked around in the pitchy black to see if they could pass. "Allry. Dis way." Jeshua climbed up the rubble and pushed through the hole at the top with his back scraping the ceramic roof. The other side of the tunnel was dark. The boy cursed under his breath. "Whole tube," he said. "Ginger walk, now."

The pools beyond were luminous with the upright glows of insect larvae. Some were a foot long and solitary; others were smaller and grouped in hazes of meager light. Always there was a soft sucking and thrash of feelers, claws, legs. Jeshua's skin crawled and he shivered in disgust.

"Sh," the boy warned. "Skyling here, sout' go, tro sound."

Jeshua caught none of the explanation, but stepped more lightly. Dirt and tiles dropped into water, and a chitinous chorus complained.

"Got dur here," the boy said, taking Jeshua's hand and putting it against a metal hatch. "Ope', den go. Compree?"

The hatch slid open with a drawn-out squeal, and blinding glare filled the tunnel. Things behind hurried for shadows. Jeshua and the boy stepped from the tunnel into a collapsed ante-

room open to the last light of day. Vegetation had swarmed into
the wet depression, decorating hulks of pipe valves and electrical boxes. As the boy closed the hatch, Jeshua scraped at a metal
cube with one hand and drew off a layered clump of moss. Four
numbers were engraved beneath—"2 1 7 8."

"Don' finga," the boy warned. He had wide grey eyes and a
pinched, pale face. A grin spread between narcissus-white
cheeks. He was tight-sewn, tense, with wide knees and elbows
and little flesh to cover his long limbs. His hair was rusty orange
and hung in strips across his forehead and ears. Beneath a ragged vest, his chest bore a tattoo. The boy rubbed his hand across
it, seeing Jeshua's interest, and left a smear of mud behind.

"My bran'," the boy said. The "brand" was a radiant circle in
orange and black, with a central square divided by diagonals.
Triangles diminished to the vanishing in each division, with a
vibrant skewedness. "Dat put dere, long 'go, by Mandala."

"What's that?"

"De gees run' me, you drop skyling on, woodna dey lissen
when I say, say dis me, dat de polis, a dur go up inna." He
laughed. "Dey say, 'Nobo' eba go in polis, no mo' eba."

"Mandala's a city, a polis?"

"Ten, fifteen lees fr' 'ere."

"Lees?"

"Kileemet'. Lee. 'Bout fi' eigh's you say mi'."

"You speak anything else?" Jeshua asked, his face screwed up
with the strain of turning instant linguist.

"Spek? Tangee I spek, melea reepera tangea somatosea psor-
pea commingla—"

"No. Anything else?"

"You, 'Ebra spek, bet I. But no good dere. I got better Englise,
tone up a bit?"

"Hm?"

"I can . . . try . . . this, if it better." He shook his head. "Blow
me out to keep up long, do."

"Maybe silence is best," Jeshua said. "Or you just nod yes or
no if you understand. You've found a way to get into a polis?"

Nod.

"Named Mandala. Can you get back there, take me with
you?"

Shake, no. Smile.

"Secret?"

"No secret. Dey big machee—machine dat tell dis me neba retourn. Put dis on my bed." He touched his chest. "Trew me out."

"How did you find your way in?"

"Dur? Dis big polis, it creep affa exhaus'—moob, sorry, afta run outta soil das good to lib on, many lee fro' here, an' squat on top ob place where tube ope' ri' middle ob undaside. I know dat way, so dis me go in, an' out no' late afta. On my—" He slapped his butt. "Coupla bounce, too."

The collapsed ceiling on the anteroom—or skyling, as the boy called it—formed a convenient staircase from the far wall to the surface. They climbed and stood at the edge, looking each other over uncertainly. Jeshua was covered with dark green mud. He picked at the caked rings with his hands, but the mud was too adhesive and would not come off easily.

"Maybe, come fine a bod ob wet to slosh in."

A branch of the Hebron River, which flowed from the Arat Range, showed itself by a clump of green reeds a half mile from the tunnel exit. Jeshua drew its muddy water up in handfuls and poured it over his head. The boy dipped and wallowed and spumed it from puffed cheeks, then grinned like a terrier at the Ibreemite, mud streaming down his face.

"Comes off slow," Jeshua said, scraping at his skin with clumped silkreeds.

"Why you interest' in place no man come?"

Jeshua shook his head and didn't answer. He finished with his torso and kneeled to let his legs soak. The bottom of the stream was rocky and sandy and cool. He looked up and let his eyes follow the spine of a peak in Arat. "Where is Mandala?"

"No," the boy said. "My polis."

"It kicked you out," Jeshua said. "Why not let somebody else try?"

"Somebod alread' tried," the boy informed him with a narrowed glance. "Dat dey tried, and got in, but dey didna t'rough my dur go. Dey—she—one gol, dat's all—got in widout de trouble we all expect. Mandala didna stop her."

"I'd like to try that."

"Dat gol, she special, like de bays 'ere stars flee, spacial like t'ree coords, she up and down legend now. Was a year ago she went and permissed to pass was. You t'ink special you might be?"

"No," Jeshua admitted. "Mesa Canaan's city wouldn't let me in."

"One it wander has, just early yes'day?"

"Hm?"

"Wander, moob, dis Mase Cain' you mumbur about."

"I know."

"So't don' let in dis you, why Mandala an' differs?"

Jeshua climbed from the river. "Appel?" he asked.

"Me, m'appel, not true appel or you got like hair by demon grab, m'appel for you is Thinner."

"Thinner, where do you come from?"

"Same as de gol, we who follow de polis."

"City chasers?" He had heard stories of them. They were ruthless savages by Ibreem's estimation.

"Thinner, you're afraid to go back to Mandala, aren't you?"

"Cumsay, afraid? Like terrafy?"

"Like tremble in your bare feet in the dirtafy."

"No' possible for Thinner. Lead'er like, snakeskin. Poke and I bounce, no' go t'rough."

"Thinner, you're a faker." Jeshua reached out and lifted him from the water. "Now stop with the incomplete tonguing and give me straight English. You speak it—out!"

"No!" the boy protested.

"Then why do you drop all 'thu's' but in your name, and change your word order every other sentence? I'm no fool. I know four tongues and how they work. You're a fake."

"If Thinner lie, feet may sole'n'curl up blow! Born to spek dis odd inflect, and I spek differs by your ask! Dis me, no fake! Drop!" Thinner kicked Jeshua on the shin, but only bent his toe. He squalled and Jeshua threw him back like a fingerling. Then he turned to pick up his clothes and lumbered up the bank to leave.

"Nobod dey neba treat Thinner dis way!" the boy howled.

"You're lying to me," Jeshua said.

"No! Stop." Thinner stood in the river and held up his hands. "You're right."

"I know I am."

"But not completely. I'm from Winston, and I'm speaking like a city chaser for a reason. And speaking accurately, mind you."

Jeshua frowned. The boy no longer seemed a boy. "Why fool me, or try to?" he asked.

"I'm a free-lance tracker. I'm trying to keep tabs on the chasers. They've been making raids on the farmlands outside of Winston. I was almost caught by a few of them, and I was trying to convince them I was part of a clan. When they were buried, I thought you might have been another, and after speaking to you like that—well, I have an instinct to keep a cover in a tight spot."

"No Winstoner has a tattoo like yours."

"That part's the truth, too. I did find a way into the city, and it did kick me out."

"Do you still object to taking me there?"

Thinner sighed and crawled out of the stream. "It's not part of my trip. I'm heading back for Winston."

Jeshua watched him cautiously as he dried himself. "You don't think it's odd that you even got into a city at all?"

"No. I did it by trick."

"Men smarter than you or I tried for centuries before they all gave up. Now you've succeeded, and you don't even feel special?"

Thinner put on his scrappy clothes. "Why do you want to go?"

"I've got reasons."

"Are you a criminal in Ibreem?"

Jeshua shook his head. "I'm sick," he said. "Nothing contagious. But I was told a city might cure me, if I could find a way in."

"I've met your kind before," Thinner said. "But they've never made it. A few years ago, Winston sent a whole pilgrimage of sick and wounded to a city. Bristled its barbs like a fighting cat. No mercy there, you can believe."

"But you have a way, now."

"Okay," Thinner said. "We can go back. It's on the other side

of Arat. You've got me a little curious now. And besides, I think
I might like you. You look like you should be dumb as a creeper,
but you're smart. Sharp. And besides, you've still got that club.
Are you desperate enough to kill?"

Jeshua thought about that for a moment, then shook his head.

"It's almost dark," Thinner said. "Let's camp and start in the
morning."

In the far valley at the middle of Arat, the Mesa Canaan city
—now probably to be called the Arat city—was warm and sun-
set-pretty, like a diadem. Jeshua made a bed from the reeds and
watched Thinner as he hollowed out the ground and made his
own nest. Jeshua slept lightly that evening, and came awake
with dawn. He opened his eyes to a small insect on his chest,
inquiring its way with finger-long antennae. He flicked it off and
cleared his throat.

Thinner jack-in-the-boxed from his nest, rubbed his eyes, and
stood.

"I'm amazed," he said. "You didn't cut my throat."

"Wouldn't do me any good."

"Work like this rubs down a man's trust."

Jeshua returned to the river and soaked himself again, letting
the chill wallop his face and back in heavy hand-loads. The
pressure in his groin was lighter this morning than most, but it
still made him grit his teeth. He wanted to roll in the reeds and
groan, rut the earth, but it would do him no good. Only the
impulse existed.

They agreed on which pass to take through the Arat peaks,
and set out.

Jeshua had spent most of his life within sight of the villages
of the expolis Ibreem, and found himself increasingly nervous
the farther he hiked. They crawled the slope, and Thinner's
statement about having tough soles proved itself. He walked
barefoot over all manner of jagged rocks without complaining.

At the crest of a ridge, Jeshua looked back and saw the plain
of reeds, and the jungle beyond. With some squinting and hand-
shading, he could make out the major clusters of huts in two
villages, and the Temple Josiah on Mount Miriam. All else was
hidden.

In two days, they crossed Arat and a rilled terrain of foothills beyond. They walked through fields of wild oats. "This used to be called Agripolis," Thinner said. "If you dig deep enough here, you'll come across irrigation systems, automatic fertilizing machines, harvesters, storage bins—the whole works. It's all useless now. For three hundred years it wouldn't let any human cross these fields. It finally broke down and those parts that could move, did. Most died."

Jeshua knew a little about the history of the cities around Arat, and told Thinner about the complex known as Tripolis. Three cities had been grouped on one side of Arat, about twenty miles north of where they were standing. After the exiling, one had fragmented and died. Another had moved successfully and had left the area. The third had tried to cross the Arat range and failed. The major bulk of its wreckage lay in a disorganized, mute clump not far from them.

They found scattered pieces of it on the plain of Agripolis. As they w lked, they saw bulkheads and buttresses, most hardy of a city s larger members, still supported upright by dessicated legs. Some were fifty to sixty yards long and twenty feet across, mounted on organic wheel movements. Their metal parts had corroded badly. The organic parts had disappeared, except for an occasional span of silicate wall, or internal skeleton of colloid.

"They're not all dead, though," Thinner said. "I've been across here before. Some made the walk a little difficult."

In the glare of afternoon, they hid from a wheeled beast armored like a great, translucent tank. "That's something from deep inside a city—a mover or loader," Thinner said. "I don't know anything about the temper of a feral city part, but I'm not going to aggravate it."

When the tank thing passed, they continued. There were creatures less threatening, more shy, which they ignored. Most of them Jeshua couldn't fit into a picture of ancient city functions. They were queer, dreamy creatures: spinning tops, many-legged browsers, things with bushes on their backs, bowls built like dogs but carrying water—insane, confusing fragments.

By day's end they stood on the outskirts of Mandala. Jeshua sat on a stone to look at the city. "It's different," he said. "It isn't as pretty." Mandala was more square, less free and fluid. It had an ungainly, ziggurat-like pear-shape. The colors which were scattered along its walls and light-banners—black and orange—didn't match well with the delicate blues and greens of the city substance.

"It's older," Thinner said. "One of the first, I think. It's an old tree, a bit scabrous, not like a young sprout."

Jeshua looped his belt more tightly about his club and shaded his eyes against the sun. The young of Ibreem had been taught enough about cities to identify their parts and functions. The sunlight-absorbing banners which rippled near Mandala's peak were like the leaves of a tree, and also like flags. Designs on their surfaces formed a language conveying the city's purpose and attitude. Silvery reflectors cast shadows below the banners. By squinting, he could see the gardens and fountains and crystalline recreation buildings of the uppermost promenade, a mile above them. Sunlight illuminated the green walls and showed their mottled innards, pierced the dragonfly buttresses whose wings with slow in-out beats kept air moving, and crept back and forth through the halls, light-wells and living quarters, giving all of Mandala an interior luminosity. Despite the orange and black of the colored surfaces, the city had an innate glory which made Jeshua's chest ache with desire.

"How do we get in?" he asked.

"Through a tunnel, about a mile from here."

"You mentioned a girl. Was that part of the cover?"

"No. She's here. I met her. She has the liberty of the city. I don't think she has to worry about anything, except loneliness." He looked at Jeshua with an uncharacteristic wry grin. "At least she doesn't have to worry about where the next meal comes from."

"How did she get in? Why does the city let her stay?"

"Who can judge the ways of a city?"

Jeshua nodded thoughtfully. "Let's go."

Thinner's grin froze and he stiffened, staring over Jeshua's shoulder. Jeshua looked around and surreptitiously loosened his club in his belt. "Who are they?" he asked.

"The city chasers. They usually stay in the shadow. Something must be upsetting them today."

At a run through the grass, twenty men dressed in rough orange and black rags advanced on them. Jeshua saw another group coming from the other side of the city perimeter. "We'll have to take a stand," he said. "We can't outrun them."

Thinner looked distressed. "Friend," he said. "It's time I dropped another ruse. We can get into the city here, but they can't."

Jeshua ignored the non sequitur. "Stand to my rear," he said. Jeshua swung his club up and took a stance, baring his teeth and hunkering low as his father had taught him to do when facing wild beasts. The bluff was the thing, especially when backed by his bulk. Thinner pranced on his bandy legs for a second, panic tightening his face. "Follow me, or they'll kill us," he said.

He broke for the glassy gardens within the perimeter. Jeshua turned and saw the polis chasers were forming a circle, concentrating on him, aiming spears for a throw. He ducked and lay flat as the metal-tipped shafts flew over, thunking into the grass. He rose and a second flight shot by, one grazing him painfully on the shoulder. He heard Thinner rasp and curse. A chaser held him at arm's length, repeatedly slashing his chest with a knife. Jeshua stood tall and ran for the circle, club held out before him. Swords came up and out, dull grey steel spotted with blood-rust. He blocked a thrust and cut it aside with the club, then parted the man from his life with a downward swing.

"Stop it, you goddamn idiots!" someone shouted. One of the chasers shrieked and the others backed away from Jeshua. Thinner's attacker held a head, severed from the boy's body. It was trailing green. Though decapitated, Thinner was shouting invective in several languages, including Hebrew and chaser English. The attackers dropped their weapons before the oracular monster and ran pale and stumbling. The petrified man who held the head dropped it and fell over.

Jeshua stood his ground, bloody club trembling in his loosening hand.

"Hey," said the muffled voice in the grass. "Come here and help!"

Jeshua spotted six points on his forehead and drew two meshed triangles between. He walked slowly through the grass.

"El and hell," Thinner's head cried out. "I'm chewing grass. Get me up and out."

He found the boy's body first. He bent over and saw the red, bleeding skin on the chest, pulpy green below that, and the pale colloid ribs which supported. Deeper still, glassy machinery and pale blue fluids in filigree tubes surrounded glints of organic circuit and metal. The chaser nearby had fainted from shock.

He found Thinner's head face-down, jaw working and hair standing on end. "Lift me out," the head said. "By the hair, if you're squeamish, but lift me out."

Jeshua reached down and picked the head up by the hair. Thinner stared at him above green-leaking nose and frothed lips. The eyes blinked. "Wipe my mouth with something." Jeshua picked up a clump of grass and did so, leaving bits of dirt behind, but getting most of the face clean. His stomach squirmed, but Thinner was obviously no mammal, nor a natural beast of any form, so he kept his reactions in check.

"I wish you'd listened to me," the head said.

"You're from the city," Jeshua said, twisting it this way and that.

"Stop that—I'm getting dizzy. Take me inside Mandala."

"Will it let me in?"

"Yes, dammit, I'll be your passkey."

"If you're from the city, why would you want me or anyone else to go inside?"

"Take me in and you'll discover."

Jeshua held the head at arm's length and inspected it with half-closed eyes. Then, slowly, he lowered it, looked at the tiled gardens within the perimeter, and took his first step. He stopped, shaking.

"Hurry," the head said. "I'm dripping."

At any moment Jeshua expected the outskirts to splinter and bristle, but no such thing happened. "Will I meet the girl?" he asked.

"Walk, no questions."

Eyes wide and stomach tense as rock, Jeshua entered the city of Mandala.

II

"There, that came easier than you expected, didn't it?" the head asked.

Jeshua stood in a cyclopean green mall, light bright but filtered, like the bottom of a shallow sea, surrounded by the green of thick glass and botanic fluids. Tetrahedral pylons and slender arches rose all around and met high above in a circular design of orange and black, similar to the markings on Thinner's chest. The pylons supported four floors opening onto the court. The galleries were empty.

"You can put me down here," Thinner said. "I'm broken. Something will come along to fix me. Wander for a while if you want. Nothing will hurt you. Perhaps you'll meet the girl."

Jeshua looked around apprehensively. "Would do neither of us any good," he said. "I'm afraid."

"Why, because you're not a whole man?"

Jeshua dropped the head roughly on the hard floor and it bounced, screeching.

"How did you know?" he asked loudly, desperately.

"Now you've made me confused," the head said. "What did I say?" It stopped talking and its eyes closed. Jeshua touched it tentatively with his boot. It did nothing. He straightened up and looked for a place to run. The best way would be out. He was a sinner now, a sinner by anger and shame. The city would throw him out violently. Perhaps it would brand him, as Thinner had hinted earlier. Jeshua wanted the familiarity of the grasslands and tangible enemies like the city chasers.

The sunlight through the entrance arch guided him. He ran for the glassy walkway and found it rising to keep him in. Furious with panic, he raised his club and struck at the spines. They sang with the blows but did not break.

"Please," he begged. "Let me out, let me out!"

He heard a noise behind him and turned. A small wheeled cart gripped Thinner's head with gentle mandibles and lifted its segmented arms to send the oracle down a chute into its back. It rolled from the mall into a corridor.

Jeshua lifted his slumped shoulders and expanded his chest. "I'm afraid!" he shouted at the city. "I'm a sinner! You don't want me, so let me go!"

He squatted on the pavement with club in hand, trembling. The hatred of the cities for man had been deeply impressed in him. His breathing slowed until he could think again, and the fear subsided. Why had the city let him in, even with Thinner? He stood and slung the club in his belt. There was an answer someplace. He had little to lose—at most, a life he wasn't particularly enjoying.

And in a city there was the possibility of healing arts now lost to the expolitans.

"Okay," he said. "I'm staying. Prepare for the worst."

He walked across the mall and took a corridor beyond. Empty rooms with hexagonal doors waited silent on either side. He found a fountain of refreshing water in a broad, cathedral-nave room, and drank from it. Then he spent some time studying the jointing of the arches which supported the vault above, running his fingers over the grooves.

A small anteroom had a soft, couchlike protrusion, and he rested there, staring blankly at the ceiling. For a short while, he slept. When he awoke, both he and his clothes were clean. A new pair had been laid out for him—standard Ibreem khaki shirt and short pants and a twine belt, more delicately knitted than the one he was wearing. His club hadn't been removed. He lifted it. It had been tampered with—and improved. It fitted his grip better now, and was weighted to balance well. A table was set with dishes of fruit and what looked like bread-gruel. He had been accommodated in all ways, more than he deserved from any city. It almost gave him the courage to be bold. He took off his ragged clothes and tried on the new set. They fit admirably and he felt less disreputable. His sandals had been stitched up but not replaced. They were comfortable, as always, but sturdier.

"How can I fix myself here?" he asked the walls. No answer came. He drank water from the fountain again, and went to explore further.

The ground plan of Mandala's lowest level was relatively

simple. It consisted mostly of trade and commerce facilities, with spacious corridors for vehicle traffic, large warehouse areas, and dozens of conference rooms. Computing facilities were also provided. He knew a little about computers—the Trade Office in Bethel-Japhet still had an ancient pocket model taken from a city during the exiling. The access terminals in Mandala were larger and clumsier, but recognizable. He came across a room filled with them. Centuries of neglect had made them irregular in shape, their plastic and thin metal parts warping. He wondered what parts of them, if any, were alive.

Most of the rooms on the lowest level maintained the sea-floor green motif. The uniformity added to Jeshua's confusion, but after several hours of wandering, he found the clue which provided guidance. Though nothing existed in the way of written directions or graphic signs or maps, by keeping to the left he found he tended to the center, and to the right, the exterior. A Mandalan of ten centuries ago would have known the organization of each floor by education, and perhaps by portable guidebooks or signalers. Somewhere, he knew, there had to be a central elevator system.

He followed all left-turning hallways. Avoiding obvious dead ends, he soon reached the base of a hollow shaft. The floor was tiled with a changing design of greens and blues, advancing and flowing beneath his feet like a cryptic chronometer. He craned his neck back and looked up through the center of Mandala. High above he saw a bluish circle, the waning daytime sky. Wind whistled down the shaft.

Jeshua heard a faint hum from above. A speck blocked out part of the skylight and grew as it fell, spiraling like a dropped leaf. It had wings, a thick body for passengers, and an insect head, like the dragonfly buttresses which provided ventilation on Mandala's exterior. Slowing its descent, it lifted its nose, and came to a stop in front of him, still several feet above the floor. The bottoms of its unmoving, transparent wings reflected the changing design of the floor.

Then he saw that the floor was coming to a conclusion, like an assembled puzzle. It formed a mosaic triskelion, a three-winged symbol outlined in red.

The glider waited for him. In its back there was room for at least five people. He chose the front seat. The glider trembled and moved forward. The insect-head tilted back, cocked sideways, and inspected its ascent. Metallic antennae emerged from the front of the body. A tingling filled the air. And he began to fly.

The glider slowed some distance above the floor and came to a stop at a gallery landing. Jeshua felt his heartbeat race as he looked over the black railing, down the thousand feet or so to the bottom of the shaft.

"This way, please."

He turned, expecting to see Thinner again. Instead there waited a device like a walking coat-tree, with a simple vibration speaker mounted on its thin neck, a rod for a body, and three legs jointed like a mantis's front legs. He followed it.

Transparent pipes overhead pumped bubbling fluids like exposed arteries. He wondered whether dissenting citizens in the past could have severed a city's lifelines by cutting such pipes —or were these mere ornaments, symbolic of deeper activities? The coat-tree clicked along in front of him, then stopped at a closed hexagonal door and tapped its round head on a metal plate. The door opened. "In here."

Jeshua entered. Arranged in racks and rows in endless aisles throughout the huge room were thousands of constructions like Thinner. Some were incomplete, with their machinery and sealed-off organic connections hanging loose from trunks, handless arms, headless necks. Some had gaping slashes, broken limbs, squashed torsos. The coat-tree hurried off before he could speak, and the door closed behind.

He was beyond anything but the most rudimentary anxiety now. He walked down the central aisle, unable to decide whether this was a workshop or a charnel house. If Thinner was here, it might take hours to find him.

He stared straight ahead and stopped. There was someone not on the racks. At the far end of the room, it stood alone, too distant to be discerned in detail. Jeshua waited, but the figure did not move. It was a stalemate.

He made the first step. The figure darted to one side like a deer. He automatically ran after it, but by the time he'd reached the end of the aisle, it was nowhere to be seen.

"Hide and seek," he murmured. "For God's sake, hide and seek."

He rubbed his groin abstractedly, trying to still the flood of excitement rushing into his stomach and chest. His fantasies multiplied and he bent over double, grunting. He forced himself to straighten up, held out his arms, and concentrated on something distracting.

He saw a head which looked very much like Thinner's. It was wired to a board behind the rack, and fluids pulsed up tubes into its neck. The eyes were open but glazed, and the flesh was ghostly. Jeshua reached out to touch it. It was cold, lifeless.

He examined other bodies in more detail. Most were naked, complete in every detail. He hesitated, then reached down to touch the genitals of a male. The flesh was soft and flaccid. He shuddered. His fingers, as if working on their own, went to the pubic mound of a female figure. He grimaced and straightened, rubbing his hand on his pants with automatic distaste. A tremor jerked up his back. He was spooked now, having touched the lifeless forms, feeling what seemed dead flesh.

What were they doing here? Why was Mandala manufacturing thousands of surrogates? He peered around the racks of bodies, this way and behind, and saw open doors far beyond. Perhaps the girl—it must have been the girl—had gone into one of those.

He walked past the rows. The air smelled like cut grass and broken reed stems, with sap leaking. Now and then it smelled like fresh slaughtered meat, or like oil and metal.

Something made a noise. He stopped. One of the racks. He walked slowly down one aisle, looking carefully, seeing nothing but stillness, hearing only the pumping of fluids in thin pipes and the clicks of small valves. Perhaps the girl was pretending to be a cyborg. He mouthed the word over again. Cyborg. He knew it from his schooling. The cities themselves were cybernetic organisms.

He heard someone running. The footsteps were going away from him, slap of bare feet on floor. He paced evenly past the

rows, looking down each aisle, nothing, nothing, stillness, there!
The girl was at the opposite end, laughing at him. An arm
waved. Then she vanished.

He decided it was wise not to chase anyone who knew the city
better than he did. Best to let her come to him. He left the room
through an open door.

A gallery outside opened onto a smaller shaft. This one was
red and only fifty or sixty feet in diameter. Rectangular doors
opened off the galleries, closed but unlocked. He tested the
three doors on his level, opening them one at a time with a
push. Each room held much the same things—a closet filled
with dust, rotting and collapsed furniture, emptiness and the
smell of old tombs. Dust drifted into his nostrils and he sneezed.
He went back to the gallery and the hexagonal door. Looking
down, he swayed and felt sweat start. The view was dizzying
and claustrophobic.

A singing voice came down to him from above. It was femi-
nine, sweet and young, a song in words he did not completely
catch. They resembled Thinner's chaser dialect, but echoes
broke the meaning. He leaned out over the railing as far as he
dared and looked up. It was definitely the girl—five, six, seven
levels up. The voice sounded almost childish. Some of the words
reached him clearly with a puff of direct breeze:

"Dis em, in solit lib, dis em . . . Clo'ed in clo'es ob dead . . . "

The red shaft vanished to a point without skylight. The unfamiliar glare hurt his eyes. He shaded them to see more clearly.
The girl backed away from the railing and stopped singing.

He knew by rights he should be angry, that he was being
teased. But he wasn't. Instead he felt a loneliness too sharp to
sustain. He turned away from the shaft and looked back at the
door to the room of cyborgs.

Thinner stared back at him, grinning crookedly. "Didn't have
chance to welcome," he said in Hebrew. His head was mounted
on a metal snake two feet long, His body was a rolling green car
with three wheels, a yard long and half a yard wide. It moved
silently. "Have any difficulty?"

Jeshua looked him over slowly, then grinned. "It doesn't suit
you," he said. "Are you the same Thinner?"

"Doesn't matter, but yes, to make you comfortable."

"If it doesn't matter, then who am I talking to? The city computers?"

"No, no. They can't talk. Too concerned with maintaining. You're talking with what's left of the architect."

Jeshua nodded slowly, though he didn't understand.

"It's a bit complicated," Thinner said. "Go into it with you later. You saw the girl and she ran away from you."

"I must be pretty frightening. How long has she been here?"

"A year."

"How old is she?"

"Don't know for sure. Have you eaten for a while?"

"No. How did she get in?"

"Not out of innocence, if that's what you're thinking. She was already married before she came here. The chasers encourage marriage early."

"Then I'm not here out of innocence, either."

"No."

"You never saw me naked," Jeshua said. "How did you know what was wrong with me?"

"I'm not limited to human senses, though El knows what I do have are bad enough. Follow me and I'll find suitable quarters for you."

"I may not want to stay."

"As I understand it, you've come here to be made whole. That can be done, and I can arrange it. But patience is always a virtue."

Jeshua nodded at the familiar homily. "She speaks chaser English. Is that why you were with the chasers, to find a companion for her?"

The Thinner-vehicle turned away from Jeshua without answering. It rolled through the cyborg chamber and Jeshua followed. "It would be best if someone she was familiar with would come to join her, but none could be persuaded."

"Why did she come?"

Thinner was silent again. They took a spiral moving walkway around the central shaft, going higher. "It's the slow, scenic route," Thinner said, "but you'll have to get used to the city and its scale."

"How long am I going to stay?"

"As long as you wish."

They disembarked from the walkway and took one of the access halls to an apartment block on the outer wall of the city. The construction and colors here were more solid. The bulkheads and doors were opaque and brightly colored in blue, burnt orange, and purple. The total effect reminded Jeshua of a sunset. A long balcony in the outer wall gave a spectacular view of Arat and the plains, but Thinner allowed him no time to sightsee. He took Jeshua into a large apartment and made him familiar with the layout.

"It's been cleaned up and provided with furniture you should be used to. You can trade it in for somewhere else whenever you want. But you'll have to wait until you've been seen to by the medical units. You've been scheduled for work in this apartment." Thinner showed him a white-tile and stainless-steel kitchen, with food dispensers and basic utensils. "Food can be obtained here. There's enough material to customize whatever comes out of the dispensers. Sanitary units are in here and should explain themselves—"

"They talk?"

"No. I mean their use should be self-evident. Very few things talk in the city."

"We were told the cities were commanded by voice."

"Not by most of the citizens. The city itself does not talk back. Only certain units, not like myself—none of the cyborgs were here when humans were. That's a later development. I'll explain in time. I'm sure you're more used to books and scrolls than tapes or tridvee experiences, so I've provided some offprints for you on these shelves. Over here—"

"Seems I'm going to be here for a long time."

"Don't be worried by the accommodations. This may be fancy by your standards, but it certainly isn't by Mandala's. These used to be apartments for those of an ascetic temper. If there's anything you want to know when I'm not here, ask the information desk. It's hooked to the same source I am."

"I've heard of the city libraries. Are you part of them?"

"No. I've told you, I'm part of the architect. Avoid library outlets for the moment. In fact, for the next few days, don't wander too far. Too much too soon, and all that. Ask the desk and it will give you safe limits. Remember, you're more helpless than a child here. Mandala is not out-and-out dangerous, but it can be disturbing."

"What do I do if the girl visits me?"

"You anticipate it?"

"She was singing to me, I think. But she didn't want to show herself directly. She must be lonely."

"She is." Thinner's voice carried something more than a tone of crisp efficiency. "She's been asking a lot of questions about you, and she's been told the truth. But she's lived without company for a long time, so don't expect anything soon."

"I'm confused," Joshua said.

"In your case, that's a healthy state of mind. Relax for a while; don't let unknowns bother you."

Thinner finished explaining about the apartment and left. Joshua went out the door to stand on the terrace beyond the walkway. Light from God-Does-Battle's synchronous artificial moons made the snows of Arat gleam like dull steel in the distance. Joshua regarded the moons with an understanding he'd never had before. Humans had brought them from the orbit of another world, to grace God-Does-Battle's nights. The thought was staggering. People used to live there, a thousand years ago. What had happened to them when the cities had exiled their citizens? Had the lunar cities done the same thing as the cities of God-Does-Battle?

He went to his knees for a moment, feeling ashamed and primitive, and prayed to El for guidance. He was not convinced his confusion was so healthy.

He ate a meal which came as close as amateur instructions could make it to the simple fare of Bethel-Japhet. He then examined his bed, stripped away the covers—the room was warm enough—and slept.

### III

Once, long ago, if his earliest childhood memories were accurate, he had been taken from Bethel-Japhet to a communion in the hills of Kebal. That had been years before the Synedrium had stiffened the separation laws between Catholic and Habiru rituals. His father and most of his acquaintances had been Habiru and spoke Hebrew. But prominent members of the community, such as Sam Daniel, had by long family tradition worshiped Jesus as more than a prophet, according to established creeds grouped under the title of Catholicism. His father had not resented the Catholics for their ideas.

At that communion, not only had Habiru and Catholic worshiped, but the now-separate Muslims, and a few diverse creeds best left forgotten. Those had been difficult times, perhaps as hard as the times just after the Exiling. Jeshua remembered listening to the talk between his father and a group of Catholics —relaxed, informal talk, without the stiffness of ceremony which had grown up since. His father had mentioned that his young son's name was Jeshua, which was a form of Jesus, and the Catholics had clustered around him like fathers all, commenting on his fine form as a six-year-old, and his size and evident strength. "Will you make him a carpenter?" they asked jokingly.

"He will be a cain," his father answered.

They frowned, puzzled.

"A maker of tools."

"It was the making of tools that brought us to the Exiling," Sam Daniel said.

"Aye, and raised us from beasts," his father countered.

Jeshua remembered the talk that followed in some detail. It had stuck with him and determined much of his outlook as an adult, after the death of his father in a mining accident.

"It was the shepherd who raised us above the beasts by making us their masters," another said. "It was the maker of tools and tiller of the soil who murdered the shepherd and was sent to wander in exile."

"Yes," his father said, eyes gleaming in the firelight. "And later it was the shepherd who stole a birthright from his nomad brother—or have we forgotten Jacob and Esau? The debt, I think, was even."

"There's much that is confusing in the past," Sam Daniel

admitted. "And if we use our eyes, and see that our Exile is made less difficult by the use of tools, we should not condemn our worthy cains. But those who built the cities which Exiled us were also making tools, and the tools turned against us."

"But why?" his father asked. "Because of our degraded state as humans? Remember, it was the Habirus and Catholics—then Jews and Christians—who commissioned Robert Kahn to build the cities for God-Does-Battle, and to make them pure cities for the best of mankind, the final carriers of the flame of Jesus and the Lord. We were self-righteous in those days, and wished to leave behind the degraded ways of our neighbors. How was it that the best were cast out?"

"Hubris," chuckled a Catholic. "A shameful thing, anyway. The histories tell us of many shameful things, eh, lad?" He looked at Jeshua. "You remember the stories of the evil that men did."

"Don't bother the child," his father said angrily.

Sam Daniel put his arm around the shoulder of Jeshua's father. "Our debater is at it again. Still have the secret for uniting us all?"

Half-asleep, he opened his eyes and tried to roll over on the bed.

Something stopped him, and he felt a twinge at the nape of his neck. He couldn't see well—his eyes were watering and everything was blurred. His nose tickled and his palate hurt vaguely, as if something were crawling through his nostrils into the back of his throat. He tried to speak, but couldn't. Silvery arms weaved above him, leaving grey trails of shadow behind, and he thought he saw wires spinning over his chest. He blinked. Liquid drops hung from the wires like dew from a web. When the drops fell and touched his skin, waves of warmth and numbness radiated.

He heard a whine, like an animal in pain. It came from his own throat. Each time he breathed, the whine escaped. Again the metal things bobbed above him, this time unraveling the wires. He blinked and it took a long time for his eyelids to open again. There was a split in the ceiling, and branches grew down from it, one coming up under his vision and reaching into his

nose, others holding him gently on the bed, another humming
behind his head, making his scalp prickle. He searched for the
twinge below his neck. It felt as if a hair was being pulled from
his skin, or a single tiny ant was pinching him. He was aloof, far
above it, not concerned; but his hand still wanted to scratch and
a branch prevented it from moving. His vision cleared for an
instant, and he saw green enamelled tubes, chromed grips, pale
blue ovals being handed back and forth.

"A anna eh uh," he tried to say. "Eh ee uh." His lips wouldn't
move. His tongue was playing with something sweet. He'd been
given candy. Years ago he'd gone for a mouth examination—
with a clean bill of health—and he'd been given a roll of sugar-
gum to tongue on the way home.

He sank back into his skull to listen to the talk by the fireside
again. "Hubris," chuckled a Catholic.

"Habirus," he said to himself. "Hubris."

"A shameful thing, anyway—"

"Our debater is at it again. Still have the secret for uniting us
all?"

"And raised us from beasts."

Deep, and sleep.

◆

He opened his eyes and felt something in the bed with him.
He moved his hand to his crotch. It felt as if a portion of the bed
had gotten loose and was stuck under his hip, in his shorts. He
lifted his hips and pulled down the garment, then lay back, a
terrified look coming into his face. Tears streamed from his
eyes.

"Thanks to El," he murmured. He tried to back away from
the vision, but it went with him, was truly a part of him. He hit
the side of his head to see if it was still a time for dreams. It was
real.

He climbed off the bed and stripped away his shirt, standing
naked by the mirror to look at himself. He was afraid to touch
it, but of itself it jerked and nearly made him mad with desire.
He reached up and hit the ceiling with his fists.

"Great El, magnificent Lord," he breathed. He wanted to

rush out the door and stand on the balcony, to show God-Does-Battle he was now fully a man, fully as capable as anyone else to accomplish any task given to him, including—merciful El!—founding and fathering a family.

He couldn't restrain himself. He threw open the door of the apartment and ran naked outside.

"BiGod!"

He stopped, his neck hair prickling, and turned to look.

She stood by the door to the apartment, poised like a jack-lighted animal. She was only fourteen or fifteen, at the oldest, and slender, any curves hidden beneath a sacky cloak of pink and orange. She looked at him as she might have looked at a ravening beast. He must have seemed one. Then she turned and fled.

Devastated in the midst of his triumph, he stood with shoulders drooped, hardly breathing, and blinked at the afterimage of brown hair and naked feet. His erection subsided into a morning urge to urinate. He threw his hands up in the air, returned to the apartment, and went into the bathroom.

After breakfast, he faced the information desk, squatting uncomfortably on a small stool. The front of the desk was paneled with green slats, which opened as he approached. Sensor cells peered out at him.

"I'd like to know what I can do to leave," he said.

"Why do you want to leave?" The voice was deeper than Thinner's, but otherwise much the same.

"I've got friends elsewhere, and a past life to return to. I don't have anything here."

"You have all of the past here, an infinite number of things to learn."

"I really just want out."

"You can leave anytime."

"How?"

"This is a problem. Not all of Mandala's systems cooperate with this unit—"

"Which unit?"

"I am the architect. The systems follow schedules set up a thousand years ago. You're welcome to try to leave—we certainly won't do anything to stop you—but it could be difficult."

Jeshua drummed his fingers on the panel for a minute. "What do you mean, the architect?"

"The unit constructed to design and coordinate the building of the cities."

"Could you ask Thinner to come here?"

"Thinner unit is being reassembled."

"Is he part of the architect?"

"Yes."

"Where are you?"

"If you mean, where is my central position, I have none. I am part of Mandala."

"Does the architect control Mandala?"

"No. Not all city units respond to the architect. Only a few."

"The cyborgs were built by the architect," Jeshua guessed.

"Yes."

Jeshua drummed his fingers again, then backed away from the desk and left the apartment. He stood on the terrace, looking across the plains, working his teeth in frustration. He seemed to be missing something terribly important.

"Hey."

He looked up. The girl was on a terrace two levels above him, leaning with her elbows on the rail.

"I'm sorry I scared you," he said.

"Dis me, no'terrafy. Li'l shock, but dat all mucky same-same 'ereber dis em go now. Hey, do, I got warns fo' you."

"What? Warnings?"

"Dey got probs here, 'tween Mandala an' dey 'oo built."

"I don't understand."

"No' compree? Lissy dis me, close, like all dis depen' on't. Dis em, was carry by polis 'en dis dey moob, week 'r two ago. Was no' fun. Walk an' be carry, was I. No' fun."

"The city moved? Why?"

"To leeb behine de part dis dey call builder."

"The architect? You mean, Thinner and the information desks?"

"An' too de bods 'ich are hurt."

Jeshua began to understand. There were at least two forces

in Mandala which were at odds with each other—the city and something within the city which called itself the architect.

"How can I talk to the city?"

"De polis no' talk."

"Why does the architect want us here?"

"Don' know."

Jeshua massaged his neck to stop a cramp. "Can you come down here and talk?"

"No' now dis you are full a man. . . . Too mucky for dis me, too cashin' big."

"I won't hurt you. I've lived with it for all my life—can live a while longer."

"Oop!" She backed away from the rail.

"Wait!" Jeshua called. He turned and saw Thinner, fully corporeal now, leaning on the rounded corner of the access hall.

"So you've been able to talk to her," Thinner said.

"Yes. Made me curious, too. And the information desk."

"We expected it."

"Then can I have some sound answers?"

"Of course."

"Why was I brought here—to mate with the girl?"

"El! Not at all." Thinner gestured for him to follow. "I'm afraid you're in the middle of a pitched battle. The city rejects all humans. But the architect knows a city needs citizens. Anything else is a farce."

"We were kicked out for our sins," Jeshua said.

"That's embarrassing, not for you so much as for us. The architect designed the city according to the specifications given by humans—but any good designer should know when a program contains an incipient psychosis. I'm afraid it's set this world back quite a few centuries. The architect was made to direct the construction of the cities. Mandala was the first city, and we were installed here to make it easier to supervise construction everywhere. But now we have no control elsewhere. After a century of building and successful testing, we put community control into the city maintenance computers. We tore down the old cities when there were enough of the new to house the people of God-Does-Battle. Problems didn't develop until all the living cities were integrated on a broad plan. They began to compare notes, in a manner of speaking."

"They found humanity wanting."

"Simply put. One of the original directives of the city was that socially destructive people—those who did not live their faith as Jews or Christians—would either be reformed or exiled. The cities were constantly aware of human activity and motivation. After a few decades, they decided everybody was socially destructive in one way or another."

"We are all sinners."

"This way," Thinner directed. They came to the moving walkway around the central shaft and stepped onto it. "The cities weren't capable of realizing human checks and balances. By the time the problem was discovered, it was too late. The cities went on emergency systems and isolated themselves, because each city reported that it was full of antisocials. They were never coordinated again. It takes people to reinstate the interurban links."

Jeshua looked at Thinner warily, trying to judge the truth of the story. It was hard to accept—a thousand years of self-disgust and misery because of bad design! "Why did the ships leave the sky?"

"This world was under a colony contract and received support only so long as it stayed productive. Production dropped off sharply, so there was no profit, and considerable expense and danger in keeping contact. There were tens of millions of desperate people here then. After a time, God-Does-Battle was written off as a loss."

"Then we are not sinners, we did not break El's laws?"

"No more than any other living thing."

Jeshua felt a slow hatred begin inside. "There are others who must learn this," he said.

"Sorry," Thinner said. "You're in it for the duration. We'll get off here."

"I will not be a prisoner," Jeshua said.

"It's not a matter of being held prisoner. The city is in for another move. It's been trying to get rid of the architect, but it can't—it never will. It would go against a directive for city cohesion. And so would you if you try to leave now. Whatever is in the city just before a move is cataloged and kept careful track of by watcher units."

"What can any of you do to stop me?" Jeshua asked, his face as set as when he'd ever come across a piece of steel difficult to hammer. He walked away from the shaft exit, wondering what Thinner would try.

The floor rocked back and forth and knocked him on his hands and knees. Streamers of brown and green crawled over a near wall, flexing and curling. The wall came away, shivered as if in agony, then fell on its side. The sections around it did likewise, until a modular room had been disassembled. Its contents were neatly packed by scurrying coat-trees, each with a fringe of arms and a heavier frame for loads. All around the central shaft, walls were being plucked out and rooms dismantled. Thinner kneeled next to Jeshua and patted him on the shoulder.

"Best you come with this unit and avoid the problems here. I can guarantee safe passage until the city has reassembled."

Jeshua hesitated, then looked up and saw a cantilever arch throwing out green fluid ropes like a spider spinning silk. The ropes caught on opposite bracings and allowed the arch to lower itself. Jeshua stood up on the uncertain flooring and followed Thinner.

"This is only preliminary work," Thinner said as he took him into the cyborg room. "In a few hours, the big structural units will start to come down, then the bulkheads, ceiling and floor pieces, then the rest. By this evening, the whole city will be mobile. The girl will be here in a few minutes—you can travel together if you want to. This unit will give you instructions on how to avoid injury during reassembly."

But Jeshua had other plans. He did as Thinner told him, resting on one of the racks like a cyborg, stiffening as the girl came in from another door and positioned herself several aisles down. He was sweating profusely, and the smell of his fear nauseated him.

The girl looked at him cautiously. "You know 'at dis you in fo'?" she asked.

He shook his head.

The clamps on the rack closed and held him comfortably, but securely. He didn't try to struggle. The room was disassembling itself. Panels beneath the racks retracted and wheels jutted out. Shivering with their new energy, the racks elevated and wheeled out their charges.

The racks formed a long train down a hall crowded with scurrying machines. Behind them, the hall took itself apart with spewed ropes, fresh-sprouted grasping limbs and feet, wheels and treads.

It was a dance. With the precision of a bed of flowers closing for the night, the city shrank, drew in, pulled itself down from the top, and packed itself onto wide-tread beasts with unfathomable jade eyes. The racks were put on the backs of a trailer like a flat-backed spider, long multiple legs pumping up and down smoothly to carry them. A hundred spiders like it carried the remaining racks, and thousands of other choreographed tractors, robots, organic cranes, cyborg monsters, waited in concentric circles around Mandala. A storm gathered to the south around Arat's snowy peaks. As the day went on and the city diminished, the grey front swept near, then over. A mantle of cloud hid the disassembly of the upper levels. Rain fell on the ranks of machines and half-machines, and the ground became dark with mud and trampled vegetation. Transparent skins came up over the backs of the spider-trailers, hanging from stiff foam poles. Thinner crawled between the racks and approached Jeshua, who was stiff and sore by now.

"We've let the girl loose," Thinner said. "She has no place to go but with us. Will you try to leave?"

Jeshua nodded.

"It'll only mean trouble for you. But I don't think you'll get hurt." Thinner tapped the rack and the clamps backed away. Night was coming down over the storm. Through the trailer skin, Jeshua could see the city's parts and vehicles switch on interior glows. Rain streaks distorted the lights into ragged splashes and bars. He stretched his arms and legs and winced.

A tall tractor unit surmounted by a blunt-nosed cone rumbled up to the trailer and hooked itself on. The trailer lurched and began to move. The ride on the pumping, man-thick legs was surprisingly smooth. Mandala marched through the rain and dark.

By morning, the new site had been chosen.

Jeshua lifted the trailer skin and jumped into the mud. He had slept little during the trek, thinking about what had happened and what he had been told. He was no longer meek and ashamed.

The cities were no longer lost paradises to him. They now had an air of priggishness. They were themselves flawed. He spat into the mud.

But the city had made him whole again. Who had been more responsible: the architect or Mandala itself? He didn't know and hardly cared. He had been taken care of as any unit in Mandala would have been, automatically and efficiently. He coveted his new wholeness, but it didn't make him grateful. It should have been his by a birthright of ten centuries. It had been denied by incompetence—and whatever passed as willful blindness in the cities.

He could not accept it as perpetual error. His people tended to think in terms of will and responsibility.

The maze of vehicles and city parts were quiet now, as if resting before the next effort of reassembly. The air was misty and grey with a heaviness that lowered his spirits.

" 'Ere dis you go?"

He turned back to the trailer and saw the girl peering under the skin. "I'm going to try to get away," he said. "I don't belong here. Nobody does."

"Lissy. I tol' de one, T-*Thi*nner to teach dis me . . . teach me how to spek li' dis you. When you come back, I know by den."

"I don't plan on coming back." He looked at her closely. She was wearing the same shift she wore when he first saw her, but a belt had tightened it around her waist. He took a deep breath and backed away a step, his sandals sinking in the mud.

"I don' know 'oo you are . . . who you are . . . but if Th-Thinner brought you, you must be a good person."

Jeshua widened his eyes. "Why?"

She shrugged. "Dis me just know." She jumped down from

the trailer, swinging from a rain-shiny leg. Mud splattered up her bare white calves.

"If you, dis me, t'ought . . . thought you were bąd, I'd expec' you to brute me right now. But you don'. Even though you neba —never have a gol before." Her strained speech started to crack, and she laughed nervously. "I was tol' abou' you 'en you came. About your prob—lem." She looked at him curiously. "How do you feel?"

"Alive. And I wouldn't be too sure I'm not a danger. I've never had to control myself before."

The girl looked him over coquettishly.

"Mandala, it isn't all bad, no good," she said. "It took care ob you. Dat's good, is it no'?"

"When I go home," Jeshua said, drawing a breath, "I'm going to tell my people we should come and destroy the cities."

The girl frowned. "Li' take down?"

"Piece by piece."

"Too much to do. Nobod can do dat."

"Enough people can."

"No' good to do in firs' place. No'tall."

"It's because of them we're like savages now."

The girl shimmied up the spider's leg again and motioned for him to follow. He lifted himself and stood on the rounded lip of the back, watching her as she walked with arms balancing to the middle of the vehicle. "Look dis," she said. She pointed to the ranked legions of Mandala. The mist was starting to burn off. Shafts of sunlight cut through and brightened wide circles of the plain. "De polis, dey are li' not'ing else. Dey are de . . ." She sighed at her lapses. "They are the fines' thing we eba put together. We should try t'save dem."

But Jeshua was resolute. His face burned with anger as he looked out over the disassembled city. He jumped from the rim and landed in the pounded mud. "If there's no place for people in them, they're useless. Let the architect try to reclaim. I've got more immediate things to do."

The girl smiled slowly and shook her head. Jeshua stalked off between the vehicles and city parts.

Mandala, broken down, covered at least thirty square miles of the plain. Jeshua took his bearings from a tall rock pinnacle, chose the shortest distance to the edge, and sighted on a peak in Arat. He walked without trouble for a half hour, and found himself approaching a thinner concentration of city fragments. Grass grew up between flattened trails. Taking a final sprint, he stood on the edge of Mandala. He took a deep breath and looked behind to see if anything was following.

He still had his club. He held it in one hand, hefted it, and examined it closely, trying to decide what to do with it if he was bothered. He put it back in his belt, deciding he would need it for the long trip back to his expolis. Behind him, the ranks of vehicles and parts lurched and began to move. Mandala was beginning reconstruction. It was best to escape now.

He ran. The long grass made speed difficult, but he persisted until he stumbled into a burrow and fell over. He got up, rubbed his ankle, decided he was intact, and continued his clumsy springing gait.

In an hour, he rested beneath the shade of a copse of trees and laughed to himself. The sun beat down heavily on the plain, and the grass shimmered with a golden heat. It was no time for travel. There was a small puddle held in the cup of a rock, and he drank from that, then slept for a while.

He was awakened by a shoe gently nudging him in the ribs.

"Jeshua Tubal Iben Daod," a voice said.

He rolled from his stomach and looked into the face of Sam Daniel the Catholic. Two women and another man, as well as three young children, were behind him, jockeying for positions in the coolest shade.

"Have you calmed yourself in the wilderness?" the Catholic asked. Jeshua sat up and rubbed his eyes. He had nothing to fear. The Chief of the Guard wasn't acting in his professional capacity—he was traveling, not searching. And besides, Jeshua was returning to the expolis.

"I am calmer, thank you," Jeshua said. "I apologize for my actions."

"It's only been a fortnight," Sam Daniel said. "Has so much changed since?"

"I . . ." Jeshua shook his head. "I don't think you would believe."

"You came from the direction of the traveling city," the Cath-

olic said, sitting on the soft loam. He motioned for the rest of
the troop to rest and relax. "Meet anything interesting there?"

Jeshua nodded. "Why have you come this far?"

"For reasons of health. And to visit the western limb of expolis Canaan, where my parents live now. My wife has a bad lung
ailment—I think an allergic reaction to the new strain of sor-
ghum being planted in the ridge paddies above Bethel-Japhet.
We will stay away until the harvest. Have you stayed in other
villages near here?"

Jeshua shook his head. "Sam Daniel, I have always thought
you a man of reason and honor. Will you listen with an open
mind to my story?"

The Catholic considered, then nodded.

"I have been inside a city."

He raised his eyebrows. "The one on the plain?"

Jeshua told him most of the story. Then he stood. "I'd like you
to follow me. Away from the rest. I have proof."

Sam Daniel followed Jeshua behind the rocks and Jeshua
shyly revealed his proof. Sam Daniel stared. "It's real?" he
asked. Jeshua nodded.

"I've been restored. I can go back to Bethel-Japhet and become a regular member of the community."

"No one has ever been in a city before. Not for as long as any
remember."

"There's at least one other, a girl. She's from the city chasers."

"But the city took itself apart and marched. We had to change
our course to go around it, or face the hooligans following. How
could anyone live in a rebuilding city?"

"I survived its disassembly. There are ways." And he told
about the architect and its extensions. "I've had to twist my
thoughts to understand what I've experienced," he said. "But
I've reached a conclusion. We don't belong in the cities, any
more than they deserve to have us."

"Our shame lies in them."

"Then they must be destroyed."

Sam Daniel looked at him sharply. "That would be blasphe-
mous. They serve to remind us of our sins."

"We were exiled not for our sins, but for what we are—
human beings! Would you kick a dog from your house because

it dreams of hunting during Passover—or Lent? Then why should a city kick its citizens out because of their inner thoughts? Or because of a minority's actions? They were built with morals too rigid to be practical. They are worse than the most callous priest or judge, like tiny children in their self-righteousness. They've caused us to suffer needlessly. And as long as they stand, they remind us of an inferiority and shame which is a lie! We should tear them down to their roots and sow the ground with salt."

Sam Daniel rubbed his nose thoughtfully between two fingers. "It goes against everything the expolises stand for," he said. "The cities are perfect. They are eternal, and if they are self-righteous, they deserve to be. You of all should know that."

"You haven't understood," Jeshua said, pacing. "They are not perfect, not eternal. They were made by men—"

"Papa! Papa!" a child screamed. They ran back to the group. A black, tractor-mounted giant with an angular, birdlike head and five arms sat ticking quietly near the trees. Sam Daniel called his family back near the center of the copse and looked at Jeshua with fear and anger. "Has it come for you?"

He nodded.

"Then go with it."

Jeshua stepped forward. He didn't look at the Catholic as he said, "Tell them what I've told you. Tell them what I've done, and what I know we must do."

A boy was moaning softly.

The giant picked Jeshua up delicately with a mandibled arm and set him on its back. It spun around with a spew of dirt and grass, then moved quietly back across the plain to Mandala.

When they arrived, the city was almost finished rebuilding. It looked no different from when he'd first seen it, but its order was ugly to him now. He preferred the human asymmetry of brick homes and stone walls. Its noises made him queasy. His reaction grew like steam pressure in a boiler and his muscles felt tense as a snake about to strike.

The giant set him down in the lowest level of the city. Thinner met him there. Jeshua saw the girl waiting on a platform near the circular design in the shaft.

"If it makes any difference to you, we had nothing to do with bringing you back," Thinner said.

"If it makes any difference to you, I had nothing to do with returning. Where will you shut me in tonight?"

"Nowhere," Thinner said. "You have the run of the city."

"And the girl?"

"What about her?"

"What does she expect?"

"You don't make much sense," Thinner said.

"Does she expect me to stay and make the best of things?"

"Ask her. We don't control her, either."

Jeshua walked past the cyborgs and over the circular design, now disordered again. The girl watched him steadily as he approached. He stopped below the platform and looked up at her, hands tightly clenched at his waist.

"What do you want from this place?" he asked.

"Freedom," she said. "The choice of what to be, where to live."

"But the city won't let you leave. You have no choice."

"Yes, the city, I can leave it whenever I want."

Thinner called from across the mall. "As soon as the city is put together, you can leave, too. The inventory is policed only during a move."

Jeshua's shoulders slumped and his bristling stance softened. He had nothing to fight against now, not immediately. He kept his fists clenched, even so.

"I'm confused," he said.

"Stay for the evening," she suggested. "Then will you make thought come clear of confusion."

He followed her to his room near the peak of the city. The room hadn't been changed. Before she left him there, he asked what her name was.

"Anata," she said. "Anata Leucippe."

"Do you get lonely in the evenings?" he asked, stumbling over the question like a child in a field of corn stubble.

"Never," she said. She laughed and turned half-away from him. "An' now certes am dis em, you no' trustable!"

She left him by the door. "Eat!" she called from the corner of the access hall. "I be back, around mid of the evening."

He smiled and shut his door, then turned to the kitchen to choose what he was going to eat.

Being a whole man, he now knew, did not stop the pain and fear of loneliness. The possibility of quenching was, in fact, a final turn of the thumbscrew. He paced like a caged bear, thinking furiously and reaching no conclusions.

By midnight, he was near an explosion. He waited in the viewing area of the terrace, watching the moonlight bathe God-Does-Battle like milk, gripping the railing with strength that could have crushed wood. He listened to the noise of the city. It was less soothing than he remembered, neither synchronous nor melodic.

Anata came for him half an hour after she said she would. Jeshua had gone through so many ups and downs of despair and aloofness that he was exhausted. She took his hand and led him to the central shaft on foot. They found hidden curved stairwells and went down four levels to a broad promenade which circled a widening in the shaft. "The walkway, it doesn't work yet," she told him. "My tongue, I'm getting it down. I'm studying."

"There's no reason you should speak like me," he said.

"It is difficult at times. Dis me—I cannot cure a lifetime ob— of talk."

"Your own language is pretty," he said, half-lying.

"I know. Prettier. Alive-o. But—" She shrugged.

Jeshua thought he couldn't be more than five or six years older than she was, by no means an insurmountable distance. He jerked as the city lights dimmed. All around, the walls lost their bright glow and produced in its stead a pale, lunar gleam, like the night outside.

"This is what I brough' you here for," she said. "To see."

The ghost-moon luminescence made him shiver. Bits of the walls and floor passed threads of light between them, and from the threads grew spirits, shimmering first like mirages, then settling into translucent steadiness. They began to move.

They came in couples, groups, crowds, and with them were children, animals, birds, and things he couldn't identify. They filled the promenade and terraces and walked, talking in tunnel-end whispers he couldn't make out, laughing and looking and being alive, but not in Jeshua's time.

They were not solid, not robots or cyborgs. They were spirits from ten centuries past, and he was rapidly losing all decorum watching them come to form around him.

"Sh!" Anata said, taking his arm to steady him. "They don't hurt anybody. They're no' here. They're dreams."

Jeshua clasped his hands tight and forced himself to be calm.

"This is the city, what it desires," Anata said. "You want to kill the polis, the city, because it keeps out the people, but look— it hurts, too. It wants. What's a city without its people? Just sick. No' bad. No' evil. Can't kill a sick one, can you?"

Each night, she said, the city reenacted a living memory of the past, and each night she came to watch.

Jeshua saw the pseudo-life, the half-silent existence of a billion recorded memories, and his anger slowly faded. His hands loosened their grip on each other. He could never sustain hatred for long. Now, with understanding just out of reach, but obviously coming, he could only resign himself to more confusion for the moment.

"It'll take me a long, long time to forgive what happened," he said.

"This me, too." She sighed. "When I was married, I found I could not have children. This my husband could not understand. All the others of the women in the group could have children. So I left in shame, and came to the city we had always worshiped. I thought it would be, the city, the only one to cure. But now I don't know. I do not want another husband, I want to wait for this to go away. It is too beautiful to leave while it is still here."

"Go away?"

"The cities, they get old and they wander," she said. "Not all things work good here now. Pieces are dying. Soon it will all die. Even such as Thinner, they die. The room is full of them. And no more are being made. The city is too old to grow new. So I wait until the beauty is gone."

Jeshua looked at her more closely. There was a whitish cast in her left eye. It had not been there a few hours ago.

"It is time to go to sleep," she said. "Very late."

He took her gently by the hand and led her through the phantoms, up the empty but crowded staircases, asking her where she lived.

"I don't have any one room," she said. "Sleep in all of them at some time or another. But we can't go back dere." She stopped. "There. Dere. Can't go back." She looked up at him. "Dis me, canno' spek mucky ob—" She held her hand to her mouth. "I forget. I learned bu' now—I don' know . . ."

He felt a slow horror grind in his stomach.

"Something is going wrong," she said. Her voice became deeper, like Thinner's, and she opened her mouth to scream, but could not. She tore away from him and backed up. "I'm doing something wrong."

"Take off your shirt," Jeshua said.

"No." She looked offended.

"It's all a lie, isn't it?" he asked.

"No."

"Then take off your shirt."

She began to remove it. Her hands hesitated.

"Now."

She peeled it over her head and stood naked, with her small breasts outthrust, narrow hips square and bonily dimpled, genitals flossed in feathery brown. A pattern of scars on her chest and breasts formed a circle. Bits of black remained like cinders.

She turned away from him on the staircase, phantoms drifting past her and through her. He reached out to stop her but wasn't quick enough. Her foot spasmed and she fell, gathering into a twisted ball, down the staircase, up against the railings, to the bottom.

He stood near the top and saw her pale blue fluid and red skin-blood and green tissue leaking from a torn leg. He felt he might go insane.

*"Thinner!"* he screamed. He kept calling the name. The lunar glow brightened and the phantoms disappeared. The halls and vaults echoed with his braying cry.

The cyborg appeared at the bottom of the staircase and knelt down to examine the girl.

"Both of us," Jeshua said. "Both lies."

"We don't have the parts to fix her," Thinner said.

"Why were we brought back? Why didn't you just let us stay?"

"Because until a few years ago there was still hope," Thinner said. "The city was still trying to correct the programs, still trying to get back its citizens. Sixty years ago it gave the architect more freedom to try to find out what went wrong. We built ourselves—her, you, the others—to go among the humans and see what they were like now, how the cities could accommodate. Then the aging began, and the sickness. The attempt finally died."

Jeshua felt the scars on his chest and shut his eyes, wishing, hoping it was all a nightmare.

"Daod the smith purged the mark from you when you were a young cyborg, that you might pass for human. Then he stunted your development that you might someday be forced to leave."

"My father was like me."

"Yes. He carried the scar, too."

Jeshua nodded. "How long do we have?"

"Not long. The city is running out of memories to repeat. Soon it will give up, like the others that are restless, and move, and strand itself someplace."

Jeshua walked away from Thinner and the girl's body and wandered down an access hall to the terraces on the outer wall of the city. He shaded his eyes against the rising sun in the east and looked toward Arat. There, he saw the city which had once occupied Mesa Canaan. It had disassembled and was trying to cross the mountains.

"Kisa," he said.

DONNAN JEFFERS *lives in Carmel, California, in the bizarre and wonderful oceanfront house built of craggy stone by his grandfather, the poet Robinson Jeffers. His first published story appeared in* New Dimensions 6; *he is still only nineteen or twenty years old, his literary career just beginning. That he has his grandfather's visionary gift is undeniable. But old Jeffers wrote turbulent, wild, violent stuff of epic scope, and Donnan's tone is gentler, more lyrical—although hardly self-effacing, as this elegant and obsessive tale of the storming of the heavens by Konstantín Vallejo in the year 2373 demonstrates.*

■

# Donnan Call Jeffers, Jr.

■

# WHEN THE MORNING STARS
# SING TOGETHER

*Faster moment spent, spread tales of change within the sound,*
*Counting form through rhythm, electric freedom,*
*Moves to counterbalance stars*
　　　　　　　—Yes: "Sound Chaser" / RELAYER

So he does it, now, at longest last. The memory is on; some year it will be heard, whether on Earth or elsewhere: *First Symphony for Unaccompanied Starship.*

◆

His name is Konstantín Vallejo. His descent is Greek and Argentine. He lives in the city and is subject to the sovereignty of the king of Buenos Aires. He was born in the año católico 2340, el año aireano 117, el catorce de julio. On the fourteenth of July 127 he was taken to the Ballet Real where he saw the revival of Béjart's "Nijinsky — El Payaso del Dios," Çe Arran's first major role. Before this it had been his family's desire that he go into cybernetics training, but his reaction to Pierre Henri's score was so intense that at the same time he studied electronics he was also apprenticed to Lázaro Serra y Justín who taught him piano and computer keyboards, technique, theory, and composition. In 133 his first major piece, *Cycle for Electrimonium and Siren,* was premiered at the Academy of Music; the same year he was graduated from his cybernetics courses and received a scholarship to study at the Institut de recherche et de coordination acoustique-musical in Paris, at that time almost four hundred years old and after a century of quiescence

199

regaining its dominance over the musical landscape of the
world and the slowly evolving Synergie Humain. In residence
at IRCAM was Michel Stephens the physicist, while Alacrán
Lûn of Tycho was a fellow in absentia; these two became his
mentors—much of his compositional work derives from Lûn
and in collaboration with Stephens he developed the theoretical model for his starship.

◆

From the beginning music was a transcendental—almost religious—experience for him. When his parents took him to the
ballet and he heard for the first time music that was not the
traditional Argentine folk-songs, simple and naïve, when he
heard for the first time instruments other than the voice and
unamplified guitar of the song-sellers, when he heard for the
first time those complicated patterns called from synthesizers,
electrimonia, percussive tape-loops, it was as though the universe fell apart before his eyes and was miraculously reconstructed within his ears. The dancers on stage were merely
motes flittering across his corneas; only the music was important. When, later, Lázaro began to show him how he could,
himself, form those chains of sound it became pure ecstasy.
Nothing could compare with the incandescent joy of performance or composition. Music was at his core; there was a string
vibrating to a pure bright tone at the center of his soul. His
training in cybernetics was important only inasmuch as it allowed him to devise new instruments; the scholarship to
IRCAM was attractive mainly because he had exhausted the
musical possibilities of Buenos Aires—there was so much more
he could learn but no one here to teach him. Music, and the
ecstasy derived from it, was his obsession, his addiction, and as
with any addiction he constantly required new and greater
inputs to reach the heights of ecstasis; eventually he could be
satisfied with nothing less than the starship.

◆

After a discussion with Michel on the physical attributes of
sound early on in his residence at IRCAM, he has a dream. He

sees a huge baroque cathedral organ somehow integrated with blocks of pre-transistor circuitry and hardware floating free in the spaces between galaxies, surrounded by a brilliant corona of astral fire. A manic Lucifer is seated at the keyboard and as his hands move across the keys and his feet press the pedalboard the universe twists and shudders about the instrument, folding and refolding, tortured by the music, propelling the demon and his instrument to an unimaginable destination. A random flake of dream imagery, superficially flamboyant though conceptually near-barren, recurrent over the next few months, out of which he evolves his theory for a starship.

◆

Despite his knowledge of computer and instrumental technology he could provide only the abstract, uncohered image; he wasn't competent to envision a concrete form for it. Eventually he forced himself to take the idea to Michel. He had little hope. It was an insane thought. He could hardly believe it himself: how could a physicist, a scientist like Michel, believe in an instrument that might be a starship?

◆

"Music is an arrangement of sounds according to the desires of the composer and performer, and the capabilities of the sound-producing instrument. Sound is an arrangement of vibrations moving through a medium and perceptible in the aural range, as light is vibration in the visible range and heat vibration in the tactile; heat and light are at a higher pitch, a higher 'octave' than sound but are similar vibrations nonetheless. Subatomic particles, atoms, molecules, matter itself is held in formation by vibration and matter is merely energy frozen—energy, matter, vibration: variant manifestations of the same 'thing.' It has long been known that crystalline structures can be disrupted by the human voice—sound—pitched at a certain level; the complementary vibration obscures and distorts the vibration which maintains the crystals' integrity. If an instrument can be devised and a music composed to produce specific tones, pitches, harmonics—vibrations—in a specific sequence and of a specific duration, the vibrations that bind a being to a certain place, time and state of matter can be obscured; the limits of mass, time, location can be transcended. That music will be my symphony and that instrument will be my starship."

◆

At first, even with the specifications already formulated in conference with Michel and IRCAM's computers, he is unable to throw off the dream of a recognizable and massive instrument for him to play, and this image makes it more difficult for him to understand and believe in plans that describe a construction involving less than a kilogram of mass, concentrated mostly in the double eleven-octave-range keyboard and its associated phase-shifters, tonal controls, volume adjusters, and other necessarily physical components of any instrument. In an earlier time it could not even have been conceived, and he is still trapped in those outmoded thought-patterns. The specially coded harmonics and pitches cannot be produced by an instrument composed solely of matter. But with the flux technologies developed within the last century, matter is no longer the only building block available. Self-maintaining magnetic fields engendered by computer and keyboard will carve from the pure force of a plasma-flux miniature sun a coherent energy construct capable of playing the music to move the universe. And as his belief grows he begins to envision a time when even the corporeality of keyboard and computer will be transcended and the performer himself will be the only matter engaged in the matrix of the starship.

◆

He began composing the symphony before he was entirely certain his theories were valid and could be implemented. It was the most difficult piece he had ever embarked on. From his long conferences with Michel and the computers at IRCAM's Artificial Intelligence Project Center came several meter-long printouts of harmonics, tonal sequences, chord changes and time shifts, and graphs and diagrams, which he had to condense, rearrange, distill into his music. And because he was more a composer than a scientist, and because the ecstasy of it would not be as great, he could not be satisfied with a strict and literal transcription of the requisites; there were two goals to be fulfilled: the creation of an artwork able to stand on its own merits and to instill in him a joy more intense than any other, and the formulization of a flight program for the starship—which must itself be formulated. The knowledge was always there; that it must be as much a musical instrument as a vehicle, as much a vehicle as an instrument, that the two must be equal, congruous, balanced. Adding to the difficulty of the composing, even were the plans for construction finalized, until the construction itself was finished everything must be tentative, capabilities could not be judged from schematics, much less the provisional ones he had; there was no guarantee that the little abstract symbols dotted across the staves on his readout screen could be realized or that the printouts, graphs, and diagrams would be accurate, that completion of either schematics or construction would not create new questions. But even so, in his IRCAM studio, on his synthesizers and pianos he went ahead with a work that could be played only once and only on the completed starship.

◆

In July of 144, ten years after theoretical work had commenced, Konstantín and Michel released a report on their progress to that point. In Buenos Aires the minister for culture read that report in his annual address to the throne. Alfonso II Rey and his council deliberated. La Nación de los Buenos Aires was too young, too precarious in its statehood to be anything but parochial, nationalistic. It was decided, *in camera,* that no research of this magnitude—if the claims for it were valid—could be undertaken by an Airean citizen on foreign ground and using foreign capital. It was decided to forbid Konstantín Vallejo the use of the commission tendered by Mohammed Sharif Al Kalif, IRCAM's major patron. It was decided to command Vallejo's immediate return to his homeland. When he was requested to present himself at the Airean consulate in Paris, Konstantín had been in the process of planning, with Michel

and the board of governors of IRCAM, a timetable for the starship's construction. The schedule wasn't firm when he learned
it must be discarded. He was given scant time to prepare for his
departure. Michel, accustomed as he was to a democratic government so well worn and of such age, raged; Konstantín could
only accept this disruption of his plans, this infringement on his
future ecstasy, this threat to the starship.

◆

At his audience with the king and the lords of the council, he
speaks of the hypothesized near-instantaneity of transition between one point and another across the universe, at least as
compared to the currently used ram-ships, still hampered by
the limiting velocity of light; of the negligible cost once primary
research is completed due to the self-maintenence of the plasma-flux; of the incalculable worth to Buenos Aires and the world
of this advance in extrasolar transportation; of the questing
spirit of humankind and the opening of new horizons; of the
fusion of art and science—but he does not mention what to him
is the greatest benefit: the unknowable transcendental experience of playing the music of the spheres, the merging with tone
and harmony, the union with the cosmos. And he is unable to
convince them. The king considers the hypothetical nature of
the project and the possibility of failure; the minister for culture
is uncertain of the worth of a musical composition that cannot
be played by conventional instruments and before an audience;
the minister for science, himself an amateur musician, dislikes
the muddling of barriers between aesthetics and physics, and is
unable to comprehend Michel's theories; the minister for national integrity is distressed that the work was funded by the
Kalifate and that, moreover, even now Michel, a French national, is able to go ahead with the construction without permission of the Airean government. Finally they decide that they
cannot support the project and, because he is a citizen of la
Nación de los Buenos Aires and Alfonso II Rey's subject, they
will not allow Konstantín Vallejo to continue his work on the
starship.

◆

"But don't you see," he wanted to cry, "don't you understand
that none of that matters? The only thing that matters is the
exaltation, the beatitude of it! Can't you comprehend, can't you
imagine the miracle of tuning oneself to the very basis of reality,
of holding the universe in one's soul? Only that matters! And I
can achieve it only through the starship."

◆

Outwardly he accepts. He is a loyal citizen. He writes asking
Michel to shelve the project. He accepts a post as resident
composer and professor at la Universidad de Entre Ríos in
Paraná. He composes chamber and orchestral works for the
university and the Academy of Music. The only outward sign of
rebellion is his refusal to undertake a royal commission for a
symphony to be prepared for the sesquicentennial in 150. But
within himself he refuses to be balked. He still dreams. On his
own time he persists in refining, perfecting the unplayable symphony. Echoes of it carry over into his simultaneous legitimate
composition. But it is not truly rebellion. Too implicit in him is
respect for the throne. The king has been misled by his council;
eventually el rey will understand; he need only wait. But it is
difficult with the vision shining in his dreams, the vision of the
starship.

◆

As time passes in contemplation and forced idleness, as the
vision becomes obsessional and central, his dream-image of it
alters, grows closer to the supposed reality of the starship. At
the center of it is the tiny crystal microchip of the computer
that will translate the impulses from each key, switch and rheo-
stat into graded pins of coherent sound. The computer is
mounted in a keyboard of fine plastics and light, tensile alloys
to withstand the enormous pressures of radiation-flux, floating
in the core of the plasma sun itself. A sphere of magnetic force
surrounds the keyboard and computer, creating a frantically
brilliant interface with the flux, which expands outward in a fire
of nuclear breakdown and fusion. The thin, unimaginably
strong skin of current could not protect the flaming Lucifer who
is bathed by it except that he is sheathed in a modified lunar

air-envelope, an intangible second skin of congealed force. To the hypothetical outside observer — which at times he is — the starship is from a distance only a star as any other until moving closer it is too small to be a true star; closer and closer: the observer realizes it is less tangible than a sun, not massive enough to sustain the continual fusion: not a star but the effect of one, imprisoned in unbreakable bonds. And because the observer is only hypothetical, only dreaming, he can hear the ineffable music, the music that moves the universe, the music of the starship.

◆

The university granted him a sabbatical in 147. He went to the moon, to the Free City of Tycho, where Alacrán was. His second week there he celebrated his thirtieth birthday by attending the premiere of one of his mentor's scores at the Lunar Ballet of Tycho. When he returned to Alacrán's rooms after the performance, he found Michel there, come from Paris to see him. Even after three years, the physicist was still angry; he argued with Konstantín, demanding that he defect, abandon his allegiance to Buenos Aires's king, acquire French or Lunar citizenship, work with Alacrán and him on the starship. But Konstantín was adamant in his refusal, sure that it was only a matter of time before Alfonso II would support the project. He could hardly understand Michel's frustration; what could it mean to him when it was only conceptual, only a thing of intellectual curiosity? He could never comprehend the meaning it had for Konstantín. And Konstantín could not disobey his monarch. Yet Michel wore at him with his constant pressuring: though he refused to compromise his loyalty, the continual referral to it brought further to the fore in his mind his need for the starship.

◆

His sabbatical is cut short when in the second week of August Mohammed Sharif mounts his insanely anachronistic *jihad* against the pagan and almost immediately afterward is assassinated. The mad Kalif's actions jeopardize the fragile stability

of the nominal Federation of Earth States and shatter the Mos-
lem hegemony. The ultranationalistic Buenos Aires government feels threatened; potentially subversive citizens like Konstantín must be accounted for and cleared. For the second time
his return is ordered, and he must present himself again before
king and council. He cannot stop himself, when he stands in
front of them; he is unable not to beg them to reconsider their
verdict on the starship — it is a matter of such importance and
urgency for him. They become angry: to intrude his wild fantasies on these vital proceedings. Yet he is so involved in con-
structing arguments, in weaving a tapestry whose central
figures are Buenos Aires, the king, himself, and the starship,
that he does not notice their anger. At length they can tolerate
it no longer. Konstantín Vallejo is charged with treasonous con-
duct and sentenced to prison, where his only solace will be the
dream of the starship.

◆

He was held at Iguazú in Misión, Buenos Aires's most north-
erly province. He would sit in his tiny cell in the stifling moist
heat playing the little mahogany recorder which was the only
instrument he was allowed for long solitary hours. When he
wasn't piping, the silence would become intolerable, because it
was not silent. Through the bone-walled caverns and corridors
of his skull the symphony reverberated until he could feel the
calcium cathedral crumbling to the rumbling bass and the
stained-glass windows of his eyes fracturing to the treble. The
program of the score had been confiscated when he was arrested, but he had it all in his mind, graved into the tissues,
singing through the ganglia. When he slept his dreams were of
stars and the symphony and the starship. The longer he was
there the more it occupied him and as, slowly, his sanity faltered
in the heat and damp and claustrophobia, so the vision became
progressively baroque, once again an organ with gleaming
pipes encrusted with rococo putti and wreaths of gilt fruit and
flowers, conducted through the galaxies by a blinding, deafen-
ing choir of angels, archangels and principalities, powers, vir-
tues and dominations, thrones, cherubim and seraphim, all re-

volving in a vast concourse about the organ as though it were
the divine light. All the elements of his upbringing in the re-
gressive Church of the True Pope in Santiago rushed together
into a gorgeous cataclysm about the beautiful seraph Lucifer,
the light bearer who played the starship.

◆

Not knowing he was imprisoned, Michel had written Konstantín several times before Alacrán of neutral Tycho learned
of it and told him. This was early in 149; Konstantín Vallejo had
been in jail for a year and a half. Michel and IRCAM's governors
with the French government lodged a complaint; it did no
good, and it was intimated that were the matter pressed much
further the Airean council might cut off relations with France.
The starship had become now for Alacrán and Michel more
than "only conceptual, only a thing of intellectual curiosity";
they knew, though not why, that it was of central importance
to Konstantín, and as they had come to be bound up with him,
so they were bound up in it. It was of central importance to
them. But it seemed there was nothing to be done, it seemed
that what had begun as a dream must end as a dream, never to
be realized, the starship.

◆

Lucifer rides the chariot across the heavens like Apollon,
drawn by two horses, the pure white Pitch and the opalescent
Harmony. The road is ruled with two parallel tracks of five lines
each. The gates of delirium crash open before him, each flange
ornamented with a single symbol: on the left ₡ and on the right
♫ . The chariot is gilded in silver and gold, its keys are of ebony
and ivory; Lucifer's robes are painted in blistering medieval
tinctures, gules and azure and vert and purpure: it is as though
the whole assemblage is the vignette of a genius monk, inked
onto the staves of the score for a Gregorian chant. The chariot
shines; it is the starship.

◆

Michel Stephens goes again to Tycho, for Alacrán Lûn cannot

come to him in Paris, trapped by the irrevocable bonds of mass and gravity as he is. What can they do, they ask each other. It is unthinkable that Konstantín be left rotting in his tropic prison, as it is unthinkable that the starship not be built or the symphony be left unplayed. Ultimately Alacrán has the idea: they will appeal to the Aireans' national patriotism. Buenos Aires's sesquicentennial is approaching; the governments of France and the Free City of Tycho will jointly fund the construction of the starship and give it to la Nación de los Buenos Aires for the celebration of its first one hundred fifty years. And Konstantín Vallejo, as the originator of the idea and the only one capable of playing it, must be released. France and Tycho agree to the proposal; negotiations with Buenos Aires are instigated through Luna, and Alfonso II Rey, against his council's wishes, agrees. There will be a starship.

◆

To see sunlight again, to breathe once more the crisp clean air of the capital, to stretch one's fingers across a keyboard and *play:* almost it returned Konstantín to full sanity. He spent most of his time in the studio at the Academy that had been allotted him. It was a small room, like but so unlike his cell; he did not require space for his work. His computer was hooked into two readout screens: one, for the continuing composition, always displaying the endless staves which, even as he filled them with the diamond points, lines, and squiggles of notation, would disappear into the memory and be replaced by more naggingly empty staves to be covered by points, lines, squiggles—the score-program had been destroyed and he had to resuscitate it note by note from the corpse in his mind; the other screen was set for direct-line communication with Michel's laboratory outside Paris where the construction was on, or, with some difficulty, Alacrán on Luna so he could cascade the elder composer with showers of sharps, flats, naturals, fragments of harmony, questions on tempo, dissonance and other matters or simply mute requests for affirmation—almost always forthcoming as Alacrán recognized how fragile Konstantín's stability was. Konstantín's favorite piano was there for him, the carefully reconstructed early twentieth-century Steinway studio grand, more for emotional reassurance than anything else. And a synthesizer, built to his specifics, with the double eleven-octave keyboard of the starship.

◆

Increasingly, as the first wall of relief thrown up by his freedom erodes with time, he finds himself in his dreams back roaming the floor of that vast limestone and jeweled dome he grew to know so well when he was jailed. Each dawn he must slam the gates of delirium on the glorious phantasm of Lucifer's chariot and concentrate on the no less glorious reality of the starship.

◆

In May of 150 he finished the symphony, at least to the extent possible without the use of the instrument for which it was written. And even when the instrument was readied, as Michel promised it soon would be, he could not test its capacities and from them mold the music to fit; for to play the starship would set in motion the irreversible reactions and counterreactions that would start its movement through and simultaneous warping of the universe. When the time came to test it, test and action would be the same; if his music, though after such preparation, proved unsuitable, he would be forced to improvise. Thus while it was a complete work it was also a sketch for the fully realized piece that could only be completed in its performance. After sending a syntheziser-redaction to Alacrán at Tycho, and a cube of his playing, he went into retreat for a month to perfect his improvisational technique and ready himself for the task, the joy, the ecstasy of playing the starship.

◆

Even in his peculiarly brilliant dreams he is unable fully to comprehend the reality of it. Now, el catorce de julio de 150, his thirty-third birthday and the sesquicentennial of his country's creation, in the center of the city it begins, to the greater glory of himself and la Nación de los Buenos Aires. The king is

present with his retinue, the president of France, the ambassa-
dors or heads of state of many other principalities, including the
Free Cities of Luna and the Communality of Ares, and the
people of Buenos Aires; several seconds lagged, Alacrán Lûn
watches via 'cast; Michel Stephens is here to help him in his
preparations and share in his long-delayed triumph. The Royal
Academy's orchestra performs an all-Vallejo program: first the
*Cycle for Electrimonium and Siren,* moving through to his last
work before the symphony's completion, the *Prison Pieces for
Recorder and Orchestra.* By himself he can carry the merely
physical matter of his instrument, the keyboard and microchip
computer, to the dais in the center of the plaza; then he goes
before his monarch to pledge, without rancor, his allegiance
and receive decorations from Alfonso II Rey and both the
French president and the ambassador for Tycho. Now, he
stands in the coldly brilliant winter sunlight, the orchestra and
the audience quiet. He disrobes, giving his clothing to Michel,
and is naked and alone. He activates the computer and its
memory. He sits cross-legged before the keyboard. He begins
to play the starship.

♦

As the first unhearable chords ring out, the mechanism comes
into being. First the envelope covers him and he is as though
aluminum-plated. Invisible magnetic fields weave a tensile co-
coon about him. The computer emits coded lasers, the visible
manifestation of the music, which thread in scintillating, com-
plicating display, becoming more dense and brilliant until the
performer is hidden within a blinding starlike effect fluctuating
to its own internal tempi, the rhythms of his symphony. And
suddenly, though the observers cannot see it through the afterimage, there is nothing but a shifting in the air where was
the starship.

♦

As his fingers, one hand on the upper and one on the lower
keyboard, activate the first chords, the instrument absorbs him
into it so that even if he wished he could not observe what

appears to be around him—though how could he wish it, with the apotheosis upon him? Now he is only another part of the small physical aspect of the being, the Angel, that is his symphony and his starship.

◆

He climbs the walls to the gates of delirium. With ponderous thunder they open. His horses, Pitch and Harmony, whicker and nuzzle him. He harnesses them with rhythm. He climbs into the chariot and sets out across the great calcine dome of night. He is Apollon, he is Lucifer, he is Archangel, he rides the starship.

◆

The music is a self-contained, self-sustaining, self-perpetuating moment. He—the computer, the keyboard—is the spark, but once begun, mass becomes extraneous, at least momentarily, to instantaneity. Labels are meaningless, in this instant of creation; what does a Principality distinguish among, in eternity? The starship is the music, the music is Konstantín Vallejo, he is the starship.

◆

As he sits at the Lord's organ he is filled with limitless power. He is Power. What can he not do? The heavenly host rises up around him to do his bidding, the greatest of the servants of the Lord. What can he not do who is Lucifer the light bearer who plays the starship?

◆

Matter does not exist in Virtue the spirit of preservation. Form is embodied in shifting rhythms, harmonics, modulations of the infra-aural vibration which is the Virtue Konstantín Vallejo who is the starship.

◆

In this durationless, timeless state the eternal and eternally modulating pitch is entangled and one with the cyclic central vibration of the universe. As they are identical and equal, yet the music, a Domination, molds and distorts the song of the universe, a Domination, creating a momentary discontinuity that has always been and always will be a part of the fabric of reality. Into it falls and has fallen and will fall the starship; falls, has fallen, will fall the universe, Dominations both and one, for they are united in the vibrations of the symphony. Universe is discontinuity is starship.

◆

Nothing and everything exist within the ever-revolving Throne. Reality is and is not a part of the divinely circular Throne. The vibration that is the universe is the music that is he who is the starship is the vibration ordered and arranged by his mind which is ordered and arranged by the universe that is the starship.

◆

It is beatitude and exaltation and adoration. He is Cherub, part of the great multitude of the second circle about the divine light of the Son. He is Cherub, the second mandala that surrounds the divine sun that is the starship.

◆

The glory and the pain are exquisite, ecstatic, unceasing for they are, have been, will be the eternal fire of the first ring that he is as Seraph. He sits behind God, he sits at the feet of God, he sits on the right hand and the left, all about, he surrounds his Lord as an infinite globe of divine radiance. He is pleasing to the sight of God, he is pleasing to the starship.

◆

The fabric of space folds according to the modulations of the symphony. He bends the universe for He is God, He is the Three-in-One and the One-in-Three; He is the universe and the symphony and the starship.

◆

In the first movement all is quiescent and nonexisting. A slow gathering of energies becoming inchoate mass as His ten fingers aggregate a ringing tone-cluster. A shattering run of crescendi and diminuendi begins the expansion, the creation. As He claws in disparate notes, matter coalesces in thin nebular drifts of dust pocked with deposits of hydrogen collapsing under their own density until they commence their spinning and their fusion to become stars. In the second movement, the tempo increases, series of hardening and eroding arpeggios. High, scattered trip-lets as each new star is stimulated to ignition, low rumbles as they decay and burn out, violent chord-eruptions if they nova. The tempo is even faster in the third movement, solar rather than galactic or universal time. Still, in its minor reaches, His music recognizes and directs everything else; but He concen-trates now on a single pocket of hydrogen and helium, tainted with trace heavy elements emitted by older stars. The pocket condenses, whirls, throws out a disk of extraneous matter, and in its core a crescendo initiates fusion. Nine orbiting motifs conglomerate as planets with their attendant satellites. One, almost as soon as it has a discrete identity, shatters from the conflicting resonances of too-close pitches; it is replaced by a wandering chord diverted from the outermost planet. The fourth movement He plays in terrestrial time as the crust hard-ens and the atmosphere forms. A pair of notes, uttered at seem-ingly random intervals as tides roll the seas back and forth, are at a certain point sustained and the spark of life is lit. That two-note chord modulates slowly, growing more complex, and finally with all its ramifications it becomes the major theme of the fifth movement, which He has set in human time, the time of Konstantín Vallejo who, in the process of the movement, will devise and play the starship.

◆

So he does it, now, at longest last, so he begins. Only He will hear it in its fullness, only He Who plays it: *First Symphony for Unaccompanied Starship.*

◆

may–august 1976
carmel, san francisco

◆

(for Chris Squire, Steve Howe,
Jon Anderson, Alan White,
Patrick Moraz, of Yes.)